This book is dedicated to my mother
Mrs. Patricia Eze Chimé
whose unwavering support has not gone unnoticed by me.

And to my son
Jidobi Ken Chimé
In my humble way,
I am making amends for the raw deal life has dealt him.

MY SONGBIRD CAN DANCE

This book is published by:
Breakfast Pictures Entertainment, Inc.
P.O. Box 322
New York, NY 10027

www.breakfastpictures.com

Telephone Contact:
646.359.0576

Email Contact:
info@breakfastpictures.com

ISBN: 978-0-615-34235-1

ACKNOWLEDGEMENTS

Front Cover Design –
Wendy Mojica-Florian

Back Cover Design –
Peter Felix
(Peter, what can I say … there are no adequate words)

Front and Back Cover Photos of Vigil –
Gilbert King Elisa

———

For ideas that added to the book –
Natasha Guruleva, Thierry Saintine, Crystal Wynn-Wise

Editors –
Raina Oberlin, Natasha Herring, Jane Bender

Readers –
Ken Chimé, Philip Chimé, Wairimu Kiambuthi, Melissa Harts

All the booksellers in Harlem, Brooklyn, Bronx & Queens –
In particular Henry Ndombo and Sidi, both at 125th Street (Harlem)

A special thanks to Gabriel Daley
With his help, what could have ended as one became two ☺

———

Friends who gave support of any kind –
Kofi John, Cinque Brathwaite, ChiChi Onukogu,
Paula Coleman, John Buckley, Mavia Louis-John,
Bonny Hart, Kene Evans & Yuriy Sheydvasser

———

I can't forget the readers –
Thank you for taking the time to pick out this book.
I hope it proves to be breezy and worth your time. Enjoy.

Books by Vigil Chimé

My Songbird Can Dance

Films by Vigil Chimé

African Dilemma, Part 1
African Dilemma, Part 2
African Youth
Manchester Bound

For information on how to get this book or these films, please contact Vigil directly:

646.359.0576
vigil@vigilchime.com
vigil@breakfastpictures.com

MY SONGBIRD CAN DANCE

a
Vigil Chimé
book

Breakfast Pictures Entertainment, Inc.
New York

RACHEL

24-year old Rachel Ofordilli finds herself sitting front row and center in a huge auditorium somewhere in Sweden. A smile is plastered on her face and her eyes are beaming with delight. She just heard the president of the Nobel Prize Committee declare to the assembled dignitaries that she is the greatest writer ever! And that it is with great honor and pleasure that he is now bestowing upon her the Nobel Prize in Literature.

Everything is moving in slow motion to Rachel. She sees and hears the hall erupt into deafening cheers and claps. The Nigerian president and his entourage, in the audience, lead the cheers because it's not every day the American daughter of two Nigerians wins the coveted prize.

Obama and Michelle are also in attendance because Michelle is Rachel's greatest fan, and got her husband, the leader of all the free world, to accompany her to pay homage to the young and brilliant writing genius.

Rachel herself is sitting between her father and her man. Nathaniel, her father, jumps to his feet and hops all over the place, shouting at the top of his lungs, "That's my daughter! That's my daughter! She's the greatest! She's the greatest!!" Then he grabs Rachel's mom, Anne, off her seat. They hold each other tight, weeping like babies at the unbelievable accomplishment of their lastborn.

Not to be outdone, Bo, Rachel's boyfriend, a world-famous painter in his own right, immediately gets on his knees. He takes Rachel's hand in his and asks her to marry him on the spot. He slips a 30-karat diamond engagement ring on her finger. It's Rachel's turn to burst into tears. She accepts Bo's proposal by implanting a long and delicious kiss on his lips.

All the dignitaries jump to their feet now, including Obama and Michelle who are surrounded by a swarm of Secret Service guards. Rachel watches in awe as everyone continues to cheer and clap for her. She is expected to get to the podium and deliver the thank-you speech she has already committed to memory.

Rachel does not intend to disappoint. She offers her hand to Bo, her engagement ring sparkling brilliantly. Bo takes the hand and lifts her to her feet. She stands 5’9”, although she appears taller than life. She is very dark in complexion, with flawless skin and a regal bearing that renders her majestic.

She appears particularly stunning tonight because she is wearing Victoria Secret silky soft black underwear and bra – and that’s all, complete with 6-inch red stilettos that lift her higher. Her massive butt cheeks peek through the barely-there panties, while her size D-cup boobs are practically pouring out of the bra that is two sizes too small.

No one reacts as if this fashion statement is in the least bit extraordinary. The cheers and claps continue as Rachel and her rippling and thoroughly moisturized flesh flow towards the podium. When she gets there, she asks for quiet. Silence descends immediately as all take back their seats to await her every word.

Rachel takes her time. A master dramatist, she knows how to build tension and increase anticipation. She smiles down on the quarter-million crowd – focusing on the smiling faces of her beloved father Nathaniel, her cherished boyfriend – now fiancé – Bo, her beaming best friend Jada, and of course on Obama and Michelle.

Michelle blows her a kiss, so Rachel returns it by blowing Obama a kiss. The Nigerian president is not to be forgotten. She throws him a kiss too, which the elderly statesman catches in the air, then directs to his heart like a love-struck schoolboy.

Rachel finally zeroes in on the scowling face of her sister Ada who is sitting all the way in the back, next to her stupid boyfriend Paul. Rachel knows her sister is dying of envy and determines to rub it in. She waves to Ada, making sure to brandish her engagement ring in a way that Ada cannot miss – although, who could miss the blinding light of a 30-karat diamond ring!

Ada looks at her own tiny engagement ring given her by Paul. She begins hitting Paul upside the head, then bursts into tears and buries her face on Paul's lapel. This appears to be the cue Rachel is waiting for. She laughs heartily then begins her speech.

"Dearly beloved," she quotes the Bible sweetly. "We are gathered here today to join this woman – that would be me – to celebrate this most highest of honors …"

No sooner is the word out of her mouth than comes crashing through the sound speakers Jay-Z and Alicia Keys' *Empire State of Mind*. No one else appears to be as distracted by the song as Rachel is. She looks about her in an agitated manner, wondering where the song is coming from. She finally concludes that the best way to deal with the intrusive lyrics is to raise her voice.

"Um, once again, thank you all for coming!" she screams. "I just wanted to take the time to thank you guys who have supported me, um, over the years, and boo the rest of you haters who haven't! I'm speaking to you Ada and Paul!"

Everyone turns to Ada and Paul and suddenly burst out with, "Boooooooooooo!"

Ada and Paul cower under the overwhelming negative energy. Rachel would be awesomely overjoyed to hear all this, except she can't hear a thing. Jay-Z and Alicia Keys' hip hop fiasco drowns everything out.

PROLOGUE

A party rages in a tidy two-bedroom apartment in the Bronx – although not so tidy now, given the merriment. The guests are all working professionals, in their mid-to-late twenties, a mixed group of whites and blacks – Americans and Africans.

The occasion is 26-year old Ada Uchenna's medical school entrance exam result. Hers was a perfect score, far exceeding anything her mother, Anne Uchenna, had prayed to all her saints for. The party is also to celebrate Ada's engagement to her boyfriend of three years, Paul Ike, whom she met at NYU. Paul was in medical school then, but is currently a resident at Harlem Hospital. The two lovebirds chose a wedding date exactly one year from the party.

The music in the apartment is higher in volume than Anne would have liked. There are certainly more people in the space than her tiny home can accommodate comfortably. Already, a vase has been broken and liquor spilled all over her light-green carpet. But tonight, Anne forgives all as she buzzes about the kitchen with the expected happiness of an African mother whose dreams and happiness are intrinsically tied with the achievements of her children.

The kitchen hums with the smell of traditional African delicacies and American cuisine. Anne's three best friends are there to assist. But what she really needs them for tonight is to bear witness to the party. She is sure that by tomorrow, the women will do what they do best – carry the gossip throughout the small Nigerian Igbo community based in New York City. In this way, her ex-husband, Nathaniel Ofordilli, will hear of it while sitting in the palace in Long Island with his second wife.

Pouring hot water over the *foofoo* flour in a bowl, Anne's mood immediately turns cloudy at the thought of the man. She quickly rattles off, *Hail Mary full of grace, the lord is with thee. Blessed art thou amongst women, and blessed is the fruit of thy womb Jesus.* As expected, thoughts of Nathaniel vanish from her mind – well, almost.

Meanwhile, the doorbell rings. Ada, a beautiful woman, standing an impressive 5'11", rushes to the door and ushers more of her animated friends into the living room. Kisses go round as she grabs coats and purses, and heads to the designated coatroom.

After moving in with Paul two years ago, Ada rarely comes round to the home she lived in since she was 8-years old. She barges into the room now and throws the coats into the darkened space. The coats land on the bed – already, a mountain has risen there. She slams the door unnecessarily loud, then returns to her friends in the living room.

The mountain on the bed suddenly moves. Coats cascade to the floor – revealing Rachel who wakes up furious. Her dream of standing on a podium in Sweden and receiving the Nobel Prize in Literature was rudely interrupted by the noise from the party. She really wanted to see the end of that dream. As she imagined it, Ada and Paul would be thrown out of the Swedish hall by Obama's Secret Service!

Rachel stumbles out of bed, clad only in panties – though not nearly as nice as the Victoria Secret one she'd been wearing in her dream. She wears no bra, so her massive boobs flop around without restraint. It's early April and nights are still nippy – the reason the radiator is overheating the room, and the reason she sleeps practically nude.

She deliberately steps on the coats, scarves and purses on the ground – items she knows belong to her sister's friends. She regrets she's not wearing shoes with shit on the soles. That would teach them a lesson for using her bedroom as the fucking coatroom, she thinks. How dare they wake me up!

Rachel's habit is to stay up all night writing. She found that her creativity is on fire from midnight to 5AM. Not that she's writing these days. Only a week before, she mailed her first completed manuscript to at least three-dozen publishers. This is the same book the Nobel Prize Committee in her dream chose as the best thing ever written by man, woman or child, hands down!

The book is about *Yasmin,* a 20-year old African girl who enters America as a sex slave, then rises through the ranks to become the madam of the very prostitution ring in Harlem that enslaved her. Her mother called the manuscript vile. Her sister could not be bothered to finish it, citing overwork and over study. Paul, the stupid fiancé doctor, said it cast Africans in a poor light.

What does he know about the immigrant struggle, Rachel concluded at the time. The guy is the son of a prominent Nigerian politician. He was raised in the lap of luxury his whole life, both in Africa and in America – with money, Rachel is certain, his family stole, and no doubt continues to steal, from the poor people of Nigeria.

Rachel herself knows nothing about immigrant struggle. She and Ada were born in the Bronx, and spent all their lives surrounded more by affluent American friends than by poor African ones. Although her parents divorced when Rachel was 6-years old, her mother single-handedly raised her and her sister better than most two-income families. Anne often went without to make sure her daughters wanted for nothing.

As for her knowledge of Nigeria, on this issue, Rachel's details are also scant – going no further than the gossip of her mother and her friends, and the summer stints she and Ada endured when they were little girls.

Rachel refused to go to Africa after her junior year because she found Nigeria abysmal: the perpetual heat, traffic jams, electrical blackouts, not to mention the lack-of-water-in-the-toilets scenario. At 16, Rachel had enough of Africa to fill a lifetime.

As she walks out of her bedroom, Rachel's head pounds from the fucking music of her sister's fucking party. She begged her mother not to host the shindig, but she might as well have been talking to a doorknob.

Anne dreamed of this very party, ever since Ada got into NYU. In fact, she went on a hunger strike when it looked like Paul wanted to have the party at their place in Manhattan. Always concerned about her mother's health, Ada could not permit Paul to hold the party in Manhattan, even though most of their friends also lived there. Showing their loyalty, everyone the couple invited to the party showed up in the Bronx.

Rachel crosses the living room to get to the bathroom. Her rude bottom, continuing to peek from barely there panties, and her flapping D-cup breasts give off the desired effect. The music comes to a squeaking halt, jaws drop and more liquor spills on Anne's carpet as the guests try – with little success – not to gape.

Rachel saunters into the space as if no one is there. Yet, her steps are deliberate and measured, each designed to pronounce and jut out her rotund butt cheeks. Her eyes are cast down, the image of feigned innocence. She stifles a yawn for good measure.

Rachel never makes it to her destination. Anne slams upon the table, the bowl of *foofoo* she grips in her hand as Rachel flows past. At 50-years old, the woman moves with lightening speed, a whir of movement that zips in and out of frozen guests, aiming straight towards

Rachel. Anne pushes her daughter roughly into the master bedroom, the room closest to the bathroom.

As her mother's door slams shut, Ada immediately collapses onto the couch, weeping uncontrollably. Paul and the guests surround her quickly, fanning her with their hands and whispering words of comfort.

"Dearest," Paul coos. "Never mind the girl, you know she's cuckoo."

"I knew she was gonna pull something!" Ada wails. "But nothing like this! She's ruined everything!"

"She didn't ruin nothing!" adds a drunken male guest, thinking Ada's shrieks a bit theatrical. He wishes Rachel would pass by again. He'd never seen anything so gorgeous in his life – she was giggling flesh in all the right places.

In Anne's bedroom, Anne is boxing her daughter's ears, hitting her upside the head and buttocks, forgetting for a moment that Rachel is not the 10-year old girl she used to visit such beatings upon. But constantly behave like a child is what Rachel does, Anne thinks to herself, as she rains still more blows on the girl's body.

"Mommy! Mommy stop!" Rachel screams, covering her head and face with her hands. Her mother is the only woman in the world from whom Rachel would accept such beatings and humiliation – otherwise, the bedroom would have been all torn up and the police summoned.

"How can you do this?!" Anne screams, in a deep African accent that always causes Rachel to burst out laughing. The girl thinks better of it now, though – if for no other reason than to stave off more blows from her mother.

"Have you absolutely no respect for yourself?!" Anne is beside herself with fury. Fearing a stroke, she grabs her wrist, pinches it tight to gauge her blood pressure.

"I have to pee!" Rachel attempts a defense. "Is it my fault the bathroom is on the other side of the living room?"

She squeaks the question out, knowing she can offer no reasonable defense for her behavior. But what balls, she thinks, going off in her mind as she often does when she cares nothing for what is going on around her. She will make sure to write a scene in which *Beatrice* – the main character in her current story – exits the closet the Congressman stuffed her in after their delightful afternoon quickie in the State Capitol. *Beatrice* must be clad only in panties before she walks into the Congressman's meeting!

"Have you no respect for your sister?" Anne's voice invades, automatically bringing Rachel out of her dream state. Any mention of her sister almost always causes a violent reaction within Rachel.

"Oh give me a break, mommy!" Rachel retorts, her face screwed up with anger and envy. "Ms. Melodrama Queen! She's out there shedding crocodile tears. You'd think she's the only person in the world with a fiancé or passed the damn MCAT! I was trying to sleep. Does anyone think about me?!"

Forgetting about her always-imminent stroke, Anne responds with a slap to Rachel's face. Rachel stumbles onto her mother's bed then falls off the other side, her legs and arms up in the air, like a roach right before it dies.

The image is funny to Anne, but she does not care to laugh. She knows this night will reach her ex-husband's ears by morning – never as it played out. It will be that Anne's useless youngest daughter paraded herself naked, like the prostitute all suspect her to be, before an audience of a hundred thousand.

"This night, Rachel Ify Ofordilli, does not belong to you," Anne pronounces. She cannot recall how she went wrong with this child. "This night belongs to your sister. I had hoped you would put aside your jealousy to stand by her."

Anne walks out the door as Rachel shakily gets to her feet. "Jealous?" Rachel mumbles to no one in particular. "What does she have for me to be jealous about? I'm going to be the famous one. It's my name that'll be remembered for all eternity."

The sentiment sounds hollow, just like the emptiness in her heart. I should go pee, Rachel thinks at long last. Instead, she stands there unmoving, since she never needed to pee in the first place.

BO

Rachel is sitting in a hair salon, one of the many that litter the 125th Street shopping strip. The African girl working on her braids is almost done. This time around, the style is longer than Rachel usually wears her hair, stopping in the middle of her back. Rachel consented to the long braids because Bo specifically requested it for his birthday today. She will be seeing him in a little while for a celebration.

The African girl nears the end of her life story which Rachel prompted her to tell, and which she listened to attentively throughout its telling. Rachel would never consider herself a plagiarist of other people's lives. Instead, she considers her interest and constant query of Africans and their life stories a form of research for her own storylines.

" … I had to run away, Rachel," the African girl is saying. "I took my baby and got into a shelter. That was the scariest night of my life, but what else could I do? That man would have finally killed me if I stayed."

"What did your people say?" asks Rachel.

"His family and my family – no one is speaking to me. I'm not supposed to leave my husband! Do I care? I love my life and my freedom more than I love someone beating me!"

"I would've cut off his dick before I left," Rachel offers.

The girl breaks into peals of laughter, giving Rachel a high-five.

"You're crazy enough to do it too," the African girl laughs. "You're so lucky, Rachel, you never have to know what we African women go through in this country. You were born here. No man would ever treat you like that."

"Just wait and see. I'll take you away from here when my book hits the *New York Times* bestseller list."

"You and your dreams!"

"Girl, don't make me burst into my dream song!"

The African girl is laughing for she is familiar with Rachel's "dream" song, rendered any time anyone mentions the word "dream" to her.

"In fact, I think I will!" Rachel opens her mouth wide and begins screaming the *Mother Abbess'* song *Climb Every Mountain* – from *The Sound of Music* – hands down, Rachel's favorite musical of all time.

"*... climb every mountain ... ford every stream ....*" This is the part in the movie where the *Mother Abbess* is encouraging a depressed *Maria*, the governess, to return to her employer *Captain Von Trapp*, to see if what *Maria* is feeling for the man is genuine love. The *Abbess* chides the young and beautiful *Maria* that she cannot remain in seclusion in the convent, hiding from her troubles. She must face them!

"*... follow every rainbow ...,*" Rachel nears the end of the song. "*... till you find your .... dreeeeeeeeeeam!*"

The African hair braiders, used to her presence at the salon – Rachel gets her hair done every three months – shake their heads in amusement, some of them anyway. Others feel she's annoying – a typical American who cares nothing for other people's peace save her own amusement.

The other customers do not know what to make of Rachel as she and the African girl fall over each other in sidesplitting laughter.

"Girl, you make my day every time you come here!"

"If you don't have dreams, girl, you have nothing!"

"True, true, true," the African girl says, becoming subdued. "I just want my son to be a good man and make something of himself."

"He will, with a mother like you? I will sponsor your green card too and you will marry a white man!"

"Ah! No white man, please. You don't watch TruTV! All these white guys kill their wives for life insurance!" The two giggle uncontrollably.

After getting her hair braided, Rachel spends the rest of her afternoon shopping for Bo. She buys him – as usual – lots of underwear, socks, undershirts and comfortable jeans because Bo rarely thinks to purchase these items for himself. The man could go a whole year without changing underwear! Fortunately, Rachel would never allow it.

In honor of his birthday, she also buys him a pair of Timberland boots. She ignores the fact Bo hardly ever wears the many expensive boots or Nike shoes she's bought for him over the 15 months she's known him. He prefers to loaf around in flip-flops – year round!

Bo's favorite flip-flops lie at the foot of the queen-sized bed he and Rachel now lie upon. A soft jazz tune fills the room and Bo's senses as Rachel slides down on top of him. She does not like him wearing a condom, which almost always causes him nervous tension. The music always helps to calm his nerves. She rocks away slowly on top of him, while he steadies her with his hands, gripping firmly her full cup of breasts.

The braids he wanted spill over his face, emanating a strong smell of acrid cinnamon. She leans towards him, kissing him long and luxuriously, then showers his face and torso with lingering kisses, light as a butterfly's landing.

He feels himself about to blow. Sensing this and not ready for him to be done, Rachel stops, withdrawing him from her. He finds it uncanny how she's always able to know. She does not allow him to come inside her – not so much for fear of planting his seed. She is religious about staying on the pill. She prefers him to pour himself all over her breasts, for her to spread on like coco butter lotion. She is weird, the girl. But he loves her mainly because she loves to fuck.

As he regains himself, he watches her atop him – she manipulates her clit with one hand, while the other fondles her nipples. She is gone, he can see, reduced senseless by pleasure. Her head is arched back, her mouth partly open as she lets out a series of moans that cause the heat between his legs to rise again.

He gently flips her over so that he is on top. She spreads her legs as far apart as they can go, revealing a nectar framed by neatly shaved pubic hair in the form of a triangle. His hand circles her small waist, as he pulls her crotch closer towards him. The look in her eyes tells him to come right in, so he does, entering her warmth with ease. Her hand works her clit furiously as he pumps himself into a feverish pitch.

She climaxes first, moaning and shivering beneath him – driving him nuts with carnal pleasure. He couldn't stop now even if he wanted to. Sensing him about to flow for real this time, she brings him out herself and pulls his whole body to straddle her torso. Because she works the tip of his penis with fast-motion friction, Bo spills himself all over her chest. She spreads his cum all over her breasts, loving the feel of the stickiness on her nipples.

As he always does, Bo is suddenly overcome by cold sweat. He shivers uncontrollably, wishing to be held but not wanting to say it. There is no need. Rachel grabs him and pulls him against her ample, now sticky, bosom. She clutches him to her warmth and smell, stroking gently his back and the back of his head. He loves this moment more than life. He fucks her, really, for this after-love repose. In her arms, he feels 5-years old all over again – a time when he had no fears, no worries, and the feeling of being loved pervaded everything.

The sound of Fela Kuti's *Lady* shrieks in Bo's bedroom. He lounges on the bed while Rachel bounces about naked, in rhythm with the Afro pop beat pounding from the speakers. It's remarkable to him her agility and flexibility. She spins, prances and gyrates in movements expected of a seasoned Alvin Ailey dancer. She dances for him, he knows, her after-love routine. He won't lie, he enjoys seeing her bouncing boobs and rippling behind.

The song's conclusion coincides nicely with her final twirl. She stands frozen – in a funky pose he could probably duplicate on canvas – drenched in sweat, her heavy breasts rising up and down. She waits for his applause. He does not disappoint, hooting and hollering loudly as he knows she likes.

She turns off the CD player and jumps on top of the bed, lying on her tummy, her bountiful bums waiting for petting. Again he does not disappoint. He loses himself in the softness of her flesh against his palm, as she goes on and on about *Beatrice*, the character in the story he knows she's outlining in her head, but has not yet begun to write. Bo half listens, desiring only to gain inspiration from stroking her ass, as if rubbing the bottle for the genie to appear and grant him his wish.

Bo Dempsey is an accomplished painter in the central Harlem community where he has lived all his life. His pieces hang in the homes of notable hip hop celebrities, in the homes of well-to-do upper echelon black denizens, in the State Capitol, and in numerous lobbies and hallways of local black businesses in Harlem. Still, Bo feels failure lurking round every corner of his nightmares. It is only a matter of time, he is certain, before he is found out to be the "poser" he believes he is at his core.

Running his hands round and round Rachel's perfect rump soothes his tortured soul, makes him forget the blank canvas in the studio – but only for a little while. Like a vulture circling dead venison, his mind returns to the problem at hand. He is stuck on the painting – writers have writers' block; painters painters' block, he figures.

The piece would be the center of the upcoming show. He is planning 25 pieces, and none have been created. He is not so much worried about his overall lack of productivity as he is about the first piece. The first piece almost always ushers forth a flood of images that will complete the remaining 24 pieces one right after the other.

Bo has never let Indira down – Indira, his manager, agent and benefactor. Her money keeps him fed, her belief in his work keeps him alive. In return, he never wants to disappoint her. Of late though – she will not say it – she too is growing anxious. Only two and a half months left before the opening of the show, it has never happened that he is stuck on the first piece. By this time, with previous shows, he would have already completed half the required pieces.

"I'm going to pattern the governor after Eliot Spitzer," Rachel is saying, flipping herself onto her back, parting her legs a bit. He knows the code – she wants him to go down on her. He resists, not in the mood, other thoughts on his mind. So Rachel spurs on to talk about the wanton whore *Beatrice*.

"She'll bring him down! I'll make him married, with three kids or something, but he has to be flawed, so I guess he can be sleeping with the pageboys in secret. *Beatrice* will find all this out. She'll have to blackmail the guy, and if that fails she'll have to fuck him, I guess. Eventually, of course – cause this has to end happily for her – she'll rise to the top and eventually be Governor of New York State!"

"Why do all your heroines have to sleep their way to the top?" Bo quips. "Why can't you empower them? Let them use their brains or something." Bo does not mean the irritation in his voice. He is tired of hearing about the story of *Beatrice*, tentatively titled *Albany Ho.*

As Rachel tells it, *Beatrice* was molested by her stepfather from ages 9 to 16, at which point the character became pregnant with his baby. Unable to face the reality of what was happening right under her roof, *Beatrice's* mother kicked her out, rather than accept the fact that her husband of a dozen years got her daughter pregnant.

Beatrice hit the streets, became hooked on crack and had her baby in a dumpster one cold November day. She managed to leave the baby at a nearby fire station in the dead of night, but her son did not survive. He died at the local hospital, his 4-pound body ravaged by drug withdrawal and hypothermia.

Beatrice wept as she read the front-page news of his death two days later. His death marked a turning point in her life. She vowed from then on to clean herself up and go back to school. She quit the drugs but continued to trick her body. How else was she to pay for her room and all the fine accessories she loved to drape on her body?

In this way, *Beatrice* found herself in the bed of the assistant to the Councilman serving Lower Manhattan District Court. She moved from the assistant to the Councilman himself. She was just 19 and by that time had forgotten all about going back to school. In no time at all, *Beatrice* stepped right over the Councilman to her next political conquest, and in this way, her path takes her to the Governor, via the Mayor.

Bo is tired of Rachel talking. It is an endless stream of chatter about *Beatrice's* bedroom antics. At 19, there was no sexual position *Beatrice* had not engaged in, no sex toy she had not manipulated, no sexual fantasy she did not star in.

Rachel's unabashed graphic sexual details often cause Bo to blush. He is not blushing now and he has heard enough. What he wants is some quiet time so he can think about the naked canvas.

"Oh where have you been, sweetheart?" Rachel laughs with eagerness. "Readers are not interested in brains. They want sex! It's all about when the woman takes off her clothes, and it better be before page six!"

It doesn't appear she's prepared to stop talking so Bo gets off the bed. He slides his feet into his worn and paint-smattered flip-flops at the foot of the bed. He looks funny to Rachel, a short and balding 44-year-old – correction, 45-years today – black man who hates clothes. Bo prefers to walk around in full-monty, wearing only flip-flops.

He heads now into his studio to contemplate what color paint to throw on the canvas. Rachel runs after him, covering her body with her robe on the bed, kept in his loft apartment for just this purpose. She senses his irritation and naturally wants to make him feel better. All her talk of *Beatrice*, really, was to get his mind off the upcoming show. She does not understand why he is so worried. He has never disappointed himself or that bitch Indira.

Rachel exits the bedroom to find Bo staring at a huge white canvas hanging on the wall. He stares at the canvas intensely as if willing it to show an image to him.

"Boo?" she calls quietly from behind him.

"Bo," he corrects her with a smile. He is fond of her particular bastardization of the name his mama gave him. She calls him *Boo* when she wants him to smile. He sighs as she circles her arms around him.

"It'll be okay, you'll see." Her voice is tender. "You'll knock 'em dead like you always do."

He sighs again, leaning his head back, to rest atop her head. He wishes he could have her same lightheartedness about the future. He loves her because she is a child. At times though, that same childishness he finds overly simple and annoying.

She is the reason he is not working, if truth must be told – at least, that's what Indira posited. The child is a distraction, the other said. Does he dare say to her now what Indira had suggested? He does not like to see Rachel upset. It disturbs him further and leaves him jittery. Still, with only eleven weeks to go, he has to admit maybe Indira is right this time around.

Bo faces Rachel, kisses her deeply, then holds her face between his hands.

"Dearest," he begins tenderly.

"Yes, my love," she answers expectantly.

"I need to work."

"And I am here to make sure you do. Do you need to fuck me again for inspiration?" She's dead serious.

He stares into the dark pools of her eyes. Really – she is the devil, he concludes. He makes his way to his desk, littered with sketches of images that could possess the blank canvas. He hates staring at the drawings for he knows none is quite right.

"I've had enough … celebration … for the day," he finally says.

"I'm not so sure I have. We'll go again after you get some rest."

This is not what he wants to hear. He seizes her forearms tight, a little too tight. "I want you to do me a favor," his voice is tense but firm.

"You're hurting me, Boo."

He lets her go immediately. "Sorry."

"What is it then?" She asks, staring at the imprint of his hands on her arms.

"I need you to stop coming around for some time." He watches her closely.

"Oh?" Rachel's body tenses, Bo's too. He does not like the way the question comes out, full of mistrust. She is very good, he thinks secretly.

"Indira's idea, I guess?"

He sighs. "Please, let's leave her out of this." He could cut the air with her contained anger. He expects her to lash out. He would have to grip her arms again. She surprises him when she visibly relaxes.

"For how long?"

Sensing a trap, he answers cautiously. "Three, four weeks? I should have the centerpiece done by then. The rest will be a cinch. I'll call you when I need you."

"You say that as if I'm your tramp for hire."

"Not you," he says with a smile. "When I give you money though, you should surprise me and give it back."

"Why would I do that, Boo? I deserve it! You're taking care of me now, yeah. But after I become a world famous writer, I'll take care of you, free you from the bitch!"

"I wish you'd stop calling her that, Ify." He likes to call her by her African middle name. She hates it.

"Rachel," she corrects.

"She's responsible for my success."

"You're responsible for your success!"

He stares at her sadly. If only her words meant something to him. He catches her staring at him intently. Her dark eyes are unreadable. "Do you love me, Boo?"

"Of course I do," he croons, easing into their familiar game. He pulls her between his legs. He notes his penis is getting hard again. She notes it too and melts.

"I would do anything for you – happy birthday." She holds him tight as she climbs on top of his hardened shaft. Her robe cascades to the floor. She goes to task, humping up and down on his lap.

Bo finds his eyes drawn to the empty canvas on the wall, giving him a reproachful look. He closes his eyes quickly, to lose himself to the pleasure filling his senses.

INDIRA

Rachel and Jada Appleton, her best friend, also 24, sit atop the "black top" – the name they've dubbed the giant rock at Marcus Garvey Park in west Harlem. The rock affords the best view of 120th Street and 5th Avenue, as far as the eye can see. It is a fatal drop should one hurl oneself off it.

Jada is a personal banker at a local bank only a few blocks from the park. They meet up for lunch on Mondays and Wednesdays. On Fridays, Rachel arrives at the bank right before Jada gets off. Thereafter, it's shopping along 125th Street, and afterwards, dinner and then movies at Magic Johnson Theater – a veritable girls' night out.

The day is Wednesday and the park shows signs that spring is holding on – here it is late June and the trees are in full bloom, the air is cool and breezy, the sun high and bright. Instead of admiring the weather and nature though, the girls are busy scrutinizing the note and a key on Rachel's lap.

"Why would he write a letter asking you to come over tonight?" Jada queries, always full of suspicion where Bo is concerned. She thinks he's only using Rachel. "He could've just called," she persists.

"Well, I called him, you know – to find out how much he was missing me, but he's blocked my number."

"Un-fucking-believable! Why do you tolerate being treated like shit?!"

"Oh, you don't understand, Jada, he does that when he needs to work, it's all part of the mystique. He is such a romantic!" thrills Rachel, acting like a child.

"Brooding artist more like it. Only a self-centered egomaniac full of himself would ask his bitch of a year and a half to come around whenever he feels like fucking!"

Rachel gives Jada a dangerous look.

"Don't be looking at me like that – you know you his bitch, blocking your number like you some ho! What if there was an emergency or something and you needed his help or some shit?"

"I'd call you."

"Well for sure, you know I got your back. But seriously, Ray-Ray, that man don't treat you right! He doesn't take you anywhere, you've never met his friends, his family. Hell, he hasn't even met your mama!"

"My mama don't need to know nothing about my personals."

"Whatever. That man's just using you."

"More like me using him. I totally wear him out!"

"I know that! Why don't you go out with someone your age, the guy's 50!"

"Girl, quit it. He's forty-five! Anyway, I love men, not boys!"

"You better go see somebody about your daddy issues."

"My daddy can kiss my ass!"

"Uh-huh. You don't think it strange Bo made a copy of his key for you? You've only been nagging him about it since you met!"

"So I finally wore him down on that too," Rachel cackles good-naturedly, putting the key and the note in her purse. Her winsome face soon takes on an anxious look, which Jada notes immediately.

"It's still too soon."

"It's almost two months, Jada. I should be bombarded with publishers' letters wanting a contract with me, right? I got to prove everybody wrong – my mama, my sister, her stupid fiancé doctor boyfriend. I wanna buy my mama the house she's been wanting since we were kids."

"Girl, you don't write for nobody but yourself, so quit the melodrama." The talk is tough, but does little to cheer Rachel up.

Jada sighs at long last, losing her appetite. "See, this is why I gave up writing. My heart can't take all this bullshit."

"It's a good story, right? Someone will want to publish it, right?"

"Damn straight it's a great story! On the level of Jane Austen!"

"Jane Austen?! That was you! I don't know what a girl born and raised in Jamaica, Queens wanna be writing English literature for. That's why you quit! What you shouda done is write about your backyard – simple, urban breezy shit!"

"So *Yasmin* the Sudanese sex slave who became a Harlem madam that you sent off to publishers, you telling me you know all about being a hooker, and being from the Sudan for that matter?"

"Girl, please – I patterned her after Oluchi the Nigerian super model. The rest is imagination."

"Girl, your imagination be working overtime!"

They burst into laughter again, their merry voices ringing throughout the park.

Rachel waits patiently as Aminata, behind the counter, rings up the half-dozen urban books Rachel is buying. Aminata is from Senegal, and chats animatedly while using a calculator to add up the sale.

"... he's going against the religion, Rachel. The Prophet said a man should spend equal time with each of his wives," the girl complains.

"But she's not his wife!" Rachel shouts in disbelief. "She's his mistress!" She cannot believe what she is hearing. She finds her temperature rising, as it always does whenever she hears of maltreatment of African women at the hands of their African men.

"What can I do?" Aminata sighs.

"Leave him!"

"Leave him?!" It's now Aminata's turn to sound incredulous. "If I do, my mother will never show her face again in the marketplace in Dakar! Everybody will say her daughter went to America to shame her husband!"

Rachel can only blink. The great divide that separates her from women like Aminata has never seemed so wide.

"All I'm asking is for him to spend three days with me and three with her," Aminata reasons. "He can take the seventh to rest!"

Rachel takes a deep breath before she answers. "I got to tell you, Aminata," Rachel says, shaking her head. "I'm so happy to be raised in this country. I would leave his cheating ass flat if it were me, and then I'd deal with her!"

"I believe you too!" the girl says, laughing. She is finally done tallying the total of the books. She relates the amount to Rachel who roots for money in her purse.

"How long will it take you to finish these books, Rachel?"

"I'll be back in three days," Rachel declares, handing Aminata double the amount quoted – from the money Bo doles out to her regularly.

"I wish I had the money and the time to sit around reading trashy books. It's work, work, work around here and then home to a cheating man."

"What you got to do is find yourself another man, one who will treat you good and be honored to lavish you with his hard earned money!"

"You are too much, Rachel." Aminata laughs. She goes to give Rachel back the change. Rachel waves her off.

"Please, Ami, keep it. Treat yourself to something nice today."

Rachel exits the store with her books. Aminata waves goodbye, then puts the healthy tip in her bra.

Sitting at her usual spot in the Starbucks on 125th Street and Lenox, Rachel reads over and over again, the same page of the new novel she's been reading for the last hour. She feels like going over to Bo's house immediately, but he'd written in the note she's to come over for dinner at 7PM. She knows him enough to know he is strict with time. It's only 5:30 now.

She saw him exactly one week ago, when he asked her not to come around for a while so he could get some painting done. She is thrilled he missed her that much. And what's this about cooking? He hardly ever cooks. She would cook for him, but he is a strict vegan – Rachel's cooking begins and ends with meat. It's Indira who sees to it Bo's fridge and cupboards are always stocked with the things he can eat.

The thought of Indira causes a sharp pain in Rachel's side. She gets to her feet, to the counter to order the rice krispies blocks she's addicted to. She could put three of those things away in one sitting. The guy who serves her fixes his eyes on her breasts instead of on her order. She smiles at him good-naturedly. She is used to men reacting to her in this manner and she enjoys it.

"You can look but you can't touch," she says, sing-songy as the guy gives her the order. Embarrassed, he looks away. Rachel takes her wafer and sashays back to her seat, swishing her bum in a way she knows he is watching.

Her purse and books hit the ground as Rachel stands dumbfounded, right at the entrance of Bo's studio, the key with which she let herself in lies limp in her hand. The blank canvas no longer hangs on the wall. It's now spread on the floor, with Bo and Indira making love upon it. The same jazz ensemble Rachel and Bo made love to a week before fills the space, the reason the frolicking couple did not hear the key at the latch.

Indira is the first to notice Rachel, and why not? She had sent the girl the key and the letter, forging Bo's handwriting down to dotting the *i*'s and crossing the *t*'s. The girl never disappoints, Indira thinks, showing up exactly as instructed.

Indira is 49-years old, though she looks 26. She is one-quarter Caucasian, one-quarter black, one-quarter Latina and one-quarter Filipino. She is, therefore, stunning to look at – with caramel skin, her body a work of fine muscle tones she maintains at her daily pilates class. As a result, she is very slim, with a little girl's buttocks and breasts. Her long dark hair, speckled with gold highlight, flows down to the middle of her back.

She pulls the hair now, around her neck, down her shoulder, to flow over her left breast. Because she is no longer involved in their lovemaking, Bo looks to see what she's looking at. Seeing Rachel at the door, a frozen image of wide eyes and open mouth, his dick goes limp inside Indira and he withdraws himself immediately.

Rachel has only one second to note he is not wearing a condom, and the second second to fly clear across the room. She does not know when her hand got round Indira's throat, or when she used that hand to lift the woman off Bo. The only thing she's intent on doing is preventing Indira from taking another breath.

Indira is caught off guard, so much so she cannot let out the scream trying to break from her lungs. She feels the girl's hand against her esophagus, marvels at the vice grip choke. Survival instinct prompts her to scratch at Rachel's hand round her neck. But her years of throwing money at a personal trainer apparently did not include increased body strength in case of strangulation.

Rachel maintains her hold of Indira's bird-like neck. It does not matter to her that Indira stands 5'10" to her 5'9" frame. She does not even feel Indira's claws peeling skin off her forearm. She is doing nothing more to Indira, save choking her to death.

Indira, on the other hand, is a mass of movement as she tries, with very little success, to break Rachel's hold. As the air about her thins, and her peripheral vision dims, Indira has a moment of clarity to think – Bo, help me!

Bo has made no move because the image of Rachel killing Indira leaves him breathless. The girl is a horror to behold. He is stunned to see Rachel's dark eyes and terse lips break into mirth as she watches Indira's eyes roll to the back of her head.

The idea for his centerpiece suddenly crashes into Bo. He will call the painting, *The Death of Yetunde* – it will be the image of an African medusa-type figure wielding a jagged dagger made of steel. The same look in Rachel's eyes will fill his character's eyes as she uses the dagger to pierce the neck of *Yetunde*, the man who has betrayed her in love. Blood will spout from the fatal wound and will form a red river upon which the dueling couple will stand.

The image in his mind and that's transpiring in his loft is so riveting, Bo's limp penis fills with blood and he ejaculates – at the same time that Indira slowly crumbles to her knees because Rachel holds fast with both hands now. Bo knows he is witnessing a potential homicide, but the animal in him is on the verge of a second ejaculation and the painter in him desires to see how the story will end, how the image will be framed on the very blank canvas Rachel grips Indira atop.

Fortunately, the animal and the painter recede and the businessman emerge. If Indira dies, his career is done. Bo jumps into the fray. At first, he goes for Rachel's hand, attempting to loosen it as did Indira – an exercise in futility. He is surprised to find he cannot, the child is that strong. He next takes the girl by the neck, a chokehold really. He pulls Rachel back, applying enough pressure to her neck to withhold the very breath she is denying Indira. Rachel staggers back and finally lets go.

Indira's whole body hits the floor. She gulps air, though painfully, into her nearly collapsed throat. She back-peddles at the same time, away from the now fighting duo. She watches in terror as Rachel bites down on Bo's arm around her neck. Bo yelps and continues to scream because Rachel does not let go. He picks her up and body-slams her on the ground. Only then does she let him go.

The skin on his arm where she bit down is broken and ringed with blood. He immediately worries about tetanus. He cannot recall if he's had one in the last ten years. He doesn't have time to think it through because Rachel reaches for Indira again, crawling on the floor towards the older woman's legs.

Indira kicks Rachel's arms and face, at the same time Bo grabs Rachel's feet and pulls her towards him. Indira grabs one of two 5-pound barbells located close by. She gets to her feet shakily, a fighting stance, wielding the barbell for dear life.

"Touch me again, motherfucka," she barks at Rachel. "And I will bash your fucking head in! Come at me again, bitch!"

"Let me go, Boo," Rachel hisses, all thrashing arms and legs. "She calling me, so I got to go to her!"

"Stop it, Ify!"

Rachel whirls around and slaps Bo. "Goddamn it, it's Rachel! Fucking Rachel!"

"Get out of my house right now!" Bo's face stings from her slap. He has had enough, he's got his image and needs to get to work at once. Images for the other 24 pieces fly past his mind's eyes, like billboards on the highway. He pulls and pushes Rachel towards the door. "I told you not to come here till I call you. Now get out!!"

"Me?! Why I got to leave?" The pain in Rachel's heart bursts out, and she breaks down. "I am the girlfriend!" she screams at Bo in tears, though it's apparent to her now she wasn't even that. "She is the manager, agent, benefactor, the bitch! She is the bitch, remember? You don't mix that up, Boo. Now, you ask her to leave so we can get to the bottom of this here nonsense. Tell her to leave now!"

"You're standing in my space, little girl!" Indira spits out. "Every inch of this square footage I pay for!"

"Shut your damn mouth, Indira!" Bo shouts. What he wants is for both of them to shut up and get out so he can get to work.

Indira ignores Bo as she continues to address Rachel. "The money he keeps you with, he takes out of the account I keep him with!

You relieve stress for him, baby, nothing more. I tolerate you because I deny him nothing!"

"I told you she wanted you, Boo!" Rachel does not want to cry, not in front of this woman. But she can't help it. Her heart is breaking, not because she caught Bo cheating – she has long suspected they were sleeping together, a charge he vehemently denied whenever she confronted him about it.

Rachel is heartbroken because she did not see this night coming. The writer in her expects to anticipate drama, even the ones transpiring in her life. She is mostly heartbroken because she knows – the way she had known her parents' marriage was falling apart long before they told her – she knows that at the end of it all, it is she who will lose … again.

Her tears fall freely as she attempts to forestall the inevitable. "Didn't I tell you, Boo? She sent me the letter!"

"What letter?" Bo is mildly intrigued as he struggles to hold onto images fleeting past his mind's eyes.

"The one asking me to come here tonight, at exactly this time. She made the key too, it's clear now. I got them in the mail two days ago."

"You should have called."

"You blocked my number!"

"Oh."

"Are we done now?" Indira interrupts, "Can she go now so we can continue where we left off? I didn't get off yet!"

Rachel makes for Indira again, but Bo holds her fast.

"She set this whole thing up. Can't you see that, Boo, she wants you all to herself!"

"I've always had him, you fucking cunt!" Indira shouts, beside herself with fury. "I was here before you and will be here long after you're gone. Now … Boo … you ask her to leave!"

"Just stop it okay," Bo warns Rachel, trying to be authoritative. His voice falls flat because sympathy for Rachel breaks into his senses. Her tears are falling on his arm round her boobs. His face, against her braided hair, smells in the acrid cinnamon with which she greased her scalp – he recalls now, for his birthday.

She has been absolutely no fuss – except on the issue of Indira, she's a werewolf. Who could blame her? Other than that, the child has always done whatever he has asked of her. Feeling Rachel's body against his, its curvy contours that he prefers to Indira's bony structure, he supposes he loves Rachel, though never more than the art. He loves nothing more than his art, not even Indira. He has sacrificed everything for it – family, children, a legitimate wife.

He has slept his way to the top, spending time with whoever will take him to the next level, sometimes with men. But no one has taken him farther than Indira, of course, the reason their "union" has lasted 15 years. Still, he tires of her and the way she ends his sidebar affairs whenever she feels the other women becoming a distraction, or he becoming attached. This done to Rachel tonight, he feels, is unwarranted.

"Ask her to leave!" Indira screams, bringing Bo out of his somber thoughts. He doesn't want to, yet knows he must. Undecided, he clutches Rachel closer, but it is she who makes a move. Rachel throws Bo off her, lifts herself to her full womanly height, and then strides towards the door.

“I’m HIV positive!” she declares to the room at large, then walks out the door.

Indira drops the dumbbell in horror. Bo proceeds to the canvas on the floor as if Rachel never spoke. He can at least get to work now.

“What, what did she say?!”

“She was lying, Indira, to fuck with you. Pay her no mind.”

“You didn’t practice safe … you didn’t use a condom with her?!”

“Like you, she doesn’t like it.”

“Oh God, oh God, oh God!” In a panic, Indira runs to the sink, runs the faucet and begins splashing cold water against her vagina.

Bo would be laughing at this image if he were watching her. As it is, he neither sees nor hears Indira, consumed as he is with sketching the image of *Yetunde,* the cheating lover, on the canvas that is blank no more.

ANNE & ADA

Completely dry-eyed, Rachel finds herself walking up and down 125th Street after she left Bo's loft. Bo lives on 131st Street and Lenox. Rachel got to 125th, headed west till she hit the Westside Highway. She wanted to cross it, to touch the river, but she deemed the dashing cars too dangerous. Therefore, she turned around and headed east.

Now, she is on the FDR Drive, another highway with dashing cars speeding by. This is her third time on the highway, having walked back to the Westside Highway twice already. She knows she will not attempt to touch the East River because the speeding cars, here also, scare her to death.

She about-faces again, intent on reaching the west side for the fourth time. She does not feel the ache weighing her feet down. She figures she will sleep well tonight. Sleeping well tonight will be necessary so she does not think or dream of Bo.

She does not see anything on 125th Street, having retreated to a corner of her mind where distractions are not permitted. She does not know what time it is, only that it is late. The only thing she is aware of is the tune in her head. She's been singing it over and over again, until her untrained voice became horse.

"Perhaps I had a wicked childhood ..." she begins the song again. She has *Maria von Trapp* and the *Captain* singing in the gazebo in her mind's eye – from *The Sound of Music*, of course. The couple is finally united and is declaring their love to one another.

"... Perhaps I had a miserable youth ...." Being a song that celebrates love, she knows the tune is inappropriate for the end of her love. She can't help it though, she finds the melody strangely soothing,

and strangely soothing in another way – she and *Maria* share the common bond of having had miserable childhoods!

"But somewhere in my wicked, miserable past ... there must have been a moment of truth ...." If truth must be told, Rachel does not really think of *Maria* or Bo as she sings the song. She thinks of her father: "... *For here you are, standing there, loving me ... Whether or not you should ...."*

Rachel remembers the movie as her father's favorite movie of all time. She has vague memories of lying on his stomach while he lay on the couch. They would sing their hearts out during each musical number, then be reduced to peels of laughter or tears, depending on what was happening on screen.

"... So somewhere in my youth or childhood ... I must have done something good ...." Rachel does not remember anything else about her father – not the bitter divorce, not her mother's relocation of her and her sister to a different apartment, not her frantic calls to her father to come get her until he changed his number and she could never find him. Rachel remembers none of those things. But the image of lying on her father's tummy and watching *The Sound of Music* remains her earliest and fondest memory.

"... Nothing comes from nothing ... Nothing ever could ... So somewhere in my youth or childhood ... I must have done something good...."

Rachel continues on, past the streetlights she does not see, past the crack head gyrating at the corner, past the wino begging for money. Her voice is totally gone, so she can only hum the song – beginning from the top all over again.

Anne stumbles into the kitchen to put the kettle on for tea. Filling the kettle with water from the sink, she begins to cry – doing it softly so neither Ada nor Paul in Rachel's bedroom can hear her. After she turns on the flame on the stove, she takes a seat at the breakfast nook, dabbing her teary eyes with Kleenex and occasionally placing a hand over her heart to feel its thumping beats. Harvard!

Anne cannot believe the boy was accepted there. The boy she thinks of is her ex-husband's last son. After she divorced Nathaniel, within the same year, he wed the very secretary he had cheated on Anne with.

Anne blames her bevy of friends for having left Nathaniel in the first place – they had encouraged her to do so, even though they remain in their own miserable marriages today. Anne conveniently forgets that in the seven years she was married to Nathaniel, he was a no-good son of a bitch who beat and berated her constantly, sometimes in front of their two daughters.

He lied through his teeth about everything and slept with every woman who parted her legs for him. In fact, he was with the secretary the last three years of their "marriage." Nathaniel and the secretary's first-born was born while Anne and Nathaniel were still technically married. For an African man, Nathaniel was particularly low.

Aaah … but I am an African woman, Anne thinks now. What sins in the hands of our husbands have African women not endured. She likes to think it is Mrs. Ofordilli Number Two, a white woman, who has to deal with all that now. But this is wishful thinking, Anne knows. According to the grapevine, the white woman transformed Nathaniel into a duty-bound husband who stays close to home, wife and children.

This phenomenon of abusive African men becoming loving and doting to their white wives and or mistresses is not unknown to Anne. She knows that the white woman is still the prized commodity upon which no sins must be visited. The African man, owing to his own sense of low self-worth, is so stunned he sneered a white woman, he immediately learns to toe the line.

A man who never saw the insides of his kitchen, suddenly helps out with dinner preparations and learns to wash dishes. A man who never knew which way the diaper fits round his kid's ass, suddenly knows which brands are best at preventing urine leaks. In Nathaniel's case, he learned all of that and a whole lot more. He learned to forget about Anne and his first-set of 100 percent black children.

Anne knows Nathaniel would never have shown his best side to her, even had they remained married for 100 years. Because they share the same culture, come from the same place, speak the same language, in short – are African together, he considered it a right given him by God to be a little god onto her. Her culture expected her to take it. America permitted her to flee.

Then came his second set of abuses. Child-support came intermittently because Nathaniel would quit work here and there to reduce what she and her children got. He unleashed the white wife upon her, and many screaming matches would they have on the phone – she citing her four children, Anne citing her two – before the number would be changed, and Anne would struggle to find it and the battle would begin anew. Her doctor cites those days as the beginning of the skyrocket climb of her blood pressure.

In the end, Anne tired of the other woman, the courts and the chase to garner Nathaniel's wages. For her health and sanity, she resolved to care for her girls on her own, and she did. She moved forward with her life, but found she could not leave Nathaniel or thoughts of him behind.

What always drags Anne down, what always causes her these very tears she's shedding is news of the achievements of Nathaniel's second set of 50 percent black children. The first son, now 21, being extremely talented in basketball, was quickly drafted to the NBA at age 18. Nat Jr. skipped college altogether and today plays for a professional team based in the south.

Anne will not utter the name of the team and prefers to think the boy does not exist at all. What no one knows, including her friends, is that she follows the boy's career, pays close attention to his statistics, his injuries, his salary negotiations and which model he's dating with the same rabid obsession that his fans do all over the world.

The boy made good and promptly installed his parents in the palace in Suffolk County, Long Island. Anne knows the house is a palace because one of her friends drove by it and snapped a digital photo, then emailed her the picture.

Anne could not open the attachment, of course, not being well versed in the use of computers. Ada had done it for her and together they stared at the impressive structure without saying a word. Anne eventually got off the computer to her room and laid on her bed for the rest of the afternoon. Ada decided on the spot to be a brain surgeon instead of the pediatrician she was preparing for.

The second son, 20-year old Brian, is at Yale studying drama. The boy wants to be an actor. Anne consoles herself with the knowledge that acting is as frivolous a career as wanting to be a great urban novelist, say. Freddy, the third son, was killed by a drunk driver two Januarys ago, as he crossed Jamaica Avenue in Queens, on his way to his baby-mama's house. He was just 17.

Although Anne sent a letter of condolence – she never got a thank you note in return – the boy did not count in her mind for he had no achievements for her to drool over. The boy had dropped out of high school, was known to regularly smoke dope and had impregnated his girlfriend at the age of 15. She would go on to give birth to a son.

That little boy, Imhotep, was abandoned by his mother right after Freddy's funeral and now lives with his grandparents in the big house in Long Island. Anne regrets Freddy's death for the specific reason that had he lived, he might have continued his life of uselessness.

Then there is N.G., short for *Nigeria*, Nathaniel's fourth and last son, the source of Anne's current imminent stroke fears. The 16-year old boy made up for Freddy's shortcomings. Brilliant straight out of the womb, the boy remained in Anne's radar for having won local and national spelling bees and science competitions.

The boy has even met the President of the United States when the President came to his school to read to them. A photo of N.G. at age 7 shaking the President's hand was on the front-page of every newspaper in New York City!

Anne will not lie, she has prayed the boy would equally be smashed on some cross street in Long Island, Queens or wherever. Had N.G. gone on to meet his maker, he never would have gotten into Harvard – at 16 no less – to study … what else, Constitutional Law.

Anne has heard through the grapevine, the boy's constant admiration for that piece of document. He has memorized the Constitution's entire content and can recite it word for word. His father and mother, Anne herself included, believe the boy will some day be

President of the United States. If her stroke does not happen before then, Anne has made a promise to God she would commit suicide at his inauguration.

Ada enters the kitchen then, interrupting Anne from her fatal thoughts. The image of her mother sitting weeping because of her ex-father – Ada likes calling him that – and her non-brothers – she likes referring to them as that – moves her to want to burst into tears herself.

Ada's whole purpose in life, she realized as soon as her parents' marriage collapsed, is to bring comfort to her mother. She is a doctor because it makes her mother happy. She is marrying a Nigerian Igbo man because it makes her mother very happy. That Paul is also a doctor is the icing on the cake. She and Paul will have how ever many children her mother requires to further make her happy. This last bit Paul does not know about, but no matter – Paul would do anything for Ada – unlike her ex-father for her mother and unlike Rachel for their mother.

Rachel has been the bane of both Anne and Ada's existence – that her mother spoiled her sister rotten as she compensated for the lost parent is not a charge Ada would ever make known to Anne. She understood her mother's desire to make everything right for Rachel. Rachel had been in love with their father. His departure was a pain Ada is not sure Rachel has ever overcome. But enough is enough, Ada thinks, as she places her hands tenderly on her mother's shoulder. It ends tonight. Ada sighs with relief and gratitude that her mother has finally seen the light.

"Everything is ready, mommy," Ada says to Anne.

"The lock?"

"Paul finished changing it just now."

"Her things?"

"All packed, he is taking them outside the door."

"Alright, my darling. Let's have some tea."

Ada gets up. They will be drinking tea while they wait for Rachel to return home.

Rachel exits the elevator, her feet weighing a ton from her six hours of walking along 125th Street. She roots for her keys with shaking hands. This irritates her, for she thought she'd banished Bo and the bitch from her mind. Bo and the Bitch – catchy, she thinks. She'll be sure to write an entire story round that title.

She rounds the corner in the hallway and stops dead in her tracks. Lining the wall against the hall leading to her door are trash bags and suitcases stacked neatly. Curious, she arrives to the bags. The suitcases – two – belong to her. She knows them from her trips to Africa way back when. But what are they doing out here, she thinks, confused. And what's in the bags?

She looks through the bags. Is stunned to find pieces of her clothing within all. There are other knick-knacks – her books, toiletries, etc. The reality of what is happening escapes her for a moment and she stares at her things with a stupid expression.

Since the key is already in her hand, she inserts it into the keyhole, and marvels that her hand is still trembling – not because of Bo and the bitch. Something else. She doesn't have time to figure it out for the key does not fit in the hole. She notes immediately the lock is shiny and golden. She's certain something about it is different – it's a little too shiny, spanking new shiny.

A new thought lands in her head. In disbelief, she tries the key again, and again it does not fit. Were it not for her clothes in the bags, she would be led to believe she's on the wrong floor, at the wrong door.

“Hey!” Rachel screams, terror in her eyes. She is reminded of when she, Anne and Ada moved to this apartment. Of the first night she spent in her bed and woke up screaming because her father was not in the house. She does not know why the fear she feels now should be the same.

“Mommy! There’s something wrong with the key … the key won’t …”

She is interrupted when she hears the bolt turned from behind the door. She takes an involuntary step back, her chest rising and falling.

Anne looks through the chain link at her lastborn. The door is cracked, but she leaves the chain connected. She does not want a scene, but knows it’s inevitable.

“Open the door, mommy,” Rachel whispers, her little girl’s eyes piercingly black. It’s been a long time since Anne has seen this look in her daughter’s eyes. There were years of sleepless nights, cooing the child to sleep in a new apartment. Her eyes then were filled with the same fear and uncertainly as Anne sees now. All she wants to do is let her child in. She knows she cannot.

“The lock is changed, baby.”

“Why? What was wrong with the old one?”

Anne gulps down the lump in her throat. “You cannot come in.”

“Why not, mama?”

“You have to go, Rachel.”

“Go where? Let me in.”

“I did this … so now I will end it.”

Her mother’s African accent is so thick, Rachel bursts out laughing, a nervous reaction, really.

“End it,” she mimics Anne. “End what?”

Anne is suddenly pulled away from the door. Ada takes her place.

"Your mother is tired of taking care of your ass, that's what she has to end!"

Rachel regards her sister coolly, while inside the house, both Paul and Anne stand around nervously. Paul does not want to be here at all, he is a doctor, not a landlord. But he dared not allow Ada to be here alone. Rachel is unpredictable, he knows. He has broken countless physical fights between the two, the reason the door is chained. If the door does not hold, he is prepared to dial 911.

As expected, Rachel does Rachel. With lightening speed, she reaches for her sister's face, a halo through the chain. Anticipating this very move, Ada slams the door against Rachel's hand. Rachel yelps, withdrawing her hand immediately.

"I don't need this shit!" Rachel spouts. She lifts a foot to bang the door, but is stunned at how heavy her foot feels. She knows better than to bang the door with it. Instead – she slams her fists against the shut door. "I don't need this shit right now! I need to get some sleep! You let me into my motherfucking home, Ada!"

"Whose home?!" Ada retorts from behind the door. "You don't contribute to anything here, you don't pay rent, not food, not gas, not electric. All you do is hang around 125th Street, with no-good thugs, then you come home whenever you want and sleep your ass off. Aren't you ashamed of yourself, Ms. Columbia University dropout!"

"Open the door and say that to my face!"

Ada yanks the door open a crack. She's not stupid, she leaves the chain link connected. "Columbia University damn dropout!" she repeats.

"Remove the chain, missy, come out here and talk to me!"

Ada knows better than to do this. She sees murder in her little sister's eyes. Ada was never a fighter. When they were younger, it was Rachel who beat the shit out of the neighborhood tough girls and boys who bullied Ada. Somewhere along the way though, Rachel turned on Ada and became the bully.

"Carry your things and go, Rachel!"

"You go! You don't live here, you motherfucking-ass cunt!"

It's Paul's turn at the door. He pulls Ada away and takes her place. Pointing his finger through the chain, he admonishes Rachel.

"Do not say such things to my wife!"

"Remove that finger from my face," Rachel hisses, "or I'm going to bite it off!"

"You are cuckoo!"

"You've been warned," Rachel deadpans. She is tired and her voice is ebbing in and out again. She tells herself to take it easy. The last thing she wants to do is burst into tears right here. "Now, be a good boy and bring back the wife."

"Go and fuck yourself, Rachel." Ada says as her face appears beside Paul's. "You don't talk to him like that!"

Neighbors have now ushered out of their apartments, or are peeking from their own cracked doors. The screaming matches between the sisters, and sometimes their mother, are legendary. They are just in time to see Rachel go for her sister's face again – a mistake. Paul receives the thrust hand through the door. He yanks Rachel forward, slamming her against the door, then he throws her back. Rachel staggers back and falls.

"Who do you think you're dealing with?!" The man is furious. He takes the link off the door, against Ada's wishes, and throws the door wide open. Paul stands in front of the door as if he owns the joint.

"Come at me again and I will show you my name is Doctor Paul Ike!" He is egged on by Ada who claps and cheers behind him.

"I don't know what the big deal is," he continues, fawning for Ada who places her hands on his shoulders. "Nobody stays where they are not wanted! We are tired of you!"

Rachel gets back to her feet, moving in the same manner a grandma would. She sways back and forth, looking at her soon-to-be brother-in-law and her sister.

"That's right," adds Ada. "Your father got tired of you real quick too," she continues wicked. "That's why he rejected your ass a long time ago!"

Rachel stops swaying, stung by the remark. She does not recognize her sister there at the door. For her closeness to their mother, Rachel loathes Ada. In their mother's eyes, Ada can do no wrong, not that Ada ever has.

A long time ago, when they were girls, Ada wanted to be a sculptor. As little girls, they did not know what the word was, all they knew was that Ada used her penknife to carve intricate figurines out of little chunks of wood she picked up all over the place. Rachel adored these figurines and worshipped her older sister.

The first stories Rachel made up involved these figures. They were her first characters. The more stories she made up, the more characters Ada completed. They lined the figures up in their room, grouped according to the stories that involved them.

The girls talked about being famous – Rachel as a writer, and Ada as the person who chipped wood. They still did not know the name of what Ada would be. Their fame would make their father sorry, and he would come back so that they would all live happily ever after. At least, that's the way it would happen in the story Rachel told.

Ada did not like that ending too much – preferring that Nathaniel should take his own life, but not before killing the white woman and her four bastard children. It wasn't often that Ada contributed to the stories. To keep her sister happy, Rachel acquiesced to the tragic ending, although reluctantly for the thought of her father dead disturbed Rachel more than she would admit. Ada cheered the revised end and immediately chipped off the appropriate figurine representations.

Not understanding what the figures in her children's room were all about, but feeling threatened by their creativity, Anne always tossed these woodcarvings in the garbage. She had higher hopes for her daughters – Ada would be a doctor, eventually a renowned brain surgeon; Rachel would be a lawyer, eventually New York State District Attorney or Judge, and then of course, be a sitting judge in the Supreme Court.

Rachel ignored these, her mother's musings – understanding them to have nothing to do with the life she and her sister dreamed for themselves. Ada, on the other hand, dutifully listened. It wasn't long before her wood creations dwindled, even as Rachel's story output increased.

Ada began to spend more and more time following their mother around and less time listening to Rachel's stories. In time, she ceased hanging out with Rachel altogether, ceased chipping wood and retired the penknife forever. Ada became someone Rachel did not know and slid into the category of "number one enemy."

"You're not the sister I grew up with," continued Ada, as if reading Rachel's mind. "I am so fucking tired of you, Rachel! And mommy is tired of you too!"

The last statement falls on Rachel like cold water – she knows she cannot take another step. "My mama needs to say that to my face," she says quietly.

Ada and Paul turn behind them. Anne approaches softly and takes their place in front of the door. She nods to them to give her room. Paul and Ada retreat into the house. Anne pulls the door closed, leaving it just a crack. Standing behind it, she faces her daughter.

"I am tired of you and your troubles, Rachel," Anne says softly.

Rachel swallows the lump in her throat as Anne extends what appear to be folded bills towards her. Rachel does not see the money, only her mother's tears falling on her cheeks. "Take the money, okay. It'll tide you over until you get a job. Make it soon."

Rachel does not take the money so Anne withdraws it. Her heart breaking, she says to her daughter, "Your father and I gave up everything to come to this country so our children would have better opportunities than we had back home. Things did not work out between your father and me, but you cannot continue to blame me for it. I raised you the best way I knew how, and now I have to let you go so you can go out there and make something of yourself. You have it in you to succeed, but I am afraid if you continue on the path you're on, you will not amount to anything. And that, my dear, will crush my heart. So please, go away. Go into the world and be good, do something meaningful."

What Rachel wants to say to her mother is, I've never blamed you for anything, mama. Instead, what she says is, "When I become famous, I won't buy you that house!"

"It's a good thing I have another daughter," Anne says with acid. "Ada will buy it for me!" With that, she throws the cash in Rachel's face, then slams the door shut. It's not the only door that Rachel hears closed. Behind her, the neighbors quietly close their doors. The entertainment is over.

Rachel walks forward and leans her head against her mother's door. For a long time, she does not move. She does not have the strength. Finally, she gathers herself up and shuffles away – neither gathering the 1000 dollars on the floor, nor the bags containing all her earthly belongings.

In the morning, the money will be gone, taken by the neighbor across the way who watched all through his peephole and prayed to God Rachel would leave the money on the floor.

JADA & CHRIS

At 2:30AM, Jada quickly opens the door to Rachel who drops into her arms, out cold. Jada's screams usher her boyfriend Chris to come stumbling out of the bedroom. Standing an impressive 6 foot 3 – all muscle and sinew – and clad only in boxers, Chris easily picks Rachel off Jada and deposits her onto the couch.

"Get her some water, baby," Jada says as she takes off Rachel's shoes, the Timberland boots she always wears. Chris runs to the kitchen to get the water, the sleep in his eyes quickly fading. The clock on the cooking range tells him what time it is. He can't understand what happened to the girl to show up at such an indecent hour.

Chris takes the glass of water to Jada. Jada gives it to Rachel who is stirring now. As Rachel drinks the water, Jada's eyes fall directly to Chris' waist, his hands placed akimbo there. She notes with discomfort the outline of his penis against his cotton boxers. He has never seemed as well endowed as he appears now.

Jada changes position. She was sitting beside Rachel, perched on the couch where Rachel's head situates. Now, Jada removes herself from that position and moves to Rachel's feet. This is convenient, for her head blocks Chris' waist should Rachel look at Chris. Rachel looks at Chris now.

"Thank you, Chris," Rachel says in a whisper, her voice hoarse. He gives her a simple nod, and finds himself moved by the sorrow in her voice. "Thank you, Jada," Rachel continues as she hands the glass to Jada, who hands it back to Chris, who takes it back to the kitchen.

"What's up with your voice, girl?" Jada asks, concerned, though wary of Chris' presence. He has arrived, once more, behind her.

"Can you give us a moment, Chris?" Rachel asks. Jada could not agree more. Chris gratefully obliges, leaving the women alone so he could get back to bed. It takes Rachel a while to compose herself and a long time to run down the events of the longest day of her life – or so it feels like to her.

By 3:30AM, she is done. She spoke in an even deadpan tone, as if she were reading an uninteresting novel. Jada listened, breathless. Long has she felt Rachel lives in la-la-land.

They met at Columbia University seven years ago, two giddy 17-year olds fresh out of high school, enrolled in the school's liberal arts program. Even then, it was hard for classmates and teachers alike to take Rachel seriously. All she wanted to do was write about life in the ghetto.

Jada tried her best to keep up with school, even though she felt woefully overwhelmed. Rachel breezed through school with dreams of grandeur, but suddenly dropped out at age 20. She felt she was wasting her time among folks who did not take her work seriously.

Moreover, she wanted to begin her masterpiece immediately. So Rachel hunkered down at her mama's house to begin the story of *Yasmin* the Sudanese sex slave. Without Rachel's presence in school, it wasn't long before Jada retired her dreams of being a writer for a more practical profession – she became a banker. This was after she got her degree from Columbia, of course. She wasn't stupid.

It took Rachel four years to write the masterpiece – this was because she did more partying than writing. There was no New York City club the girls did not visit in those days, no dance floor they did not shake their booties on. Men were naturally drawn to Rachel. So the girls, more often than not, were sprayed with free drinks from admirers lusting after Rachel.

In the mornings, Jada rolled into work, while Rachel slept off hangovers till late afternoon, pretending to write every now and then. During these transition years, Rachel filled Jada's ears with phone calls placed to her at work with gripes against her mother.

Anne never seemed to give her daughter enough money to live as Rachel wanted. That Anne was taking care of paying back Rachel's school loans with her social worker job was not a point Rachel wanted to consider. To Jada's suggestions that Rachel go out and get herself a job, Rachel quipped she already had a job – writing!

Jada was somewhat relieved when Bo finally came into the picture. By that time, she had Chris and rarely hung out after 10PM. Bo became Rachel's convenient access for booty and spending money. This quieted Rachel some but flared Jada's own gripes against Bo. She was proven correct tonight. Rachel and Bo were no more.

A shame it had to happen on the same night Rachel's mama kicked her out. That too, Jada thinks, was long overdue. Rachel has no choice now, Jada concludes, but to grow up and join the rest of us struggling folks out here. But then again, maybe the story of *Yasmin* – appropriately titled *Pass the Hoochie* – might hit it big with the publishers and its writer become an overnight sensation.

"Get some rest now, okay," Jada says to Rachel, who appears to already be asleep. "Everything will be alright in the morning," she concludes.

Jada rises to a nearby closet, retrieves a blanket with which she covers Rachel. Turning off the light, she quietly enters into the bedroom. She does not want to think about the sudden unease rising in her heart.

The morning dawns with Rachel lying on Jada and Chris' couch. She looks morose and despondent. It doesn't seem as if she's moved from it since arriving 26 days ago. Her routine is to wake at dawn, remain on the couch until Jada runs out to work around 7:30AM.

She makes hollow promises to Jada about going to look for work. She even stumbles into the bathroom as soon as Jada slams the front door shut. But after taking care of her personal hygiene matters for the day, Rachel stumbles back onto the couch where she remains watching senseless television until about 11AM.

She leaves for one hour, walking round the neighborhood in search of a "job." Of the job prospects, she has no idea. She enters no place of business, asks no employer about positions, or even cracks open a newspaper's classifieds.

She might stumble into a coffee shop, take a seat, plop a notepad onto the table, and proceed to jot down notes on character development and or plot points. Most of the time though, the notes turn into doodles – her cue to rise and exit the shop. She returns "home" to plop back on the couch to continue her mindless television watching.

When that exercise thoroughly exhausts her, Rachel finds herself sitting at Chris and Jada's tiny dining table, trying to finally bang out the story of *Beatrice*. Printed copies of the manuscript litter the table, all over Jada's old computer from her days in high school.

Rachel uses the machine with its keyboard covered with coffee stains and debris between the keys. Rachel cannot stand the old contraption, but she will not return to her mother's house to retrieve her more sophisticated one. She made a vow upon entering Chris and Jada's house that she will never see her mama again – at least, not until she actually wins that Nobel Prize in Literature.

That prize was a long way in coming because Rachel has not quite managed to move forward on the story of *Beatrice* – beyond *Beatrice's* early childhood abuse at the hands of her stepfather. *Beatrice* has come in contact with the Councilman, but nothing more than this. And so, day in and day out, Rachel finds herself staring at the monitor, re-reading a page she has practically memorized. For sure, she has writers' block – stuck on whom in her life to base the Councilman's character on.

Depression will not permit her to continue, so she will stumble off the table and back onto the couch. There, she will wait for the mailman to arrive – the mailman whom she likens to God. He will bring to her the long awaited response from the publisher(s) that her first book is finally going to be published.

Rachel imagines there will be a bidding war. She will be hailed the next "it" girl in the publishing circles. Her work will be studied in universities across the country, she will be set up in some cottage somewhere in Connecticut with a fat genius grant to last her till the end of her dying days.

Each day, however, the mailman brings bills – Chris and Jada's, and now hers – well, only a cell phone bill, the only bill in her name. Her mother dutifully forwards this bill and other irrelevant mail to her current location. Chris dutifully brings up the mail before he leaves for work around 3PM.

Speak of the devil – Chris stumbles out of the bedroom and into the kitchen. Since Rachel moved into the apartment, he has ceased parading in his boxers – Jada made him do this for Chris was unaware of such things.

Jada made him wear underwear too, to hold his manhood somewhat at bay, and cover that up with pajama-pants and a top.

Fortunately, he does not have to sleep so caged. He only has to "cover up" once out of the bedroom.

"Hey, girl," Chris mumbles to Rachel. "You good?" He always says this to her, and each time, she answers, "fine." He knows she's not fine at all. To distract her as he always does he asks, "What my girl *Beatrice* up to now?"

This usually brings her up, but of late even this is not working. She mentioned yesterday she had writers' block. He tried to help but she had nodded here and there in a weary fashion, so he shut up. He wonders if he should keep his mouth shut today.

Looking at the concern in Chris' sleep-fogged eyes, a light bulb immediately goes off in Rachel's head. She doesn't know why she didn't think of it before, but there stands her Councilman!

Chris makes his way to the kitchen and to the fridge. He takes out condiments for an omelet – specifically spinach, his favorite. Chris is an assistant chef at one of New York City's renowned restaurants in midtown, catering to the business elite and tourists.

He keeps late hours, returning home mostly after 2AM, and crawling into bed next to Jada. He is tired of working these hours for someone else. His dream is to one day open his own Caribbean restaurant.

"I don't think she's going back to school," Rachel says. She gets off the couch, to hover near the kitchen door. Chris is pleased to see her off that couch. Her body's indentation seems already etched on the poor thing.

Rachel watches Chris grab a chopping knife and zip through the cutting of the spinach. He works lightening fast, his hands a blur of movement. It never ceases to amaze Rachel how he could cut so fast without chopping off a finger or two.

"That's what you were stuck on?"

Rachel shrugs, says nothing. To keep her talking, Chris quickly asks, "Why not? Thought you said she saw school as her only way out."

"Not anymore," Rachel says, admiring Chris' physique. "She's figured out other, faster ways to get to the top," she adds, a twinkle in her eyes.

Chris gets her meaning and howls with laughter, the sound is booming and genuine, a 29-year old man who has no secrets, perfectly content with who he is. Rachel listens to the laughter and concludes her Councilman must have such a laugh.

"I heard that!" Chris finishes, as Rachel looks him up and down discretely. She wonders why she's never really taken a good look at him. She knows why – it's taboo, of course, to check out one's best friend's man like this but she feels it's okay since she's suddenly conducting research.

Her Councilman, Rachel decides, will be 6'3" exactly, Chris' height. He will be slim in build, chocolate mocha in color, with a deep set of light brown eyes, like Chris. His body will be divine to behold, like Chris, and also like Chris, he will be bald. Perhaps that would be too obvious, she reasons. Better give him a full head of hair, though cropped close to the scalp.

"You hungry, girl?"

"I'm always hungry," Rachel says, meaning nothing more than that. She gauges the kitchen. It is small and narrow, only a small pathway in the middle. It is almost impossible to have two bodies working in there comfortably – if lovers, cozy; if strangers, awkward. They are not strangers, however, merely good friends.

"Don't worry, girl, I'm an assistant chef, remember? I don't need help in a kitchen!"

"Please, Chris, I can't have you cooking for me. You guys have done so much for me already, letting me stay here. I should be cooking for you!"

Chris can't stop her, so he moves his body against the counter since it appears she wants to get by him to the range.

"Knock it out," he chides. "You'd do the same for Jada or me."

Rachel passes by him quickly. Their bodies touch momentarily. Each acknowledges the other's physical warmth and comfort in silence. The love they have for the woman between them – Jada – is enough of an obstacle to keep them in check.

Rachel retrieves a worn skillet from the nearby dish rack and places it on the stove. She adds olive oil, then cracks and beats four eggs she got from the fridge. This is not the first time they are in the kitchen together, nor is it the first time Chris will pepper her with all sorts of questions regarding *Beatrice.* They will not admit it to the other, but their days in this way have become a sort of routine, a pleasant one at that.

"Don't you think it's a cliché for *Beatrice's* mother to have thrown her out instead of the bastard?" he is asking. "I mean, you hear about shit like that a lot – women who'd rather get rid of their kids than risk losing their man. That shit is messed up!"

The question amuses Rachel. No one in her life questions her as much as he does about characters in general and their motivations in particular.

"Well," she begins. "There are women who throw their children out for the man. Their stories should be told."

"True," he agrees.

"But what do you suggest?" she asks lighthearted. She's enjoying their banter.

"What if she doesn't throw *Beatrice* out? What if she throws him out? Then the mama hugs her child, apologizes for not knowing what was going on, and then marches *Beatrice* to an abortion clinic to get an abortion."

"There'd be no story."

"True, true, true. Not the story you're writing now – *Albany Ho* and all – a different story, yes."

"It'll be a different story alright, an after-school special."

Chris is laughing as he takes over at the range. He pours the beaten eggs into the skillet, while Rachel readies to dump the cut spinach, tomato and feta cheese.

"I guess you don't want to write an after-school special."

"Not this year."

"You're a great writer, Rachel," he says genuine. "I hope you know that. I bet you could make a story out of a leaf falling off a branch!"

She is touched by his confidence in her. It lifts her higher than it should. "Thank you for saying that, Chris."

At this point, they are done with the omelet. He scoops it out of the skillet and onto two standing plates. She spreads butter on already toasted bagels that popped from the toaster. Chris takes the plates to the table, while Rachel follows him there. She clears the table of printed-paper and her numerous notepads. She feels a tad guilty for treating this particular piece of furniture as if it too, like the couch, belongs to her.

"You're welcome!" Chris beams, pleased with himself for Rachel appears in a lighter mood. They take a seat – only for Chris to rise almost immediately for the phone is ringing. Both know who it is – Jada. She calls frequently these days, every forty minutes or so.

Jada's obsession with calling home coincided with Rachel's arrival – as soon as it became clear to her that Rachel did not spend as much time out of doors actually looking for work. Jada begins her calls almost always at 12:30PM, when she expects Chris to rise from bed. Sitting in her office now, she drums her fingernails impatiently on her desk.

She rushed through helping her last client open a checking account just to get the man out of her office. She cannot understand how you can be 43-years old in this day and age and not have a bank account. She knew she was forfeiting points in her annual bonus package by not suggesting to the man he also open a savings account.

She wanted to mention to the man to look into life insurance while they were at it, to help support his two small children in case of tragedy. She didn't. At the moment, Jada could care less about other people's children. Before another customer sits in her guest chair, she's determined to hear from Chris.

Chris picks up the call, laughter and a carefree attitude in his voice. Jada immediately stops drumming her fingernails. She decides, quite irrationally, he must be naked in the house, and that he and Rachel must have already fucked.

The image of her man riding her best friend in their bed fills Jada with such horror, she promptly hangs up the phone. She bounces to her feet, her hand over her mouth, against a sudden urge to vomit. She rushes out of her office at the same time the bank manager is bringing a young client in.

"Excuse me!" Jada barely manages, as she rushes towards the bathroom.

At home, Chris calls into the dead phone, "Jada?" There is no response, only the dial tone. He immediately dials her back. The bank answers. He requests her direct connection, which he is given, but the line goes straight to voicemail. He hangs up and dials her cell phone.

As he has been feeling of late, it is important to call her back when she attempts to make contact with him. The caretaker in him understands the importance of reassuring her. He does not know why he needs to reassure her, or even what he is reassuring her about, but he understands he needs to do this.

Fortunately, Jada picks up her cell phone.

"What's up, mama?" Chris asks into the phone. His voice is serious now, no more light-heartedness. It is unusual for her to call and then hang up. Even if a client walked into her office, she would still say a word or two to him, and then hang up, with promises to call back later.

"Hey," Jada answers guarded. This strange element to her voice causes Chris to listen closer. She informs him she is in the bathroom. She will call him later.

"You okay?" He asks concerned. "You just called here, right?"

"Yeah, but then, a client came in and I had to go pee. You okay?"

"Yeah, I'm cool." He looks across to the table and sees Rachel reading a page of her printed manuscript. He knows she will not start eating until he rejoins her at the table. But he knows he cannot rush Jada off the phone either to sit with another woman.

Chris' eyes fleet away from Rachel as he focuses all his attention to Jada. Trying to sound casual and reassuring, he begins on the tale of *Beatrice* – really, to make her laugh, and get her sounding normal again. The suspicion he's reading in her voice intrigues him. She has nothing to worry about.

"Rachel was just telling me about that ho she writing about. That's some funny, mad shit, baby."

"She's a ho, huh?" Jada hisses, the muscles in her stomach tightening again.

"Yeah, *Beatrice*!" Chris corrects quickly. He is growing a little irritated now for he is suddenly aware he is being accused of something.

"Uh-huh." Jada is not listening to his words, only to the tone of his voice, looking for telltale signs of deceit. She finds none, but is sure he is masking it.

"You sure you okay, babe? You sound …"

"I'm fine, Chris! Listen, I got to go. I got a client in my office." She hangs up and sits quietly on the toilet.

Chris rejoins Rachel at the table, his face screwed up in worry and annoyance. Rachel is her damned girlfriend, Chris thinks. If she didn't want her in the house in the first place, she shouldn't have asked her to stay.

Rachel reads Chris' face loud and clear as she scoops small amounts of omelet into her mouth.

"She's overworked," Rachel begins. "That's what it is."

"You think so?" Chris asks, not wanting to talk about Jada, but too irritated to keep quiet.

"Yep! I know y'all have dreams – kids and the white picket fence and all, but you got to be alive to pursue them. The girl works 70 hours a week, Saturdays and some nights! You can't sustain a relationship working like that!"

Chris is quiet as he shoves food into his mouth. He really doesn't want to talk about Jada or their relationship – something his mama taught him. Never, ever speak about your woman to another woman. He can even hear his mother's voice in his head saying this very thing. Lines get all blurred and stuff, and before you know it, Chris …

Chris does not want to finish his mama's thought. He does not want to stare at Rachel's breasts either, the cleavage of which he can glimpse across the table. He maintains his attention on her eyes, fiery now as she waits for him to respond.

He is attracted to her, he's articulated that much in his mind. The only way to deaden it – again, lessons from his mama – is to think of Rachel as his sister. No easy feat for he has no sisters.

"I don't see how anyone with barely a high-school education can go on to be governor of New York City!" Chris begins, as he deftly steers the conversation away from Jada to *Beatrice*.

"I mean, Rachel, that's a bit of a stretch, you've got to admit it."

"True, true, true," Rachel admits while full of laughter. "I didn't say she's never going to get her degree, just not right now. She'll probably end up doing some online correspondence or some shit like that, or take night classes at CUNY or something. Now Chris, I hope you don't mind but I'm thinking of basing the Councilman on you."

"On me?!"

"Uh-huh. It won't be you exactly, I'll just take details here and there, from this person and that person, but the dominant character would be based on you."

"Wow."

"Do you mind?"

"Nah, girl! What you wanna know, and he better be good in bed!"

"Trust me – he will be!"

Chris laughs nervously. Jesus Lord, he thinks. Is that a twinkle in her eyes? He looks down immediately to shove food in his mouth. He did not mean to take the talk there. An image of his face buried in Rachel's breasts suddenly flashes past his mind. Jesus Lord! That was his mother's voice, she'd seen the image too.

Later that afternoon, Chris runs back into the apartment. He holds a bunch of mail in his hands, but none is more important than the one addressed to Rachel – with its bold logo of a publishing house.

Inside the apartment, Rachel lounges on the couch watching *The Matrix*, Chris' favorite film of all time. She never saw the flick, so she decided to watch it since the Councilman's favorite flick would be the same.

She flies off the couch at the look on Chris' face as he bursts through the door, shoving the piece of mail into her hands. He does not wait for her to completely tear it open before lifting her in a bear hug. He sets her down to read over her shoulder.

Their faces cave in simultaneously as they both absorb the shock of the rejection. Signed by a Mr. Marks, the letter thanks her for her submission, but that the company is choosing to decline her novel at this time. No further explanation is given.

Rachel forlornly hands the letter to Chris as she heads to the couch. She lies upon it, turns off the movie with the remote, and then covers her body with the blanket that's been draped there since she arrived. Chris doesn't know what to do, although he wishes Jada were here. Jada would know what to say.

He makes his way to the couch and takes a seat at the end where Rachel's feet lie. He takes her feet in his hands and begins massaging them. He does this for Jada on the rare occasion they are off on the same day – he works six days a week, and often seven to cover someone else's shift.

His mama would no doubt frown that he's touching a part of another woman's body but under the circumstances, he's not even aware he's doing this. Rachel's sorrow touches him greatly, as does the grief of all women.

"Mr. Marks, huh?" he begins softly. "He sounds white. He's not gonna get *Yasmin* or her troubles."

"A good story is a good story, Chris. It shouldn't have to matter what color the guy is."

"You're kidding, right?"

Rachel sighs.

"The good news is," continues Chris, "now you're hearing from them. I bet the rest will be coming soon. Mr. Marks is gonna be really sorry he didn't sign you first."

Rachel disentangles herself from the blanket. Before Chris knows what she's doing, she makes her way into his arms and he finds he's holding her.

"Thank you for saying that, Chris." She starts crying softly against his chest, her head under his chin. He smells in her hair which badly needs a wash. His mother's voice in his head is quiet, surprising him. He thought for sure she'd be screaming, "Get away from that girl,

Chris!" But his mother has nothing to worry about for she's raised a good son. He loves only one woman and her name is Jada.

Chris is right about one thing – the publishers' responses begin to pour in, one right after the other, as if in concert together. If the arrivals do not show an uncanny synchronicity, the rejections sure as hell do. Without exception, the companies reject the manuscript. With each rejection, Rachel sinks further and further into the couch, to the point it is difficult to tell where the blanket ends and her body begins.

She ceased going out for her hourly walks altogether, ceased working on the story of *Beatrice.* Most alarming of all, she ceased bathing and taking care of her physical appearance. She's gained 11 pounds in 30 days for consoling herself with buckets upon buckets of chocolate ice cream, ice cream that Chris dutifully stacks in the refrigerator for her to consume.

Neither Jada nor Chris wants to mention the rancid odor that's hanging around in the living room. The smell bothers Jada so much, she's taken to throwing up in the toilet upon entering the apartment from work. She walks in now, at 2:15PM, not at 7:30 when she usually saunters in. Jada's nostrils promptly cringe at the odor pervading the space.

Coming from the kitchen with a new gallon of chocolate ice cream, Rachel should be surprised to see Jada home so early, but she barely notes her there at the door. Instead, she takes her pitiful place on the couch and tears into the ice cream with a vacant look typical of someone who doesn't give a damn about anything anymore.

Jada takes a moment to size up Rachel on the couch, the couch that she and Chris spent 2500 dollars on upon moving into the apartment some three years before. How she loved that couch – but no more. Rachel disfigured it with her body and her stench.

Without warning, Jada rushes to Rachel, snatches the ice cream, slams the container on the center table. She pulls the frayed blanket from under Rachel and throws that on the nearby love seat. Rachel's eyes, no longer vacant, stare at Jada stunned.

"Jada!" Rachel cries, her mouth full of ice cream.

"You got to go now! Today!" Jada is a whir of movement as she pulls Rachel off the couch, not an easy thing to do due to Rachel's sudden weight-gain.

All the commotion summons Chris from the bathroom, a towel around his waist and shimmering water beads glistening on his well-formed torso. He stepped out of the shower and into a fracas. In Jada's eyes, he is practically naked, a condition that heightens her already high-decibel fury.

"Baby!" shouts Chris, frozen at the door of the bathroom. His mother's voice in his head lets him know in a subdued monotone, You going be late for work today.

With a hand round her waist, Chris pulls Jada away from Rachel. "Jada!" he calls again. "What's come over you? What you doing home so early?!"

"Why you asking me that, Chris? What the two of you doing while I'm at work, huh?! You all naked and shit!"

"Huh?" Chris is confused.

"Whoa!" Rachel begins, "I can't believe you wanna go there, girl!"

"Yeah, I wanna go there!" She's in Rachel's face now, and the proximity to the other makes Jada want to vomit – Rachel's body odor is that overwhelming. Jada takes an involuntary step back, closer to Chris who smells like the Irish Spring bar soap he just used in the shower.

"You think I don't see the way you look at her and shit!" She's in Chris' face now. She pronounces each word with a poke at his naked torso. "It's either me or her, baby, you can't have us both!"

Her last jab against his chest was quite painful. He winces as he massages it, while too stunned at the turn of events to actually utter a word. All he can hear is his mother's voice in his head cautioning him to step lightly.

Boy, you know to never, ever engage a woman when she's foaming at the mouth like this. Don't even answer the question if you can get away with it. But if she insists, better see your tone is calm. Make her think she's not out of her fucking mind for asking the question in the first place. Give her the impression she's making a whole lot of sense.

"It's you, Jada," he says, in a voice mellow with love and tenderness. His mother would be proud.

"There is no one else, there never will be," he finishes.

Jada is momentarily disarmed by the love she sees in his eyes, but is intent on making a scene – she forges on.

"Quit lying to me, Chris! I know you've been rolling around with her in our bed!" She snatches the towel from round his waist and grabs his balls.

Chris lets out a fatal yelp because she's holding him so tight. "Just tell me the goddamned truth!" Jada's shrieking, then she gushes into tears. In some dim distance of her mind, she's aware of her pitiful actions but seems unable to stop herself. She can't let go of his balls as

Chris dances precariously, his hands on her hand on his balls. He dare not yank her hand off for fear she'll rip him apart.

In his head, his mama is also shrieking with insanity for the disrespect happening to her son. You better knock her out, Chris! I can't believe she's doing this to you! Quit dancing around, goddamn it! Hit her on the damn head!

It's Rachel who saves the day. She throws Jada off Chris in one mighty swoop so that Jada lands onto the much-abused couch. Chris quickly gathers the towel round him, though he limps with pain.

"Are you fucking out of your mind, Jada!" Rachel blurts out, standing over Jada. "What the fuck is wrong with you? Why the hell you going accuse us of something like that?! Didn't I tell you I don't do boys!"

"Boys!" Chris yells. "You calling me a boy?!"

Of course, neither Rachel nor Chris means the incense in their voices. They are in collusion in wanting a distraction from the intensity of the moment. It is better that they appear to be insulting each other than they appear to be angered by Jada's actions.

"Yeah. Boy!"

"If you wasn't Jada's best friend, girl, I'd be hitting you upside the head right about now."

"Yeah, I'd like to see you try, motherfucka."

Jada chuckles. Their play of words works … but only momentarily. She becomes subdued again. The tempest she was riding on seems suddenly spent. She's ashamed of herself and finds she can't look at either of them. She cleans the tears falling still on her face and finally blurts out the truth.

"I'm pregnant."

Utter silence.

Finally, "Say what?" from Rachel.

"Baby …" Chris manages in a whisper.

"Yes. A baby."

Chris quickly limps his way to Jada on the couch, while in his head, his mother bursts into tears.

"Are you sure?" he asks breathless.

Jada nods. "I'm five weeks along," she says softly. "I just found out today, that's why I came home."

"Oh, baby." Chris doesn't know what part of her to hold or kiss.

"You want the baby, right?" she asks him, a little fearful. They planned to have a baby two years down the road. They're piling up cash now in anticipation of that future date, the reason they both work over-time.

"Oh yes, baby, oh yes! A baby is a gift whenever it comes, my mama always says." They are hugging and kissing and carrying on.

Watching them, Rachel knows her stay here is over. It's only a matter of time before they remember she's still in the room.

She is remembered alright, in a not so flattering way. The stench in the room finally catches up to Jada. She suddenly bounces to her feet, the need to throw-up overcoming all other needs. She rushes to the bathroom to do just this. And so finally, finally, Chris turns his eyes on Rachel.

"You have to go fix things with your mama, Rachel." And that's that.

NATHANIEL

After leaving Jada and Chris's apartment, Rachel finds herself at a local bank, where she withdraws the last of her cash from the ATM machine, 60 dollars. She leaves a 10-dollar balance. A sense of decency will not permit her to zero the account. The money is from the last stash given her by Bo a long time ago. She leaves the bank with no clear direction of where she's going and is surprised when she finds herself inside the deli across the street from Bo's gallery.

Bo, she thinks, how did he sneak up on her like that? She did not know she still thinks of him. She even remembers the day of his art opening. How about that? It's strange how the mind works. She realizes now – staring out the deli's window, at the troupe of high-society folks streaming into the gallery – that she was biding her time at Chris and Jada's, not so much waiting for mail, but waiting for this day.

She expected Bo, in the end, to call her to come tonight. And maybe he tried. Her phone was turned off only two days ago for lack of payment. She doubts that he tried though. If he wanted her, he would have called long before two days ago.

In the time she knew Bo, she attended every single one of his art openings. He always invited her to serve as one of the bartenders. She knew nothing about mixing drinks, but she always watched what the other bartender was doing and then got things right. Bo loved that about her, her ability to quickly learn new skills.

She never minded being in the background in this way. Nor did she mind that he never introduced her to his savory friends and contacts. She was merely content to be in his space, watching him mingle so charmingly in and out of guests. She tucked all the colorful folks she saw at these events in her mind for future use in her stories.

Nor did she mind Indira about at these events either. Ever the busy bee, Indira would fleet here and there, deftly steering guests to the more expensive of Bo's pieces. Rachel has to give the woman her kudos. Indira is very good at selling Bo.

No, Rachel did not mind Indira at the art openings. She willed the woman out of her psyche anyway and didn't see her at all. Of course, those were the days when Rachel believed she alone was sleeping with Bo.

Rachel rejoiced then in what she thought was the secret knowledge that no matter how the night ended, it was she with whom Bo would go home. So she did not mind standing behind the drink table, pouring liquor into whatever glasses were thrust in her face. Sometimes, it was Indira whose glass she had to refill. She would always brandish a killer smile to the other, then flick her the bird when Indira turned to walk away.

Now, Rachel watches the gallery from across the street, the gallery with its floor-to-ceiling windows that permit her the perfect frame to glimpse the happenings within the packed space. She makes Bo out immediately. She could spot that man anywhere. He is dressed in African garb tonight, and why not? The theme of his show bounces off his centerpiece painting, *The Death of Yetunde*.

The painting is prominent to Rachel for it hangs directly against the wall that practically faces the deli. The rendition came out even more alarmingly striking than what was in Bo's head. The piece's most dominant colors are black and red – the red, of course, being the flow of blood from the wound inflicted on *Yetunde* by his lover. The black from the darkest of nights, the time of day the two lovers chose to duel it out, and is also the color of the canoe the lovers are standing in.

Though Rachel has a great view of the piece, she can barely make it out for guests are constantly standing in front of it. Each time someone moves off – permitting Rachel a tantalizing glimpse – another guest immediately takes over the space. Rachel's irritation steadily mounts because of this. She feels it yet another personal slight by God, on this day He has already heaped on so much.

To add injury to her pains, she tries not to think of what Bo is wearing. She gave him the dashiki last spring, on the occasion of his 44th birthday. He hated the thing – she knows for he never wore it. Yet, there he is, beaming in it, a champagne glass in his hand. Indira stands very close to him, Rachel sees, massaging his back with friendly pats that declare to the room at large — she's the one permanently in his bed now.

Rachel lowers her head for unbidden tears brim in her eyes. She knows she's drawing attention yet again from the cashier at the counter. The guy, from Yemen, has already thrown her wary looks. She has been standing there far too long, pretending to drink the apple juice she bought at least an hour and a half ago.

"You okay, miss?" the guy asks. He's not really concerned about her well being. He wonders if she might be some sort of lookout, perhaps keeping an eye on the comings and goings in his deli. He was robbed eight months ago in broad daylight. He had a pistol pointed at his head as he emptied the contents of his cash register to a masked assailant. The assailant rushed out with the breeze, a blur of movement that occupies the man's dreams at night. The experience left the deli owner jarred and paranoid.

"Yeah, I'm cool," Rachel answers. She's not cool at all for every image in all 25 pieces hanging on those walls across the street – at least, those she can see – every face on the numerous paintings is her face, even the lover stabbing *Yetunde*.

If you stood Rachel beside any of the paintings, in truth, you would not see Rachel, merely a caricature of her. The caricature is a private joke between her and Bo. Any time Bo sketches Rachel into his work, he draws this figure. He told her so when she queried him about it – once upon a time, as they laid on top of each other, after a mid-afternoon quickie.

The figure is a black girl with dreads, Rachel has braids. Her breasts are quite large, just like Rachel's. The figure, though, is narrow in every other way where Rachel is full-figured. Bo said to her that whenever he means to put her in his work, he would use this character.

Staring at this caricature image of herself now, plastered all over his pieces, Rachel feels as if he is mocking her. He must surely know she is close by, watching. Why else would he be wearing the clothes she gifted him and which he loathes? What did she ever do to this man to deserve such maltreatment? All she ever did was love him.

No longer able to take her face staring back at her and no longer able to take the deli owner's hostile glances, Rachel makes her way out of the deli. At the corner, she stops to look back at the gallery, skewed now for her vantage point is not ideal. She walks away in silence – unaware, again, which direction she is headed. She will not go to her mama's, of course not.

In time, Rachel finds herself in front of her father's massive home in Long Island. Of how she got here, she is not entirely clear. She knows, though, she spent money on the Long Island Rail Road. She shelled out still more money to the cab driver who drove her here. She does not know how much she gave the man, but it was money wisdom cautioned her against spending.

Whatever she is seeking searching for her father, wisdom told her as she began the journey, she most assuredly would not get from him tonight nor on any other night. But there is nowhere else to go, really. In truth, she doesn't want to be anywhere else. Nathaniel is her father and she chooses to believe he loved her once.

Nathaniel Ofordilli is a man of short stature. His children, both the males and the females, are taller than him. His current wife is taller than him – standing an astonishing 6'2" to his barely 5 foot 8 inches. Even his past wife Anne stands 5 foot 10. This stature impediment – he sees it as that – has ruled his psyche for as long as he can remember.

He chases after women who are taller – believing that in bringing them down, he would some how measure up. In the world of men, he is a bulldog – how else could he command their respect?

He is lithe to boot, having finally abandoned in his 40s, all manner of exercise and dietary regimen to add bulk to his frame. He is one of those men who can never amass muscle no matter what he puts in his mouth.

For his petite frame and youthful face, he is often mistaken for a child, a big problem in his 20s and 30s. Now 57, his dazzling and sparkling eyes can never be confused for youth because experience, hardship and tempered rage belie them. He is seething now.

He is angry because his second son Brian, his wife's favorite, is dropping out of acting school to relocate to Los Angeles to pursue the stupid craft for real. Nathaniel is not a man who requires his children to do as they are told, as his own father required. He knows that in

America, this won't do. Beat them, and the very children might even call the cops to send you to jail.

Nathaniel recalls at least once a day, the abuse he endured in Africa. Tough-love they called it there. His body is covered with scars of the countless beatings delivered onto him by his father. He shudders now recalling the face of his father. For this reason and only this, Nathaniel refuses to set foot in Africa 30 years after his arrival to America.

When his mother died ten years ago, he sent the cash that buried her. But he himself did not go back. His father then branded him a bastard and ceased all communication with him. Nathaniel would have it no other way. The person he cared for the most in the world – his mother – was dead. He has no more ties to his brothers and sisters than an ant has to a goat, say.

His quarrels with Anne began, not because he was a wanton womanizer – and he was – the quarrels began because Anne insisted on sending the girls to Africa every summer, as soon as the girls were born. Nathaniel did not want this. And so for defying this most important of his edicts, Nathaniel began to misbehave even more.

He did not want his children to have anything to do with Africa, that land he had abandoned though still carried around in behavior. He started sleeping with the temp, whom he quickly promoted to his secretary. This was after he fired the previous secretary, of course.

He began the affair with the temp because she was white, primarily, and because she would let him. But he was also sleeping with her because she seemed, quite honestly, to listen to the things that were important to him. That Maureen was 19 then and was therefore very impressionable was a fact he failed to take into consideration.

It was a no-brainer to Nathaniel to leave Anne for Maureen. Anne's children – which he came to see the girls as – were becoming unknown to him. They seemed to cling more to their mother than they did to him. He considered this brainwashing – and not attributable to the fact that he was hardly ever home.

Determined not to lose children twice, and not wishing to have his marriage to a white woman also fail, Nathaniel turned himself around. He doted on Maureen and the boys. Yes, he occasionally stepped out on her, but never so indiscrete as to create too much friction in the home.

As soon as they married, Maureen quit the company to be a stay-at-home mom, a status Anne felt was beneath her. A pity, for this move alone bonded Nathaniel to Maureen. If for no other reason, Nathaniel cherished Maureen for this critical organization of his home in the early years. She doted on his boys the way his own mother had doted on him. Maureen complained – and continues to complain – very rarely, and does almost always everything Nathaniel wants – the same as his mother did to his less-deserving father.

If there was one thing he could say against Maureen it was that she loved the second son more than the rest. His own mother had shown no favorites with any of her children, treating them all in much the same manner. Each child, however, felt she loved him or her more than the rest. This took a great skill, a skill Nathaniel came to realize all women do not possess – as he witnessed with Maureen and the boys.

It was because Maureen spoiled him rotten that Brian ever had the audacity to think he could become an actor. She praised his acting "prowess," comparing him to Brando, Eastwood, Newman and recently, Sean Penn. That Yale accepted the boy into its renowned acting program, Nathaniel could care less. The best he hoped would come out of it was a degree from the prestigious school.

But now that the brainless whip is dropping out, Nathaniel hit the roof. If the boy were near him, he would choke him to death – all 5 foot 11 inches of him. Since Brian is not, Nathaniel, instead, heaps all manner of verbal abuse upon Maureen – this is the most he can do, since he has never laid hands to her flesh in a harmful way.

"You did this, Maureen!" he's screaming at her in bed. Maureen has her back to him and is trying to sleep. She is 42-years old, blond with blue eyes. She is a beautiful woman – made even more beautiful by grief, the grief of having lost a son.

Grief should have bowed her, for the loss of a child was never anything she could have imagined – the thought, quite honestly, never crossed her mind that she would outlive any of her children. No, grief did not bow or diminish her – instead, it froze her in its awe. She became wise overnight, then mellow, then graceful.

Nathaniel became the obverse. Grief hardened him to the texture of wood. He will not discuss Freddy and chooses not to mourn the loss emotionally by focusing on all of Freddy's shortcomings. He's painted Freddy so black in his mind's eye that the kid no longer even existed. Nathaniel's two shining rods are Nat Jr. and the basketball career, and of course N.G. and the entrance into Harvard. In considering Brian now, he wonders if he would have to paint that son black too.

"Why did you have to encourage him," he's barking at Maureen, "to stick with this acting thing?"

"Can we talk about this in the morning, darling?" Maureen says, in a soothing voice. This quality crept into her voice the day of Freddy's funeral. Seeing his casket lowered into the ground, she used the same tone of voice to soothe Immy (Imhotep), Freddy's 2-year old boy, now almost 4.

The boy was particularly fussy that day, as if he understood in a way that only a toddler could, that he had lost his father forever. Immy would only become quiet in his grandmother's bosom, listening to her soothing voice talking about clouds chasing each other in the sky. Because the boy is around her day in and day out, Maureen's voice has become permanently soothing, even when speaking to her husband.

"It's almost midnight," she says, hoping that would end it.

"That boy adores you!" exclaims Nathaniel, not ending it at all. He's referring to Brian. "All you had to do was point him in the right direction. You could have gotten him to do anything! Be anything!"

"Acting makes him happy, Nat." Having lost one son, the last thing Maureen would do is thwart the remaining three's passions – well, four. She and Nat adopted Immy after the boy's mother left him with them one weekend and never returned.

Shemeeka, the boy's mother, still lives in Queens, but there is a non-verbal understanding she "gifted" the boy to them. At least, she did not fight the adoption, and readily signed off all her parental rights.

"Happy?!" Nathaniel cannot believe his ears. "Goddamn it all to hell, Maureen, you useless woman! In my country, no parent in his right mind would let —"

"You don't love your country, remember, darling. And anyway, the Nigerian film industry is doing very well. I read an article the other day, it said parents are now thrilled at their children who choose to become actors."

To say that Maureen is an avid watcher of Nollywood films would be an understatement. The woman is obsessed with them. Her personal theater, located in the basement, is stuffed with over 3000 films. The African DVD sellers in Brooklyn, Bronx and Harlem look forward to her weekly visits. She purchases every new title, no matter how many, and no matter which Nigerian celebrity graces the jacket.

She would linger in the stores, discussing with whoever is around, the merits of this or that actor, the repetitious story lines (which never bore her), and always, always, what to look forward to next. She credits the films as her greatest teacher in understanding Nathaniel and the culture that shaped him. From them, she learned to be the wife he needed her to be. Then somewhere along the line, she got hooked on the films as pure entertainment.

In honor of the films, therefore, and in honor of the country that produces them, it was her idea to name her last son *Nigeria*. Nathaniel hit the roof when she told him, but had no choice but to acquiesce. He named the three previous children. When Maureen became pregnant with N.G., he promised she would name the child – whether boy or girl. And to her, whether boy or girl, *Nigeria* would be the name.

"Why are you talking about the Nigerian film industry, you foolish woman!" Nathaniel fumes. "This is the reason I don't like you watching that garbage, goddamn it!"

"Please keep your voice down, honey. I don't want the baby to wake up, and N.G. has an interview tomorrow." In no time at all, she is snoring.

She sleeps peacefully because she takes no offense to Nathaniel's sometimes nasty words thrown at her. Many of the characters in the movies speak this very way to their wives and or girlfriends. In Nathaniel's case, Maureen knows this persona of his is a defense mechanism he uses against losing control.

She knows that her husband is a man who feels he doesn't deserve anything good that's come his way, the result of the emotional and physical abuse he suffered at the hands of his father. With his own hands, Nathaniel destroys whatever good he creates – as in the case of his first marriage.

He would destroy the life they have made together too except that Maureen would never allow it. She is his rod, the only entity on earth that balances his destructive nature. In turn, he has given her everything her heart has ever desired – and of course, he loves her dearly.

Nathaniel knows if he stands there watching her angelic face in sleep, he is bound to lose the anger in his head, so he marches out of the room. He storms into the kitchen to pick at leftovers in the fridge, his routine whenever the night is ruined for him.

His head is in the fridge, in fact, when the shrill sound of the ringing phone interrupts him. So startled is he that he almost drops the plate in his hands. He heads for the phone, wondering if Brian is calling his mother to see how he took the news. Naturally, she had waited until bedtime to spring the news on him.

Reaching for the phone, Nathaniel is puzzled reading the ID as coming from a local pay phone.

"Hello!"

Rachel almost drops the phone. The voice is her father's, to be sure, but the wave of bitterness with which the word comes out makes it feel like a curse flung at her.

At about the same time her sister and her mother viewed Nathaniel's mini palace for the first time on the computer, Rachel took the opportunity to locate and to visit the actual house. She sat for two hours across the street, in the back seat of the cab that drove her there.

She never got out, nor did she see anyone going in and out of the house. Of course, it was in the middle of the day and she knew that her father must be at work.

She returned to Long Island four more times - each time, never getting out of the cab. No one knew she made these visits, not even Jada. She couldn't bring herself to tell anyone because, like everything else about her father, it was her own private pain – never to be opened up for discussion before any other mortal.

On her last time across the street, the week before she sent out the story of *Yasmin* to the publishers, her father unexpectedly returned home from work. Rachel ducked to the floor of the cab, an act that made the driver think her even more of a lunatic than he already believed her to be, evident by the look he gave her once she resurfaced. She requested to be driven back to the train station, and with speed – he obliged.

For the rest of that day and all of that week, Rachel slumped on her bed, drowning herself in gallons of chocolate ice cream. She recovered the following week to throw multiple copies of *Yasmin* into the mailbox. And a week later, Ada and Paul threw their engagement party.

Getting the phone number of the mini-mansion was easy enough for Rachel. Nathaniel no longer hid his public details. Ada and Rachel were now young adults, and Anne ceased long ago to pursue him for child-support. Rachel never called the number – until now.

"Hello!" Nathaniel demands again, on the other end of the line. "Brian, get home right now so we can discuss this thing man to man!

"Um," Rachel begins. She prayed he would pick up and not anyone else in the house. Hearing his voice now though, she is scared shitless. "This is not Brian, um, daddy, this is —" Rachel cannot say her name. For a stupid second, she doesn't know what it is. And then she remembers. She remembers he calls her *Ify*.

"It's, um, Ify."

"Ify!" He says it as he said "Hello!" To Rachel's ear, a curse.

"Uh … how are you, um, daddy?" The word "daddy" feels wrong to her, as if she is calling someone else's father daddy.

"How did you get this number?! Why are you calling here?!"

Rachel's heart sinks. She feels like a burglar who has broken into his house, only to be caught red-handed before she could steal anything.

"Well, I was thinking if I could, um, come stay with you." Had she been speaking to anyone other than her father, Rachel would have commended herself on her bravado. She would have immediately thought of ways to incorporate the scene into *Beatrice's* life. But right now, she is stripped bear, is reduced to her core, does not feel brave at all. She is 6-years old all over again, a time when she was too young to build up any defenses against the pain he represents.

"What?!" Nathaniel has never heard anything more outlandish in his life. "You want to come stay here?! Are you kidding me?! How old are you?!"

Rachel is not sure if this is a rhetorical question. Is he asking her this because he doesn't really know how old she is, or is he mocking her? She decides to treat the situation as innocently as possible.

"Um, I will be 25 in November, sir." Yes – *sir* feels better in her mouth.

"I know how old you are!!"

"Oh." So he meant to mock her.

"What happened to your mother's house, did it burn down?"

"Burn down?" She thinks the question absurd – preposterous, in fact. "Why would it burn down?"

"I can think of no other reason for you to be asking me something so stupid, you should have your own place."

Rachel says nothing.

"You don't have your own place, I guess." He knows very well she doesn't. Just as Anne keeps up with his life, he also keeps up with theirs.

"No, sir," Rachel answers, for once – ashamed of herself.

"So then …" Nathaniel's voice takes on a lighter quality, giddy almost. All thoughts of Brian are out the window. "… that must mean your mother finally threw you out? I heard you disgraced yourself at your sister's party. Is that true?"

Rachel is silent.

"Something about an orgy in the middle of the living room floor? You with multiple partners? That side of you comes from your mother's people, you know that."

It would do no good to correct or debate him. She can hear that much in his voice – along with wickedness.

Yes – Nathaniel is enjoying himself. But the merriment masks unbridled anger. He is angry that a part of his life he has buried – as deeply as he buried Freddy, both literary and figuratively – had the audacity to pick up a local payphone and call his number in the dead of night. He does not want it to ever happen again.

"I would not let you stay here if your mother's house did burn down, and all the other houses in the world burned down except for mine. I do not harbor lazy, no-good-for-nothings who should be ashamed of themselves for dropping out of one of the most prestigious schools in America."

That Freddy dropped out his junior year in high school and was not banished from the home, Nathaniel chooses not to dwell on. Nor does he want to dwell on Brian with now a similar issue. He wonders distantly what it says about him, the propensity of half of his seed for dropping out of school.

"And furthermore," Nathaniel continues to hiss at Rachel. "I do not harbor prostitutes, call girls, hookers, or anyone else who works in the sex trade. Remember this, Ify, you have no father in me, so never call here again!!"

He bangs the phone on her ears and promptly bursts into heart-wrenching wails. It was the thought of Freddy that did it. He remembers the day he and Maureen brought him home. The kid had weighed an unprecedented 10 pounds 1 ounce, the biggest baby in the hospital all that year, the biggest baby of his four boys, certainly, and the whitest looking of his children.

Freddy had a blond afro, and was imbued with the palest of blue eyes. Freddy, his shortcomings notwithstanding, was Nathaniel's favorite son, not that he let the other three boys know this. Nathaniel picked that much up from his African mother.

He loved Freddy most of all because the boy was daring and fearless, like Nathaniel in his youth. Freddy bucked authority all the time and did whatever he damned well pleased. He was even prone to cursing out both his mother and his father whenever the need arose – not that Nathaniel appreciated that last bit, but the point is – Freddy was a work in progress, and Nathaniel cherished him.

He knew the boy only needed more time in life to eventually find his way. Instead of time, the boy was unceremoniously torn apart on the road. After the first car hit Freddy, he was thrown into the path of another, then a third and then a fourth. His limbs were scattered for miles.

Nathaniel spared Maureen the identification process in the morgue, but the image of his beautiful son's splintered carcass is by far the most horrendous piece of information Nathaniel has tried to bury as he strove to banish the boy entirely from his memory. But now, here was Freddy:

Freddy's first attempts to walk as a baby; Freddy's first attempts on his tricycle as a 5-year old; Freddy's refusing to comb through his afro which grew and matted into long dread locks; Freddy and Nathaniel practicing a jump shot at a local basketball court – a funny image considering Nathaniel's short frame against Freddy's 6 foot 2.

There are many more images, all too painful for Nathaniel. His tears fall freely now, mixed in with snot and spit. He weeps, really, because underneath it all, he feels responsible for Freddy's death – that boy had been taken from him as punishment for his sins against Anne. Instead of mending with God and with Anne (and of course with her children), he threw them all out of his heart.

"Paw-paw," calls a tiny voice from behind Nathaniel, which belongs to Immy. Nathaniel freezes, then quickly pulls himself back together. He cleans tears and snot off his face with the back of his hand, smearing all on his white wife-beater.

"Hey, pal," Nathaniel says, trying to sound cheerful as he faces the boy. Immy is slightly darker in complexion than was Freddy, owing to the fact that his mother Shemeeka is dark-skinned. But in everything else, Immy is Freddy personified – down to the walk, the temper, the afro, the pale blue eyes and Freddy's smile.

Nathaniel is grateful for this, of course, even as he tries hard to forget about Freddy. He picks the boy up now. "Why is a big man like you walking around at midnight?" he asks the boy. "Maw-maw will have your hide if she finds out."

"You have a boo boo, paw-paw?" the boy asks, ignoring the warning about his grandmother. He knows she will do no such thing. "You were crying."

"No, I wasn't."

"Yes, you were," the boy answers, smiling. This is a familiar game with them.

"No, I wasn't."

"Yes, you were."

Nathaniel does not answer but instead, stares at the boy with a goofy expression. Seeing his grandfather's funny face, Immy bursts into one of his Freddy laughs. Nathaniel's heart melts. He throws his head back and laughs as well.

And what of Rachel? Aaah, yes … she has remained standing without moving the entire duration of Nathaniel's outburst in the kitchen. Long after her father took Immy back to bed and tucked him in a second time that night, Rachel stood in the phone booth holding the dead phone in her hand.

She eventually regains some form of consciousness due to the cold. It is the first week of September, fall is giving way to an early winter. Out in Long Island, the air is colder still, more so than it would be were she in Manhattan. She is not prepared for it, having abandoned all her clothes at her mother's, over two months before. She is wearing the same outfit she had worn when her mother kicked her out – jeans and a short-sleeved blouse. A light jacket, belonging to Jada, covers the blouse.

She has no more money, certainly not enough for a cab. It never occurred to her Nathaniel would not let her stay, although as for that – him letting her stay was wishful thinking on her part. At the moment, she is not worried about anything because she is not able to feel anything – not fear of the night, nor fear that she might freeze. She feels absolutely nothing.

She replaces the phone on its hook then starts walking, not due to a need to get anywhere. Rather, she walks for affirmation that she is still alive, even as she feels she is not. She has come to Long Island often enough to know the way to the train station. She doesn't know what she will do once she arrives, but she resorts not to worry about that until she gets there.

And so it is that she has walked some 45 minutes on the highway, with passing cars giving her a wide berth, when a nondescript automobile pulls beside her and slows down in rhythm to her gait. By that time, she was nearly rattling out of her body with shivering from the cold.

Brett Story hits the automatic button that winds down the passenger's window of his SUV. He is a 23-year old white boy with dark hair and lazy eyes – the eyes are a misrepresentation of his character, for he is not lazy or even sinister. What he is is kind, and that compassion is what makes him pull up alongside Rachel.

He has no clue whether she will be a friend or a foe, and knows he puts himself at great risk in this day and age if she turns out to be the latter. Still, he could not pass her by without inquiring if she needs a ride. It is almost 1:30 in the morning, a time of the night when no reasonable person should be walking alone on any highway in America.

He came upon her about ten minutes ago, and slowed down considerably to study the situation. Because her walk showed no fear or care or drunkenness – she did not once look back nor look around at her environment – he decided to finally approach her. He was certain that if she proves to be a lunatic, one look into her eyes will tell him so.

"Hey!' he calls out the window. Rachel turns her head towards him, permitting him the opportunity to carefully scrutinize her eyes, which are lit by the highway lamps hanging on the shoulder.

A part of him knows it would be very rude to suddenly peel off if he discerns signs she's an idiot, or signs she's of an evil nature – he is, nevertheless, prepared to do this. He receives information she is neither. Her eyes are deep-set and expressive. From their bottomless depths he gauges she is tired and is in need of great sympathy.

"Where're you going?" he asks softly. He does not want to frighten her in any way, nor give her the impression he's a no-good son of a bitch – of which, Brett knows, the world is filled with plenty.

If Rachel were in her right state of mind, she would recall the wisdom of not talking to strangers, even ones who appear as harmless as the man in the car. Since she's not in her right state of mind, she is more concerned about the effort required of her to actually respond. The effort seems heavy, too much to ask of her right now. But the question itself is a simple one, surely, she can manage to talk.

"The station," she answers at long last.

"Do you need a ride?"

"I'm good, thanks."

"You sure cause your teeth are chattering."

She considers this with slight surprise. She was not aware her teeth are chattering.

"Get in, alright. I won't hurt you," he adds finally. The utter sincerity in his voice causes Rachel to stop. Brett hits his breaks and opens the door. Without hesitation, Rachel climbs into the SUV.

In the car, Brett cranks the heater to its highest level. He sees she's still shivering, so he takes off his jacket and carefully drapes it over her body, tucking it in firmly on the sides. She allows him this closeness to her body without flinching.

"Thank you," she says, then leans her head against the passenger window and closes her eyes.

"You're welcome," Brett answers as he drives at a moderate speed down the road, making sure to avoid any bumps. He takes her closed eyes as indication she's asleep and thus says nothing so as not to disturb her.

He marvels at the trust she has placed in him, a total stranger. Determined that their encounter should begin and end with no harm to her as he promised – and, hopefully, no harm to him too – he intends to deposit her at the station, though it is a considerable distance out of his way.

He drives for a long while when she asks, "What's your name?" He's almost startled hearing her voice. Her eyes are open and staring straight ahead.

"Brett Story. Yours?"

She shrugs, an indication she does not want to give it, so he lets it be.

"Am I taking you out of your way?"

"No," he lies. "Um, where were you coming from? I mean, you're far from everything!"

He has that twang of speech typical of native Long Islanders. Rachel remembers her mother and her accent, but quickly throws Anne out of her mind to give Brett a shrug.

Brett chooses not to press her about her details. He is content enough to talk about his own. "Do you wanna know where I was coming from?"

"Sure." She doesn't really care.

"My bachelor party, it was wild." He laughs at the memory.

"So, are you drunk?" To Brett's ears, she does not sound in the least bit concerned even if he were. She might as well have asked, what color are your eyes – which are hazel, by the way.

"Not tonight."

"Oh?" Again, she shows nothing resembling genuine curiosity.

"Yeah, I promised my girl I wouldn't. She didn't want me losing control with strippers around." He laughs heartily.

"How old are you?"

"Twenty-three."

"Why are you getting married?"

"Huh? Why not?"

"Twenty-three seems young to me."

"You don't seem much older. How old are you?"

Rachel shrugs. Brett leaves it alone, saying, "If you knew my girl, her name's Stephanie, you'd want to marry her too!" He is cheery remembering Stephanie, then rattles off his history with the girl, also 23 – beginning with when they met in high school. He didn't go to college, though she did.

Rachel listens without hearing a word he says – it hurts her head to stay focused on the details. She hangs on his tone though, which confirms to her that he is good people. She knows he will make Stephanie very happy, and that hopefully – Stephanie too is good people and will make him very happy.

They will probably have two point whatever children, and he will be amazing to them. His children will love him till the end of his dying days and will grow up to tell nostalgic stories about their dad to their children.

Rachel decides right there and then she wants to sleep with Brett, in his SUV, at the back of the train station's parking lot, or wherever she can get him to stop the car. So she leans her head against the window again and begins shedding crocodile tears, tears that aren't real.

Since Brett knows nothing about crocodiles or their tears, he assumes she is genuine, and maybe Rachel is. But she also knows that the quickest way to raise the protector in a man is to act just this way.

Brett automatically stops talking and grips the steering wheel. He doesn't know whether to stop or to keep driving. He feels like the gum under a shoe for not recognizing how fragile she is. It's apparent to him now that she's been through some tough times.

"I'm, I'm … sorry," he says. The apology seems inadequate.

"It's okay," she manages, cleaning the tears on the very jacket he's used to cover her body. She realizes what she's doing and appears regretful.

"Sorry," she says very genuine.

"It's nothing. Please."

She sighs, moving the jacket away from her so she does not use it to clean her tears again.

"I'm … I didn't mean to go on and on about —"

"Don't worry about it. You're happy, is all. There's something very, very sad about happy people," she finishes.

He doesn't know what she's talking about, so he thinks it best to keep quiet.

"Can you pull over at the gas station?" The station in question is just up ahead, as is the train station, which can be glimpsed. Brett obliges quickly and pulls the SUV into the station's parking lot. Both remain quiet for a long beat.

"I need something from you, Brett," she begins. "And I can understand if you won't give it. It would bring me great peace, though, if you would let me have it."

He has never heard anyone speak as she just did. It reminds him of some stories he used to read in English class back when he was in high school. Moreover, the request, whatever it is, he knows will be heavy. He tries to anticipate what it could be and finally concludes it has to be money. She wants him to give her money. He wouldn't mind, if the amount were reasonable.

"Um, okay." His voice is a whisper.

"You should hear the request first before you say yes."

"Well, um, I was saying yes to … you can ask me, then I'll see if I can —"

"I need you to sleep with me." She throws the full weight of her eyes upon him, and he sees he will do it even before he fully comprehends what she just asked. He looks away from her eyes, which brim with dignity, even as the question is indecent. If he did not look away, he is afraid he will take her right there before first understanding why. And to think, he has never done anything out of the ordinary in his whole life.

The bachelor party flashes in his mind. It was his best friend's idea to hire half a dozen strippers who arrived with as many stripper poles. Everything went swimmingly well, even without him drinking. Everyone else was. He kept his head about him at all times, in deference to Stephanie and how much he loves her. The closest he came to touching the strippers was when each gave him lap dances. And so he passed whatever test of future devoted husband bachelor parties are purported to gauge, and now this? How did the evening turn into this?

"Something happened tonight," Rachel is saying to him. "I can't go into it, but it's left me … frozen. I can't feel a thing." She is very quiet and then finally, "I just want someone safe and good inside me right now. That's all I want."

Stunned at the words, he stares into her eyes again and sees she means every word. He swallows the lump caught in his throat and thinks of Stephanie. Rachel anticipated this and blocks the thought with these words:

"If this were about you, I can understand why you're thinking about Stephanie. But this is about me and what I need right now. If you can't do it, as I said, I will understand. I can see the station from here, I can get there on my own."

She finally turns from him, fixing her eyes forward. Her profile is regal, and he sees her skin is flawless. He follows the bridge of her nose to her bosom and sees she is ample, and her hips on the seat, wide. He did not notice these things initially because he knows better than to regard women as objects.

Now that he has noticed, though, he wonders what her warmth would feel like. He has never made it with a black woman before – in fact Stephanie is the only woman he has ever slept with, given that they've been together since forever. He has often wondered what another woman would feel like but has never acted on the curiosity – never had a need to.

Brett suddenly opens the door and gets out.

"Where're you going?" Rachel asks, for the first time – actually curious.

"I gotta get a rubber," he says.

The smile she gives him wins his heart as he strides into the gas station.

Brett parked the SUV behind the gas station. They are lying naked in the back seat of the SUV. Though he is average in height and in looks, Brett's physicality is something else altogether. An avid sportsman, his body – though pale – is testament to its well-kept nature. He is muscle everywhere, with a six-pack to boot.

Rachel took all this in in appreciation as she personally undressed him, then folded his clothes neatly and put them on the front seat, away from her. She said she did not want her scent to linger on any of his clothing, against Stephanie finding out.

She also made him promise he would take a shower upon arrival home, before he lies down beside Stephanie. He assured her not to worry about any of this, since Stephanie is spending the last couple of days of her single life in her parents' home.

Rachel felt better hearing this. All the same, she informed him she would avoid kissing him too deeply or roughly in order not to leave any hickies about his neck and torso. All her talk of hickies and kisses got him excited and he could not wait to begin.

He watches the dark glow that is her skin in the dark. She busies pulling the condom over his penis. Her hands handle him with care, exciting him further. He caresses her skin, then begins nibbling her earlobes and neck. He can't take his hands off her breasts, which are fuller and softer than anything he has ever held.

Done with the condom she says, "You can take over now. Please, Brett, make me feel good, okay." He hears the need for him in her voice and is determined to please her as much as he can.

As it turns out, Brett Story is an experienced lover – even given that he has made love to only one woman the whole of his life. This is because he and Stephanie are no prudes. They are experimental in lovemaking, making love often, and consulting porn websites regularly.

Brett places Rachel on top of him, guiding her bottom down until he has totally disappeared within her. He makes no moves within her, keeping as still as possible, allowing her to fully feel him, as she had wanted.

It is Rachel who moves first. She flexes and unflexes her muscles around his penis, which is extremely compatible to her vaginal cavity. He fills her in a way that Bo never did. She sighs with relief that this physical connection, on a day that has pushed her further and further to the brink, is exactly what she needs.

Brett is transfixed by her face, which is slightly lowered, as if she's thinking about something. He knows she's deep in concentration, as she continues to grab his penis within her with her pelvic muscles. This sends ripples of pleasure through him. If not that he is well restrained, he would have released already.

She looks deeply into his eyes and says, “Call me baby.” Her voice is sultry, causing him to release a moan laced with pleasure.

“Oh, baby,” he moans. “Can you feel me?”

She responds by squeezing his penis, holding the pressure without breathing. He nearly evaporates. In response, he flexes his muscles in her vagina. They go back and forth like this – flex and release, flex and release, balancing each other in perfect rhythm.

Rachel searches out his mouth and digs her tongue in. She tastes sweet and sugar, as of soda. He did not lie. There is no trace of liquor on his breath. Brett grabs a hold of her probing tongue with his tongue, and equally eats out her mouth as she eats his out. He grabs her by the butt cheeks and lifts her up and down against him, showing amazing strength and dexterity.

He watches her carefully, as he fills his mouth with her breasts. He licks and cajoles her nipples into tautness. He slows down a bit to gently circle her small waist with his arms, then flips her over so that he is on top. This is the position in which he is most superior. He rams into her pelvic space with firm though gentle thrusts. Rachel responds by circling his waist with her legs. She wants him to pound some more, so he obliges, licking and kissing her all over.

They go on like this for a while, grinding against each other. There are no other sounds save Brett’s measured moans and the whirl of the car’s heater. Rachel remains quiet throughout, as she concentrates on the sensation running through her body. She is aware that she should be feeling pleasure, but what she feels is … nothing. The condom doesn’t help, but she knows it is potential suicide without it.

Nathaniel’s words invade into her psyche: no-good for nothing, never call here again, you have no father in me; never call here again, no-good for nothing, no father in me; no father in me, no-good for nothing, never call here again!

These thoughts go round and round in her head, causing her to move more and more aggressively and urgently against Brett. He responds immediately, building himself to a point of no return.

Rachel knows now Nathaniel had seen something in her that all the publishers must have seen in her work – she is no good, her work is no good; she is no good, her work is no good; her work is no good, she is no good!

Bo saw the same thing and chose Indira over her. Her sister saw the same thing long ago. Her mother held out for as long as she could, but even she saw it eventually and cast her out. Jada and Chris were gracious, but in the end, the truth of what she must be got to them too and they too asked her to leave.

Rachel knows now she will never be a writer. She was a joke, her work was a joke – what respectable piece of work would be called *Pass the Hoochie* or *Albany Ho*? Her professors at Columbia told her as much about her writing, in veiled languages used to spare her feelings against permanent bruising.

Her mother said go out into the world and do something meaningful. By no stretch of the imagination would anyone consider her work "meaningful." It was all vile, as Paul, the stupid finance doctor – not so stupid now – stated long ago.

Her work would never be held on the same bookshelf as a Chinua Achebe, Buchi Emecheta, Flora Mwapa, Nadine Gordimer, Ama Ata Aidoo, Jane Austen, Edgar Allen Poe – hell, Stephen King!

If Ada can retire her penknife forever, so too Rachel her pen. She sees that now. But if she retires herself as a writer, what then will she be living for? Writing has been a state of mind more than a profession. If she is not writing, she is not living. She would not be living for anyone either, that's for sure. Bo has Indira. Ada has Paul. Her mother has Ada. Her father has his second family. And Jada has Chris. She has no one. So for whom would she be living, and why would she be living?

The answer comes to her then of what she must do. The thought had arrived and hovered over the phone booth after her father banged the phone on her ears. She realizes now she had been frozen holding the phone because she had been trying to identify the thought, which was alien to her. It is stranger no more!

Relief blazes all over Rachel's body for life makes sense to her once again. She slows down against Brett even as he quickens his thrusts. The main veins running along his neck bulge. He arches his head back, his eyes fluttering. Rachel expects his ride to be over in a matter of seconds but is pleasantly surprised when he does not release. She understands he is waiting for her. This touches her a great deal, so she quickens her own pace, giving him the impression she's about to quiver.

"Oh Brett! Brett!" she screams, in a way she knows men love. She grabs his neck, holding him tight, and would have scratched him all over his back but that she remembers Stephanie. Stephanie would notice that.

Brett finally releases, as he finds her mouth again. Their tongues roam each other's mouths hungrily until Brett is finally spent. She makes sure to shiver against him, so that he too is holding her tight.

"Are you okay, baby?" he asks exhausted. "Are you okay now?" He's drifting into a power nap.

"Oh yes," she answers softly, lying. She notes the smile on his face as his features take on a serene quality. All his muscles relax, though his hands wrapped around her continue to hold her tight.

Rachel is happy for him. She does not mind she did not climax. She's not clear she would have felt it if she had. She lies securely beside Brett, listening to him breathing quietly in his sleep.

When Brett wakes up half an hour later, she would be gone. So too would be most of the money in his wallet. She'd taken 80, and left him 10 dollars. His jacket would also be gone. He didn't mind the theft of the money so much, but Stephanie had given him that jacket on his birthday last year. She would remember to ask him about it months after their wedding.

His explanation that he must have lost it during the chaos of the wedding itself, or during the reception, or on their honeymoon in Canada – they're snowboarding freaks – would constitute the one and only lie he would tell his wife during the five decades they would be married. And because of that, he will harbor ill will towards Rachel for a long time to come.

MY SONGBIRD CAN DANCE

| 1 |

Marcus Peyton hears the girl before he sees her. He catches whips of words – lyrics, actually: *"... cream colored ponies ...."* And what's that? *"... crisp apple strudels ...."*

He carries an African drum on his back as he practically runs through Marcus Garvey Park in west Harlem, on his way to Excellence Charter School to pick up his children – Aaliyah and Marcus Jr.

Marcus' quick and nimble steps do not betray his 42-years, certainly not his youthful features and toned arms, peaking through the t-shirt he wears. He has maintained his top-form physique through years of dancing and beating *kembe* drums. He is a light-skinned African-American brother, standing a little over 5 foot 10.

The lyrics are coming in more audibly now,*" ... girls in white dresses with blue satin sashes ...."*

Marcus' trot slows to a walk as he rounds the trail. The foliage in the park is still in full bloom, obscuring the girl before he finally comes upon her.

She sings, " *... snowflakes that stay on my nose and eyelashes ...."*

He sees that she's sitting atop the rock, overlooking a fantastic view of 120th Street and 5th Avenue. She has her back to him and he notes her long braids, which fall close to the middle of her back. She is indeed singing, of all things, Rogers and Hammerstein's *My Favorite Things* from the movie *The Sound of Music.*

Marcus is in complete amazement, for the song seems totally out of place in this park, in this section of New York City, and at 2:45PM. What's more, the girl is black.

"... silver white winters that melt into springs ...." The girl nears the end of the song. *"These are a few of my favorite things ... When the dog bites ... When the bee stings ... When I'm feeling sad ... I simply remember my favorite things ... And then I don't feeeeel so baaaaaaaaaaaaad!"*

Her voice is not bad, Marcus thinks. With a little training it could be good. Regardless, Marcus would have clapped, but what he really feels like doing is reprimanding her.

Why Rogers and Hammerstein, he feels like asking. Why not Marley? Fela Kuti? Hell, Muddy Waters? Did it have to be *Maria von Trapp* singing about cream-colored ponies and crisp apple strudels?!

He's brought out of his pan-African haze when he notes with a shock, the girl is crying. She's trying to repeat the song, but her sniffles and tears will not permit it. At last, she gives up and breaks down completely. Marcus now feels immense guilt for the thoughts he held against her only moments before.

Maybe the song is her favorite, he thinks, nothing wrong with that. It is called *My Favorite Things* after all. The girl was obviously singing it to make herself feel better over whatever it is that's making her feel sad now.

"Hey," Marcus begins.

The girl spins around, startled to find she's not alone.

"That was really nice," he finishes, hoping he sounds believable. He notes her face is pleasant, though plain. She's obviously African for her features tell him so. Her skin is dark, the type of hue his parents would have objected to back when he was still dating. Though her eyes are besmeared with tears, appearing child-like, he places the girl's age to be around 22, no more than 24.

He subconsciously does with her what he always does whenever he comes upon a woman for the first time. He compares her to Yvette, his wife of 11 years. He finds with relief, his wife is more attractive than she – thus nullifying whatever attraction he could possibly feel for her.

The girl looks away from him and cleans the tears from her eyes with the sleeve of her blouse. His wife would not have approved of that. Yvette's ultra-feminine nature demands every woman's purse be filled with odds and ends, including the kitchen sink. There should definitely be Kleenex in there.

"You okay?" he asks the girl. She turns towards him again and nods slowly. Happy that she's at least communicating, he asks quickly, "You African, right?"

Rachel takes a moment to consider the question, since that has nothing to do with anything. Still, she is thinking, out of nowhere, I can be African. So she nods again. She knows he's looking to her to say something, but she wants to adjust her tongue for the inevitable accent. She imagines how her mother would say it.

"Yes, yes, I am," she finally says. Her accent is deep.

And because of that accent, Marcus is pleased with himself for having guessed her Africanness. His main gripe against God (in particular) and humanity (in general) is not being born on the continent of Africa. His secret bitterness against his parents and his four siblings is that despite his attempts to bring them into the light, they laugh at him whenever he ventures all discussions to Africa and the blasphemy that was committed by the slave masters when they ripped him and his future generations from the motherland.

In his youth, he had insisted his family call him *Kwame*, which they obliged occasionally, to keep his wrath at bay. He was *Kwame* all through out college, and up until he met Yvette.

Yvette had asked him to make a choice – either change his name to *Kwame* for good, or drop the whole Africa-name shit, her exact words. She accused him of not really being serious about *Kwame* otherwise he would have legally changed the name long before he met her.

He supposed she was right and reluctantly gave up *Kwame*. He reverted back to *Marcus*. His namesake is none other than the same *Marcus Garvey* the very park he's standing in is named after.

At least his daughter has an African name, he consoles himself, although Yvette agreed to it because it was the name of the late singer Aaliyah. His twin children were born the day after the singer died in the plane crash.

As to what to name their son, Yvette wasn't feeling *Kwame* in the least. To keep peace, he readily agreed to *Marcus Jr.* for his one and only son.

Marcus sees that the girl is not looking at him so he takes a quick look at his watch. His kids will be getting out soon. Should he just move on as he planned? Everything about the girl's body language is telling him to do just that. Still, his parents take great pride in how he was raised, he supposes he does too.

There's no getting around it, he concludes, he has to make sure she's okay before he can move on.

In retrospect, Marcus should have moved on, for atop that rock overlooking Harlem sat his destiny. Nothing here on out will end well for him.

On that fateful day, in early September, when he should have hurried on to pick up his children, Marcus Peyton made the fatal decision to be a gentleman. He interrupted a lonely woman's determination to take her own life by hurling herself off the rock.

| 2 |

Rachel was not really going to kill herself – she realized that once she got to the black top that afternoon. After coming in from Long Island, she had spent the night at 42nd Street Port Authority. She wandered around the cavernous station until she found a hidden nook that looked appetizing for sleeping.

She made herself as comfortable as possible inside the nook, covering her body with Brett's warm jacket. She promptly fell into a deep sleep, a sleep that was not interrupted even during the morning's rush hour.

Eventually, she woke in the early afternoon, and felt strangely well rested for someone who had slept on concrete all night. Then the events of the previous night came crashing into her consciousness and reminded her of her appointment at Marcus Garvey Park in Harlem.

So she made her way into a bathroom in the station where she washed her face, and washed out her mouth. She felt she should at least look descent when the cops or whoever found whatever remained of her at the bottom of the black top.

Because she was hungry and felt she shouldn't leap to her death on an empty stomach, she grabbed a quick lunch in midtown with some of the cash she'd pilfered from Brett, then went up to Harlem on the number 3 train.

Finally, she got to the rock in Marcus Garvey and walked atop it without hesitation. Her intent was simply to step off it and into the air. The view, as it always does, caused her pause. It was indescribably beautiful – rows of brownstones lining the street as far as her eyes could see. She appreciated once more urban planning, the singular neatness of it, even the color brown which blended well with the environment.

On the actual drop itself, she had not taken into consideration how terrified she would be contemplating it. It would be painful, she could see that, all the way down. The jagged edges of the jutting stones would tear her to pieces, but what a dramatic way to go! She thought it a pity she had not incorporated such a scene for any character in the story of *Yasmin*, the Sudanese sex slave. Nor would she now in the story of *Beatrice* since she would not live to write it.

Rachel edged ever closer and closer to the tip of the rock. What is the big deal anyway, she thought, it would be over in a matter of seconds. She stood there for a long time without making any more moves forward. She was losing her nerve, she could see that. Does this mean, she wondered, in this too, she was no good?

Tears brimmed in her eyes, blurring the horizon, and she suddenly swayed. Catching herself, she took an immediate seat on the rock for fear of accidentally teetering over and bashing her brains in. Feeling suddenly flushed and hot, she took off Brett's jacket and placed it beside her.

What a pitiful sight she appeared to herself, a soon to be 25-year old woman with nothing to her name, unloved and unwanted. *Maria von Trapp* popped into her mind then and she wished more than anything, she was the actual character. Everything had turned out well for the nun. What has being *Rachel* ever gotten her anyway? No wonder she was trying to kill *Rachel*!

She closed her eyes and saw herself as a beautiful white woman with short blond hair, spinning about on an Austrian mountain, and singing her heart out. So, Rachel opened her mouth and bewailed the afternoon, "*The hills are alive with the sound of music ... aaaahhhhh aaaahhhhhhh ....*"

She sat there on that rock, singing all the songs from the *Sound of Music*, in scene order. Her singing was mixed with bitter-sweet tears for she was trying to block out her father's face, her mother's face, Ada's face, Bo's face, Jada's face ... all the faces of everyone who has ever meant anything to her.

It's when she got to *My Favorite Things* that Marcus Peyton walked into her life.

| 3 |

"Is it bad news from home?" Marcus asks the girl out of nowhere – in reference to why she'd been crying.

The girl gives him a look he cannot interpret because Rachel detects that for whatever reason, Marcus really *needs* her to be African, so she answers, "It is bad news, yes." She offers no details whatsoever, thinking that the fewer words she speaks, the less chance she will have of incriminating herself. She's afraid of dropping the accent.

So to fill the silence that suddenly drops between them, Marcus rushes in with details of his own. "My name is Marcus Peyton," he says. "I'm the theater director at the Black Group Theater, you know it? It's only a couple of blocks from here."

The girl shakes her head and continues to stare at him deadpan. Something about her eyes upon him makes him want to talk more.

"I run the whole place," he brags.

The girl does not appear as impressed by this bit of news as he had hoped. This is because Rachel is busy stringing together details of her life as an African in America. She knows the questions will be forthcoming in a minute.

"If you don't mind my saying," Marcus continues – wondering what time it is but not daring to look at his watch now that she's looking at him – "My feeling about bad news is, see if there's any opportunity to make something good out of it."

"Opportunity?" the girl asks, sounding mystified.

"Yes!" he nearly screams, delighted she's speaking again. "I've known a lot of Africans in my day, and it seems bad news is always coming from there. I wish I could go there and change everything for you guys." He laughs nervously.

It takes everything Rachel has not to burst into laughter herself. What gall, she's thinking, but she keeps quiet to see how far the man will run his mouth.

"If it's money your people want," Marcus speeds right along. "The most important thing to remember here is you. You've got to take care of yourself first before you can help anybody else! Am I right?"

"I guess so," the girl says.

To Marcus, she seems preoccupied with private thoughts, and he is right. "You probably don't have your papers, right?" He is one of those people who mask statements as questions.

Rachel quickly looks away from him for fear he will detect the sneer on her face. In disgust she wonders, is the first rule of thumb that every African must not have papers?

To Marcus, her action of looking away means only one thing – the girl is embarrassed she does not have her papers. She is also proud, he can see that, but it's the type of pride that masks profound vulnerability.

To leave family and home to a land unknown, a land where you are often not wanted – the choice itself takes balls, balls Marcus knows he does not have – otherwise, he would have gone to Africa years ago to change the continent for the better as he has always pontificated.

This strength in Africans is what has always drawn him to their women. Before Yvette, there was a string of them in and out of his bed (among others). He did not settle down with any because, in the end, they had seemed too unknown. There was always a part of them he could never understand.

All the same, he is driven to helping them whenever their paths should cross – so long as he derives some benefit from the encounter, of course, no matter how small. In the case of this girl now, he sees an immediate opportunity.

"Unfortunately," he sympathizes. "I can't help with the paper thing, but if you need a job …." He trails off, hoping she will take the bait.

Rachel does, out of curiosity. "A job?"

"Yes, my wife and I are looking for a, um, a live-in nanny?"

The girl gives him that look he cannot interpret again because, at that point, Rachel is trying not to sprint towards him to bury her fingernails into his eyes.

Ever a sucker for long pauses, Marcus rushes in to extol the virtues of his children. "Well, not really a nanny," he explains. "My kids are not toddlers or anything. They're boy and girl twins, 8-years old. And they're great, no problems at all. It's just that we recently moved here from Jersey, so Yvette and I can be closer to the theater. She's my wife, she's an amazing actress and the star of the show. The lady we had taking care of the kids was going back and forth, from Jersey to Harlem, but she recently told us she couldn't do it anymore cause of the commute. We've been trying out other nannies, but haven't quite found the right fit. We pay what everyone else pays, plus vacation, sick days and everything. You'll have your own space. Hell, the basement, it'll practically be your own apartment!"

Marcus runs out of words. He stares at the girl anxiously. She stares right back at him coolly. He is feeling the weight of the drum on his back, so he preoccupies himself taking it off and placing it on the ground. When he looks to the girl again, she takes his breath away.

Rachel has gotten up on the rock, all 5 foot 9 inches of her. She does not approach him, nor does she face him directly. Her side-view is perfectly silhouetted against the Harlem bright sky. He notes her body immediately – she carries an ample behind, a half moon curve, made all the more shapely by the tight jeans she wears.

Her chest is the second half moon, protruding from her chest in D-cups, perfectly scooped by the low-cut blouse she wears. She's putting on a man's jacket, leaving it unzipped, thereby permitting him visual access to appreciate her well-formed boobs.

Rather than stare, Marcus looks beyond her for he feels the muscles jerk between his legs. His spirit tells him the proposal was a bad idea, but he thinks to himself he cannot take it back now. But of course he could, if he wanted to.

There's no sin against changing one's mind about a job offer, and a menial one at that. Instead, he convinces himself retracting the offer would not be a nice thing to do, now would it? So he finds himself hoping beyond hope that she accepts.

Rachel sees that the man is taken in by her, and is trying not to stare. What she can't believe is why she's led him this far. She is mystified by the excitement that's surging through her body.

"But I've, I've never been a, um, a nanny," she stammers, lowering her voice to sound vulnerable.

Marcus takes the bait. He likes the stammering. It shows uncertainty, even concern about her abilities. It also shows she's interested.

"But you are good with children? I've never met an African woman who is not!"

Jesus Christ! Rachel wants to scream, How do you people think this is okay to say?! What she does say to Marcus is, "Yes, yes! I am good with children!" She makes sure to sound desperate. She even takes a couple of steps towards him.

"That's the most important thing!" Marcus responds delighted. He is loving her reactions. "What have you, um, done since you got here? We will need a reference."

Rachel is momentarily quiet, thinking fast. She's never held a job in her life, but this should be easy.

"I don't know if my old boss will give you a reference," she begins slowly and sadly. "I was in a sweatshop in Queens. They fired me two days ago because I fell asleep on my sewing machine. I was working 16-hour days!"

She knows he will swallow these details hook, line and sinker because she knows all too well the sort of African he needs her to be.

Marcus notes only that the more words the girl utters, the more pronounced is her accent, becoming thick around the edges. She is West African, for sure, though he is not able to place the exact country. Ghana? Nigeria?

Marcus shakes his head sympathetically at her latest revelation. These are stories he has heard before – the baptism by fire that is the typical immigrant experience.

"Did you work anywhere else?"

She shakes her head no. "I've only been here three years," she is saying. "And I was in the sweatshop that whole time. This will not work, I'm so sorry. I just want to go home. My mother is dead. No one had the heart to call and tell me about it. We were so close, you see. Oh I want to go for her burial but if I leave, I can't get back in because of the stupid paper thing. Isn't that terrible? I think I should just go home, right? I am so tired of pursuing the stupid American dream!"

Rachel is proud of herself for her imagination. She breaks into fresh tears, though of the crocodile sort and turns her back on him.

Marcus is drawn to her backside, which he imagines sliding up against and giving a good squeeze. He chastises himself for the thought. But he feels awkward just standing there as her shoulders rock with tears. He looks about him nervously, wondering if anyone else is around. They are indeed very much alone. He goes to her then and places a tentative hand on her shoulder.

"Don't cry okay," he says. "Everything will be okay, you'll see."

"Thank you." She at least stops crying. "You're kind." She faces him again, her baby doe-eyes staring up at him. "I don't know what to do." She appears lost. "Should I return to my country or should I stay?"

Marcus, for his part, is lost in her eyes, which are mesmerizing. As a man, he knows he is in trouble. "Well," he begins, choosing his words with care, "this is not something anyone can answer for you … dear." He adds the last word as an afterthought, to give her the impression his interest in her is innocent and professional.

"This is your mother we're talking about," he continues. "There's only one!"

Hm, Rachel thinks, respect for the man is rising.

"What you have to ask is," continues Marcus. "What would she have wanted? Did she want you to make something of yourself in America?"

"She sold all her earthly belongings for the money I used to come here," Rachel admits, working herself into an excited and distraught state. "Her enemies said she was wasting her money, that her only child would never amount to anything in America!"

"See! There's your answer!" Marcus declares, seeing a way out. "You have to prove them all wrong. Your mother would want that! She would want you to stay!"

Wow, Rachel thinks, does a man really only think about what's dangling between his legs? "But I have no job!" she blurts out.

"I just offered you one!"

"I have no references, you said I need them!"

"Do you have anyone who can vouch for you?" He doesn't really care about these questions, only looking into the dark pools of her enchanting eyes. But he knows Yvette would ask, and thinks it best to know the answers now.

"Just the friends I made at the sweatshop, one of them is my roommate."

"Okay, listen, I want you to come to my home tomorrow morning for an interview. My wife would like to talk to you. We need someone really badly because we are both so busy. We are preparing for the company's debut performance in January. Can you get your roommate to pretend to be your boss at the sweatshop, to give you a glowing review?"

Rachel stares at him dumbfounded. Oh my God, she's thinking, I could be a serial killer!

Marcus does not flinch by her surprise. He hopes – without admitting to himself he's hoping it – that this complicity will make her pliable later on.

Rachel lowers her eyes and squeaks out a barely audible, "Yes."

"Alright then, that'll be our secret," he adds. "But I really have to go now, I have to pick up my kids from school!"

"Oh! Sorry!"

"It's okay. If all goes well, you'll be the one picking them up!"

He takes his wallet out, scribbles his address on the back of his business card, then hands it to her.

"Alright then, I guess I'll see you tomorrow." He runs over to the drum, hoists it once more upon his back.

"Come at 10, okay," he says to her. She nods.

"See you then!" he exclaims, then makes to run off.

She calls after him, "Do you want to know my name?"

Marcus stops short, embarrassed he hadn't bothered to ask. "I'm sorry, what's your name?"

"It's okay, you're in a hurry … Ify, my name is Ify."

"How do you spell it?"

"Like it sounds."

"E-e-f-e-e?"

Without hesitation she says, "You got it."

"*Eefee*. That's nice. Where from?"

"Nigeria." Let that fact be true, she reasons. She is familiar with the Nigerian landscape – from years of having spent summers there – to furnish him with details should he ask about the country.

"Some of my best-friends in college were Nigerians," he says, thrilled that he had almost guessed her country.

Rachel receives this bit of irrelevance with a smile, which Marcus is pleased he was able to coax out of her. Her face is not as plain as he had initially thought. She is beautiful, in fact. What had he been thinking. He looks her up and down again.

"Eefee, I have one more request … please don't take it the wrong way."

"What?" she asks, making sure to look worried.

"Oh no," he rushes in, wanting to reassure her. "Don't worry, it's nothing, honestly. Please don't be offended but can you, um, dress appropriately for the interview? Yvette, um, she … well, you know how women are."

She gets him immediately. "Don't worry, sir." She's acting as if she's blushing. "I understand perfectly and I'm not offended."

"Oh no! No *sir,* please. Call me *Marcus*."

She smiles demurely as Marcus finally readies to go. He disappears down the trail, moving very quickly despite the drum on his back.

Watching him disappearing down the trail, the smile in Rachel's eyes fades. Why are you doing this, she asks herself. Well, she answers, I have no place to go. Didn't he say something about a basement apartment? Plus, it's a job. Needless to say, I need the money. Really, Rachel, is that all?

Well, for sure, the man is an idiot, for all his varied and down right insulting assumptions about Africans and their lives in America. Yeah, and? It's not my fault he ran off with his own fantasies. I just didn't correct him. But Rachel, as you know, he is neither the first nor the last American who will hold such views.

Her mouth puckers in a pout. She doesn't want to think about the truth – the truth being: she wants to see how far she can go with this.

Most important, she wants to have a little bit of fun, a fitting climax to these several months that have been froth with misery.

She does not want to admit these truths to herself. Instead, she convinces herself of this: I don't want my old life back. I want a new life, not as a nanny, of course, but I need to lie low for a little while, to think what direction to take my life. And anyway, I'm sure I won't last a day cloaking myself as somebody I'm not. He's going to find out and then he will fire me.

These reasons seem most justified to her and so she chooses to believe them. She marvels at the turn of events. The afternoon started with her fatal thoughts and quickly turned in the opposite direction. She looks down at Marcus' business card in her hand. If one believes these things, he is indeed Theater Director of the Black Group Theater.

She inserts the card in the pocket of her jeans and grabs her ample butt, giving both cheeks a squeeze. As he had requested, she will dress down to cover up her ass for wifey. This, his second request, will be their second secret.

As to the first request, Rachel quickly heads towards the bank where Jada works, assuming Jada has returned to work. If not, she will have to call her at home. She plans to convince Jada to play the role of her ex-boss down in the Queen's sweatshop. She is sure Jada will not refuse if it means Rachel will be gainfully employed and will continue to be out of her and Chris' place.

As Rachel rushes through the same trail that Marcus did only minutes ago, she concentrates on remembering all the details of her so-called African life.

| 4 |

Marcus need not have worried about what impressions Rachel would make on his wife. Yvette's mind is completely elsewhere. She is a 36-year old woman so dazzling in her light-skinned color she might as well be white. She is 5'6" and wears colorful, comfortable attire that accentuates her petite and slender frame.

Yvette sits with her back straight, across from Rachel who is dressed in conservative clothes: a long dress shields rather than accentuates her bountiful assets, both on the bottom and at the top.

An African-print scarf covers Rachel's hair, which is no longer in braids. The scarf is knotted at the back of her neck, giving her a more Aunt Jamima African look. The entire ensemble renders her pious.

Yvette barely notes Rachel's attempts at piety, nor the fact the girl arrived a whole half-hour early for the interview. Marcus pointed this fact out to his wife. He went on to declare to both women, in his attempts to make small talk, that people showing up on time for anything these days seems relegated to the past. He then complimented Rachel on the scarf.

"Thank you," Rachel says sweetly, alarmed that he's being so forward with his wife around.

If Yvette were thinking straight, she would also be wondering why her husband is talking so much. Why details such as what time the girl arrived or the color of her scarf are suddenly of great interest to him who generally cares nothing for such things.

For her part, Rachel maintains eye contact on Yvette, avoiding Marcus altogether. She does this for two reasons: first, she does not want to encourage Marcus in any way as he sits there beside his wife on the couch. Second, she does not want to threaten Yvette by fixing her gaze too long on her husband.

If there is one thing Rachel knows in the whole wide world, it is women. Married or single, African or non, white or black, women are the same when it comes to perceived feminine threats towards their men. She thought Jada exempt and was unpleasantly disappointed there.

Rachel need not worry where she is throwing her eyes because Yvette is not concerned about that at all. While Rachel blabs about life as an only child in an African village, Yvette struggles to remember what the girl's reference had said on the phone only minutes before. More important than her past history in Africa, Yvette still retains some sense of reasoning that Rachel's immediate past in America is far more important.

Yvette recalls, although foggily, that the previous boss from the sweatshop gave the girl one of the most glowing reports a boss could give an ex-employee. Rachel could do no wrong and in fact, the ex-boss intimated, the only reason Rachel was let go was because the girl no longer desired to work 16-hour days.

Yvette knows very well the brutal wear and tear on the body that sustaining long-term inhuman rigor inflicts. And so pain – as it is with her 24/7 – is what Yvette Peyton is thinking about.

At the moment, the pain radiates from her center, creeping throughout her body, settling on her joints, her knees in particular. She can feel her kneecaps throbbing, imagines that the throbbing can be seen. She is anxious that Marcus not notice – hence, she moves about on the couch, often readjusting her position, looking for a comfortable pose. It helps to sit rigid, her hands over her kneecaps, covering them against her perceived perception the throbbing is noticeable.

On the outside, Yvette's body is a work of art. She is tiny and compact. Because of yoga, she's built and fine-tuned it to a tautness expected of women in their 20s. On the inside, however, she is all but destroyed, due to 20 odd years of modern dance and acrobatics, jumping around numerous stages across America.

In her youth and in her 20s she felt indestructible. Now in her 30s, the on-set of early arthritis, on top of everything else, is about to do her in – coming at the worst possible moment in her life with Marcus.

At the beginning of the year, they finally managed to scrape the necessary funds – loans from banks, family and friends – to open the theater, fulfilling a long-held dream Marcus nurtured since they met and married. While his home is the theater, Yvette's is film. She wanted to be a renowned and respected Hollywood actress, on the level of Meryl Streep and Jodie Foster – hell, even Halle Berry.

Over the past ten years, she has appeared in numerous independent films, always as a minor character and never ever catching enough of a break to actually break through – causing her self esteem irreparable damage.

To make matters worse, Marcus refused to move out to Los Angeles. He hated the place and everyone involved in the business. He promised her, though, that if she broke through, they would pack up the children and move out west.

As the years flew past, however, and as Yvette spent more and more time on the stage, Marcus upped the lobby to forget about California and to nurture their own theater in New York. He wore her down, promising he would make her a star – on the stage, at least. The play he has written to debut the theater in early January would make the company and thereby catapult her into the heavens.

Yvette acquiesced and let go of her Hollywood dreams, a dream she's held since she was a little girl. Not long after that, she threw painkillers into her mouth – initially, to dull the pain of the broken ankle she'd sustained in March. Eventually, though, she threw the pills into her mouth to also dull the pain that suddenly crept up from deep within her spirit.

The rest of her body soon followed suit – buckling under the demands of the rehearsals, hastened by the first symptoms of arthritis. After each rehearsal session, her body would take days to recover.

She noticed her recovery time was faster with the more tablets she threw into her mouth. She has no idea how many pills she consumes a day, losing count whenever she gets to around 50. The bottles are hidden in the basement, out of reach of the children, of course, and Marcus' wary eyes.

Yvette is thinking of her beautiful array of bottles now. Because the interview was scheduled for 10 and because Marcus did not hasten to the theater after dropping the children off at 8 as is his usual routine, Yvette made the critical error of thinking she could get through the interview without taking her usual battery of pills. And so she suffers. She cannot recall anything Rachel just said. To give herself something to do, Yvette readjusts her position on the couch.

Rachel notes Yvette's motion and wonders if, perhaps, the tale she is spinning is boring to the dazzling woman. She's telling the couple of how she came to America on a fiancé visa. The fiancé turned out to be a creep who was involved with someone else as he was keeping house with her. Rachel found out and walked out on him.

"Good for you!" Marcus retorts, not at all happy to hear about a fiancé. He wonders if the girl still carries a torch for the man.

Rachel ignores Marcus' exclamation as she goes on with more made-up nonsense about her life. She got the idea of the cheating fiancé from Bo, naturally, but specifically from Aminata, the African girl who works in the bookstore at 125th Street – whose husband is openly spending most of his time with his mistress instead of giving equal time to both women.

After convincing Jada to pose as her ex-boss, Rachel went to the bookstore to ask Aminata if she could spend one night on her couch. She did not want to put Jada on the spot by asking if she could spend the night at her and Chris' place again.

Fortunately, Aminata agreed. She agreed because, for one thing, it looked like her cheating husband was never going to come home from the mistress' house. And another thing, Aminata never forgot the fat tips Rachel used to give her.

Aminata and Rachel stayed up all night taking the braids off Rachel's hair. Aminata went on and on about what Allah will do to her husband at the end of his life, while Rachel added a few words of support here and there. It was also from Aminata that Rachel borrowed the dress and the scarf she's wearing now.

Aminata was instrumental in one final way – she took Rachel to Mohammed, the Senegalese master of counterfeit Social Security cards and fake IDs. Mohammed created a fake ID with *Eefee Okoli* stamped next to Rachel's face and Aminata's bookstore as *Eefee*'s home address.

Neither Mohammed nor Aminata queried Rachel on why an American would need such an ID.

"I found full-time work in the sweatshop," Rachel rattles on for Yvette and Marcus. "But then my mother got sick, so I doubled my hours to send money home for her care. Then she …"

Rachel trails off here, lowering her head to strike a sad pose. " … she passed away a couple of days ago." She says this in barely a whisper, thinking they must surely ask her to leave now. They have to know all this is made up.

Marcus sees no imposter. In fact, he is thoroughly taken with the girl's feigned tragic tone. He wants to hold her in his arms and make everything bad go away.

The same image moves Yvette out of her mental fog. "I'm so sorry to hear that, Eefee," she says.

Rachel is happy to hear from Yvette who had, until now, seemed distracted. The woman had uttered only cursory remarks – "How old are you?"; "Do you like America?"; "Can I see your ID?" – things of that nature, but she was mostly quiet.

Rachel looks at her now, zeroing in on Yvette's face. She sees that Yvette's eyes and features are genuinely filled with concern, offering just the right level of reaction expected over news of a dead mother.

"Thank you," Rachel manages softly, shifting her gaze to Marcus. She sees in his eyes she's doing very well. He is even proud of her. Rachel quickly looks away from him and back to Yvette whom she notes appears distracted again.

Yvette is thinking of when would be the appropriate time to end the interview. She's heard enough, the girl will do. What she needs is her fucking medication!!

Yvette hears her scream in her head and cringes, wondering if she spoke out loud. The other two appear not to react to a loud yell, so she's certain she did not call out loud.

"When can you start, Eefee?" Yvette asks this, the most diplomatic phrase to indicate the end of the session.

"Oh, today if you like," Rachel answers, not too desperate.

Marcus and Yvette exchange a quick glance. He answers for both of them. "That will be fine." He is smiling very broadly, which, if Yvette were once more in her right state of mind, would set off all the red bells of caution in her head.

"Good," Rachel states matter-of-factly. "I will go back to my place and get my things." She has no "things" to bring, but knows it would appear odd if she doesn't go away and come back with "things."

She will borrow a few more clothes from Aminata, and the rest she will buy with the last remaining cash she stole from Brett. She does not mind spending all her money in this way, since the couple should, hopefully, pay her something in two weeks.

Yvette practically jumps to her feet, since the other two are moving much too slowly for her. She grabs Rachel's hand in a handshake.

"We're happy to have you, Rachel!" Yvette declares, a little too loud. Rachel rises and curtsies, taking her hand back. Yvette's grip was a little too tight.

| 5 |

Marcus' study is located on the fourth floor of the Peyton brownstone. The room might be considered large, save that it's stuffed to capacity with exercise equipment he has abandoned over the years, preferring instead to bang on African drums as a way to relieve stress and stay fit.

There are numerous drums jockeying for space in the room, which also fits his massive desk made of oak on which he does all his writing. But by far, Marcus' favorite drum is the one he calls *Malika*, the one he carries back and forth everyday, from the theater to the house.

The drum is 36-years old and is his first drum ever. It was given to him by his father when Marcus was 6 years old. And it was his father who taught him how to play all drums, as a way to connect to the little boy whom he acquired when he married Marcus' mother.

Marcus does not actually play drums at home, given the noise factor. And on the rare occasion he does, it's usually when the children are in school. Of late, however, he's been dropping the children off at school and immediately running off to the theater, *Malika* strapped to his back.

Why does he do this? It would be most convenient to leave the drum in the theater where he gets a chance to beat on her no matter what type of day he's having, no matter how busy. Beat on *Malika* at some point during the course of his day is for Marcus like taking lunch for most people.

The thing is, Marcus does not consider the drum an inanimate object. She is as alive to him as are his children and his wife. Wherever he is *Malika* must be. So he carries her back and forth everyday without even thinking about it.

It is, therefore, just as well he brought the drum home when he met the girl because, with the children away at school this morning, Marcus has been beating on the drum since Rachel ran off to bring her things.

Marcus jumps up and down as he pounds on the drum. Sweat pores off his forehead, drenches his face, trickles down his neck to his exposed torso. Sweat beads his arms and glistens off his hands that strike the drum. He pounds with an intensity that's similar to if he were trying to wake the dead.

They know each other well, *Malika* and Marcus. She will never question him nor protest the heavy-hand he uses on her now. She knows he burns off the heat that surges throughout his body, which he will never admit is brought on by the thought of the girl. So *Malika* bends and booms, hollers and screams, yielding to his will. Her cacophony bounces off the walls and echoes throughout the house.

Meanwhile, Yvette creeps into the basement. It's not really the basement – actually the ground floor apartment. Everyone in the house calls it the basement because they only come down here on their way to the actual basement. Yvette uses the entire space as a yoga studio and practice space.

There is a bedroom off to the side and a bathroom across the way. The real basement door is beside the bathroom. When Rachel returns, she will occupy the bedroom and have full use of the bathroom. A washing machine and dryer occupy the section near the bathroom.

Yvette can hear Marcus' muffled drumming, coming all the way from the fourth floor. She generally requires peace and quiet in the house but doesn't mind the noise now. The sound is her audible cue to Marcus' actual position in the house. She knows she is safe, so long as he continues beating on *Malika*.

Yvette stealthily enters the medium-sized bedroom with plain furnishing. She eases onto her knees then reaches under the bed and pulls out a large plastic container filled with orange pill bottles in all manner of sizes. A cursory shake of one bottle tells her it's empty. She sets this aside and picks out another one – only to find it too is empty.

With trembling hands, she searches through empty bottles and finally finds one that's almost full. Visibly relaxing, she uncaps the bottle and pours four pink tablets onto her palm. She throws the pills into her mouth. Eyes closed, features enraptured, she crunches the pills as though pieces of hard candy.

Yvette moves quickly after that, running about the room and collecting pill containers from inside and outside the pieces of furniture strewn in the room. With Rachel moving in, she has to find another location for her precious commodities. Yvette sets the empty ones to the side, while placing filled ones inside the master container from under the bed. She is alarmed that so many of the bottles are empty.

She runs out of the room with the master container, heading to look behind the washing machine. She notes the container will not fit at the back of the machine, nor will it fit behind the dryer. From upstairs, Marcus' drumming increases in tempo, almost projecting the anxiety broadcast in her eyes. She wonders what to do.

She suddenly dumps all the pills on the floor, then pushes all behind the washing machine. Pill containers clatter about, one bottle rolls away from her. She chases after it, her hands filled with bottles that invariably also clatter to the ground.

Her eyes give a furtive and frightened glance up the stairs she just came down from, as if anticipating Marcus to come down the stairs. Since the sound of the drumming never breaks or diminishes, she appears to relax.

Yvette picks up all the fallen bottles and stuffs them behind the washing machine. She uncaps the last bottle and pours some of its contents straight down her throat. The bottle is now empty. She shakes it out thoroughly, anxious that it too is empty.

She runs into the bathroom and reappears with not only a glass of water, but with more pill containers. After drinking the water, she throws the cup back into the bathroom, then returns to the washing machine to hide the new pills.

She runs behind the dryer and distributes more bottles there. She next grabs the hamper, resembling a tall garbage can, and pushes it against the washing machine. The space behind the machine and the dryer is now hidden from the naked eye. She appears pleased with herself, then remembers something.

Back in the bedroom, Yvette picks up all the empty bottles she'd set aside. She rushes from the room and runs out the back door leading into the backyard – really, a clump of earth in total disarray since neither she nor Marcus has the time to beautify it.

Yvette opens one of two large garbage cans. She roots in the bin until she locates a plastic bag. She inserts all the empty pill containers into the plastic bag, then buries the bag as far down in the bin as she can, all the while furtively looking around.

Even outside, *Malika's* echoes are audible. Yvette worries if the neighbors are disturbed by the noise and are now looking outside their windows. Will they see her burying orange pill containers? She hopes no one is watching.

Satisfied she's buried her problems, Yvette recovers the bin and walks back inside. She heads to the yoga exercise space and takes off her sweatshirt, revealing an exercise outfit. She hangs her head low, listening to the muffled echo of the drumming.

Marcus has settled into something less urgent, almost soothing. Yvette closes her eyes and starts moving to the tempo. The transformation is never immediate, but she has learned to allow the pills the time to do their work. Her gentle moves and the gentle echo of the drum help to relax her body, giving her a focal point away from the pain.

She thinks about her role in the upcoming play Marcus has written – *She Who Bears Light* he's calling it, a play that takes place in a far away kingdom in Africa, a time before the coming of the missionaries. The echo of the drum strangely sets the tone as her mind travels to that far off kingdom.

The play tells the story of *Light*, a married woman and mother of six. *Light's* only desire is to fight in her nation's war. The only problem is her nation does not permit women to bear arms or to be anywhere near conflict zones. So *Light* is relegated to the home front, tending to her children and the sick soldiers who return home.

The sick soldiers are her only source of information on the ongoing conflict, which has raged on for 25 years. With an uncanny ability for military strategy, *Light* knows the war would come to a speedy end if their side does this or that.

Understanding the brilliance behind her suggestions, one sick soldier mends and returns to war. There, he assumes command and carries out *Light's* strategies, swaying the battle to their side. He never lets it known the ideas are not his.

Because *Light* is not actually on the battleground, the commanding soldier soon runs out of ideas and decides to secretly send for her. As much as *Light* would love to be at war, she knows she cannot leave her six small children to be watched over by others. So the commanding officer personally maims her husband by cutting his Achilles tendon with a sword. Useless now in battle, the husband is forced to return home to tend to his children. *Light* immediately takes his place in battle, disguised as his brother.

On the warfront, *Light* is not content to remain on the sidelines, whispering strategies to a man who has maimed her husband and who continues to take the credit for what should be her great achievements. If she reveals her gender, however, the men will cut her down for it is a great taboo for a woman to carry a sword.

Eventually, *Light* and the commanding officer duel it out on an open field and she kills him. She reveals her gender then, daring any soldier to lay a sword on her. They do not for they are afraid of her after she managed to kill a man in a fair duel.

She challenges the soldiers to fight beside her in the still ongoing battle with the other side. She promises to lead them to success or her name isn't *Light,* she who bears arms! The soldiers have no choice but to fight beside her or perish.

As promised, *Light* leads her people to victory and is carried home on the shoulders of her men. From then on, the law is changed to permit women to fight – but after they've found suitable replacements to take care of their children, of course.

Marcus wrote Yvette to be *Light*. She connected with the character immediately because she knows a thing or two about desire! His drum beats from upstairs flow with Yvette's movements as serenity spreads throughout her body.

Yvette knows the pills are finally doing their work because she feels free and young, bouncing with unlimited energy without pain, as light as a feather, yet powerful and firm. She moves her body to a dance as old as time.

| 6 |

Yvette adds *Eefee Okoli* to the administrative form at Excellence Charter School that would permit Rachel to bring the children home. It's about 15 minutes before school lets out, so the two women walk back outside to wait in front.

Rachel moved into the bedroom on the first floor two hours ago. Though the room boasts no windows, she loved it immediately for it is larger than her room at her mother's house. Also, it is the only other room she's lived in since she was 6 years old.

Yvette and Marcus showed her around the brownstone, filling her head with the history of the house. It belonged to Yvette's grandparents and Yvette was raised there. She moved out when she went to college.

Her grandmother then willed the house to her when the old woman passed away five years ago. Yvette and Marcus did not live in it all that time, renting the place out instead. They preferred to raise their children in Jersey. But when they acquired the theater in January, they decided to officially move into Harlem to be closer.

Yvette and Marcus treated Rachel to a lunch of sandwiches and soup in their expansive, state of the art kitchen. Yvette's grandmother kept the house in tip-top shape with money left her by her husband who died four years earlier.

Rachel assisted Yvette in the lunch preparations – a simple affair since the soup came out of a can and the sandwiches peanut butter and jelly. Marcus watched the two women closely, feeling a tinge of jealousy as he listened to their animated conversation.

Rachel was most fascinated with the dull backyard. She asked permission to "till the earth back there" — her exact words which caused both Marcus and Yvette to chuckle. They gave her the go-ahead, although Yvette made it clear to the girl her services involved only the children and not outside as gardener.

All three left the household – Marcus with *Malika* – about a half hour ago. They got on the bus on 143rd and Amsterdam and rode down to the children's school near 125th Street. Marcus went on to the theater to continue the tedious audition process to fill the rest of the cast for the play, while Yvette and Rachel entered the charter school to introduce Rachel to the staff.

In front of the school now, Yvette breaks the silence by humming a song. Rachel listens carefully, liking the mournful tune. When Yvette's hum comes to a lull, Rachel breaks in, "What was that?" she asks. "It's beautiful." She's proud of her African accent which seems more and more natural to her.

"Oh that," Yvette says dismissive. "It's an old Negro Spiritual I learned from my father. *All Gods Chillun Got Wings.* It goes something like this, "... *I got-a wings, you got-a wings."* Her voice is mellow and mournful.

"... *All o' God's chillun got-a wings ... When I get to heav'n I'm goin' to put on my wings ... All o' God's chillun got-a wings."* Yvette reverts back to the hum and in time, the tune ends.

"My dad was a preacher," Yvette confides. "The fire and brimstone type. He traveled all around the south, spreading the word of the Lord to heathens, he used to say."

"He's not a preacher anymore?"

Yvette shakes her head, saying in a deadpan voice, "Nah. He took God's word to some folks who didn't wanna hear it down in Tennessee. They found his body hanging on a tree, a noose round his neck. I was 16 years old. The murder's still unsolved."

"I, um, I am sorry to hear that." This is all Rachel can manage to say. She stares into Yvette's light brown eyes, which communicate absolutely nothing. Yvette might as well have compared apples to oranges. Rachel shudders ever so slightly, noticing the street is too quiet, the air suddenly colder.

"It's no biggie," Yvette says with a shrug. "Ghosts of our fathers, they're harmless. And *My Favorite Things?* Why were you singing that on the rock?"

"Marcus told you about that?"

"Yes."

So they talk, thinks Rachel.

"You like that musical?" continues Yvette curious.

Rachel treads softly here, wondering what she should say. Instinctively, she wants to steer clear of having to remember details about two parents. What are the odds anyway? Two black women standing on a quiet Harlem street, haunted by the thoughts and actions of their fathers.

"I just love it," Rachel finally admits. "Who doesn't like *The Sound of Music*?"

Yvette chuckles, saying, "Some more than others, I guess. "

Seeing that Yvette is livelier, her mood more upbeat, Rachel adds quickly, "Thanks for hiring me, Yvette. This job really means a lot to me."

“Oh come on, girl, we’re happy to have you. You like your room, right?”

“I love it! It’s very comfortable.”

“Good. If it gets cold, we can get a space heater down there for you.”

“Thank you, I’m sure it’ll be fine.”

“I’ll try not to practice down there too much.”

“Oh come on! You won’t disturb me at all. Really.”

Silence falls between them again which makes Rachel slightly uncomfortable. She prefers Yvette lively. “What’s Aaliyah like?” she asks, rushing on. “And Marcus Junior too?”

“You’ll see them soon,” Yvette answers. Her face lights up in an inward smile as she talks about her children. “They’re both great kids. Aaliyah’s smart as a whip, wise beyond her years. MJ’s pretty impatient, precocious. You got to keep an eye on him.” Yvette says nothing more for a beat, her face thoughtful.

“To tell you the truth,” she says at long last, “I don’t know where they came from. They’re so much better than I deserve.” There’s a sad quality to her voice now.

Rachel is touched by these words, so much so her thoughts go to her own mother. She is certain Anne would never say any such thing about her!

“What’s wrong?” Yvette asks, noticing the girl’s solemn face.

“I was thinking of my mother just now.”

“I bet you made her proud.”

At first, Rachel is unclear why Yvette is using the past tense, then discovers with a shock she had told them her mother is dead. This is gonna be harder than I thought, she thinks. She looks away from Yvette to hide her shame.

"I'm sorry. I didn't mean to remind you of … your, um, mom," Yvette says.

"It's okay," Rachel adds quickly. She does not like all the talk about dead parents. Everybody knows that if you talk about something long enough, it's bound to happen. No matter how mad at Anne she might be for casting her out, Rachel does not want anything to happen to her mother. She hopes Yvette would change the subject.

For her part, Yvette does not remember her mother, who committed suicide when Yvette was 4 – hence, why her grandmother raised her as her father traveled the South.

One fine afternoon in the fall, Yvette's mother threw herself in front of the number 2 train at the 125th Street stop and Lenox. Instead of the third rail, the woman thought she saw the ocean down there and jumped in to take a swim, right as the train roared into the station.

She was hallucinating because she was high on some good stuff, stuff she began to take because she believed she was no good. She believed she was no good because her preacher husband, Yvette's father, told her she was no good.

He told her she was a no-good motherfucking bitch who opened her legs to the whole of Harlem when he was out in the world saving God's children. She did not open her legs to anybody else in Harlem except for him, by the way, but she believed she had to be no good otherwise why would she have married him. So she began to take the good stuff to stop hearing his mouth in her head.

Yvette's grandmother never told Yvette how her mother died, only that she fell asleep and never woke up. Yvette believed her – that is, until she turned 12 years old and her grandmother's sister let her in on her mother's swan dive in the train station.

The sister kept from Yvette the crucial fact that Yvette's mother had been a crack head. The sister felt it might have been too much information for the little girl. A shame because, had anyone told Yvette her line had a propensity to abuse drugs, she might have stayed clear of the stuff.

Yvette suddenly extends neatly folded bills towards Rachel. "Here," she says. Rachel stares at the money, wondering if this is an advance of her salary. "Please, Yvette," she pleads. "I don't need an advance."

Yvette smiles as she puts the money into Rachel's hand. "It's no advance, girl. It's for your mom's, um, stuff. Marcus and I, we know you can't go home and help with her funeral and stuff. It's only 200 dollars, but we hope it will help."

If Rachel is as light-skinned as Yvette, Yvette would see the red hue of shame rise from Rachel's neck to her cheekbones. What she does see in Rachel's eyes she interprets to be humility and immense gratitude. Yvette chuckles. Her hand in her pocket is feeling the rest of the cash.

Marcus handed Yvette 500 dollars for Rachel as they walked out of the house that day. But Yvette kept 300 of it, with intent to pay Terrence, Mindy and the "boys" – the legion of folks she employs to keep her supplied with her poisons of choice.

Rachel opens her mouth to say something, which Yvette expects to be a deafening "Thank you!" But in fact, Rachel is about to divulge everything – that she was born and raised in the Bronx, that Anne is not dead, that she is a Columbia University dropout, that she was never engaged to any slime ball, and that she is slime herself for having misled the family thus far.

At that exact moment, however, a sudden piercing noise rises in the air – of children exiting the school building – a sure declaration that school is out.

| 7 |

Marcus had written the role of *Light's* husband for himself. However, he has become overwhelmed with all the different hats he's wearing these past few months: theater director, casting director, director of the play, writer, promoter, administrator, accountant – the list goes on.

Certainly, he has a "partner" who runs the business aspect of things, while Marcus is supposed to concentrate on the creative. But Marcus is the type of man who has his hands in other people's cooking pots. A consummate perfectionist and devout workaholic, he honestly believes no one can do half of what he can do.

As a result, the partner – Theo Downing – keeps out of Marcus' path by holing up in the theater's main office, located in the back. Theo makes sure the bills are paid, the actors are happy, and interns busy. Of late, he has skillfully taken on more and more of the advertising and marketing from Marcus. They communicate via the Blackberry Marcus has strapped to his waist at all times.

From the start, Theo thought it a bad idea for Marcus to direct himself in the play – as if Marcus doesn't have enough to do. Just an hour ago, Marcus announced the news to Theo, via Blackberry, that he is giving up the role. What Marcus failed to mention to Theo is his reason for stepping down. He is conceding the role because of the girl, a conclusion he came to while beating on *Malika* that morning.

The last thing Marcus wants while the girl is about the home is to remain in his study either bent over lines or, well, beating on the drum. He will not openly admit he's doing anything out of the ordinary because of the girl. His mind is not yet ready to look at the meaning behind these things. He does not want to know he's taking the necessary steps to set certain actions in motion. Like many men who do not think things through, Marcus believes at this very moment, it is possible to bake ones cake and eat it too.

And so, although the casting call went out for soldiers, he finds he's auditioning good-looking men for the role he had reserved for himself. Marcus has not shared this fact with Yvette, but feels she will not mind. Yvette does not mind very much these days, that much he has noticed on the home front.

Marcus sits front and center in the audience seats. The theater is cozy, seating 75 chairs. He, Theo and Yvette intend to have the place packed on opening night, people standing in the back and on the sides, stuffed to the point of bulging out onto the street.

At the moment, Marcus eyes an actor on the stage, a chap so stout in appearance and mannerisms, he reminds Marcus of a gorilla. The actor would make a great soldier, but the guy readily jumped at the chance for a speaking role.

Marcus' primary intern, Luis, sits to his left – Luis, black and in his early 20s, is gay. Because Marcus hates gay people and gay black men in particular, he can't stand the intern whom he's secretly referring to as *Louise* – as in the character in the movie, *Thelma and Louise.*

Out of the corner of his eyes, Marcus catches Luis' manicured fingers holding the play on his lap. He looks away from the fingers that remind him of Yvette's. He notes uncomfortably that Luis is checking out the actor on the stage.

By day's end, Marcus knows the intern will chatter like a woman with the other interns – mostly female – about the physical attributes of all the actors who will float by on the stage that day. He believes the reason Luis has stayed on this long – despite personal abuse from Marcus – is because *She Who Bears Light* is a play made up of 98.3 percent male actors.

Luis' obvious lust for the actor reminds Marcus of the actor. He wonders impatiently if the guy is finished with looking over the lines. The actor's head is buried in the sheet in his hands and he is mouthing the lines.

"Ready!" the actor suddenly barks, as he puts the paper aside.

"Alright then," Marcus gives the go-head to the actor. Then nods to Luis to say the first line which will prompt the actor to deliver his.

Luis gets to his feet, and reads from the page of the play he's holding. "You are maimed, dear husband," the intern quotes, speaking as *Light*. Luis is even trying to speak in a high tone, like a woman. "You cannot return to war!"

THE ACTOR (roars): I am a man!

Marcus interrupts the actor. "Hold up, brother." Then turns to Luis, whispering, "Can you cut that shit out?"

"Cut what shit out?" asks Luis.

"Speaking like a damn sissy! Use your normal voice."

"Whatever."

Marcus gives the intern a measured look, causing Luis to quickly look down on the page. Marcus nods to the actor to continue.

"Can I have that first line again?" the actor asks.

LUIS (in his normal tone): You cannot return to war!

"I meant the whole thing," the actor says, appearing apologetic. "Sorry."

LUIS: You are maimed, dear husband. You cannot return to war!

THE ACTOR (even more menacing): I am a man! My place is to fight! I cannot remain indoors cleaning snot from the noses of colicky children!

LUIS: It's our children you're talking about, hubby!

THE ACTOR: A thousand …

Marcus holds up his hand, indicating the actor should hold it. He then turns to Luis. "Are you kidding me?!" he nearly screams. "Do you see *hubby* written on there?!"

"Sorry," says Luis, then prepares to repeat the line.

LUIS: It's our children you're talking about, husband!

THE ACTOR: A thousand pardons, wife!

The actor begins to pace on the stage, building up annoyance and irritation.

Marcus interrupts again. "Excuse me, why are you pacing?"

The actor startles, breaking out of character. "You don't want me to pace?"

"The guy's maimed," quips Marcus.

"Maimed how?" the actor asks.

"He got his Achilles tendon slashed on his right foot," Luis says out of nowhere.

Marcus seizes him with a look that forbids him to speak unless spoken to.

"Would it have hurt?" intrudes the actor.

Marcus does not answer right away, wondering what that has to do with anything. "Yeah, like murder," he finally says.

"Does it still hurt?" the guy asks, actually looking pained thinking about it.

“You betcha,” Marcus answers. “So if anything, you should be limping.”

“It doesn’t say anything here about him limping,” the actor says, consulting the page he had put aside.

“Don’t move, okay brother man,” Marcus says, ending the discussion.

“Sure,” the actor responds, putting the page aside again. “You’re the director.”

It’s the way he said it. Marcus decides on the spot the guy won’t do. Luis sighs, and takes back his seat.

| 8 |

Rachel sits behind the glass, in a small room filled with parents and other caregivers like herself. Most of the adults in the room appear bored, while others occupy their time by reading books or magazines. Since this is Rachel's first time in the karate studio, she's focused on watching the twins at work in front of the glass.

Aaliyah and MJ are as fair in complexion as both of their parents. Other than this, they bear no other similar detail between each other for fraternal twins. Aaliyah is slightly shorter than her brother and wears glasses. MJ does not wear glasses and is stockier in build.

Aaliyah's hair is long and bunched up in a tight bun at the top of her head, as if she's a ballerina. A yellow belt is tied round her waist. Her brother is a little more advanced than she. He has a yellow belt with orange stripe tied to his waist.

At the moment, the children – along with 11 others, varying in age from 7-years to 13 – sprint round the dojo doing laps. They are led by the principal trainer, a Latino man as skinny as a rod, himself a black belt. All are dressed in the standard karate uniform – starched white top and pants.

Rachel took an immediate liking to the children primarily because they took an immediate liking to her. She brought them home while Yvette went out to run errands.

After Rachel fed the children the same peanut butter and jelly sandwich/soup combination she and their parents ate that afternoon, the children changed into their karate uniforms and all walked the few blocks to the karate studio.

On the way, the kids peppered Rachel with questions about life in an African village. Rachel filled their ears with the usual stereotypical landscape – everyone lived in huts, there was no running water in those huts, laundry was in the river, and everybody ate monkey brains.

She'd told them that last bit was a joke and they responded with laughter. But she saw in their eyes they still believed it. Rachel felt a tinge of guilt for contributing to keep Africa in the dark ages to impressionable African-American children but felt she could surely not deviate from the story she has already spun for their parents.

Now in the dojo, she watches with great interest the children kicking and punching the air, as commanded and first illustrated by the karate master. Admiration for the teacher soon blooms in Rachel's heart. She likes the way he is gentle with the children and the obvious discipline he exhibits as a karate teacher.

Rachel wonders if she might some day become a karate teacher. Why not? She had taken the job with the Peytons to lie low and think of what she wants to do with the rest of her life. She has no intention of sticking with the nanny thing as the new year dawns. She figures September till December a long enough time to find a new direction, then use the money she will earn to follow that direction.

So why not a karate teacher, she asks herself? She might even begin taking classes with the children. It all looked like fun.

When they get home at 6PM, there is nothing suitable for dinner – only canned foods and peanut butter and jelly. Aaliyah enters then, dressed in her dainty nighty.

Rachel saw to the children's baths. She hovered outside the bathroom as each child took turns to splash in the tub. She was reluctant to leave the doorway, knowing that children drowned in tubs of water. She did not want that to happen during her watch, even though there was little chance 8-year olds would drown under a showerhead. Still, she was taking all necessary precaution to protect her charge.

With a concern that projects calamity, Aaliyah now watches Rachel rooting for food. Rachel sees the child, notes how she pushes again and again, the glasses up on the bridge of her nose, even though the glasses are not falling off. Rachel is amused by the child, wonders why she's looking on with the eyes of an old woman.

"There's nothing, huh?" the child asks. Like her father, it appears she also masks statements as questions.

"I can whip up something in a jiffy," Rachel says to reassure her.

Rachel is worried now herself. Her cursory search determined there wasn't much in the house to whip up a nutritional meal. She would have to run to the store for groceries. But the children are washed and dressed for the evening. Should she have them change back into outside clothes, or just throw coats over what they have on now? She knows better than to leave children alone in a house.

Aaliyah breaks into Rachel's thoughts by heading to the cupboard. The child takes out two cans of corn, then waffles from the fridge.

"We got waffles," she says with relief. The relief in the child's voice baffles Rachel.

Just then, MJ bursts into the kitchen and blurts, "I can't concentrate on my homework if I gotta eat waffles again!"

"Again?" Rachel asks as innocently as possible.

"Yeah!" the boy declares unabashed.

"We don't eat it all the time," Aaliyah adds defensively. Rachel wonders who she's trying to defend.

"Uh-huh!" continues MJ, not caring to defend anyone but only speaking the truth. "We had 'em yesterday, day before and day before!"

"Waffles aren't so bad," squeaks Aaliyah.

"Can you make something else, Eefee?" the boy is done with the discussion.

"I'll do you one better," Rachel says cheery. "We're going out, guys. Get your clothes back on."

"Going out?" Aaliyah is immediately worried.

"Where?" MJ's delighted.

"Chinese restaurant," Rachel answers. "You like Chinese?"

"Yeah!" cry the children in unison. MJ rushes off to put his jeans back on. Aaliyah lingers.

"Did mama give you money, Eefee?" she asks softly. "I got some in my piggy bank if, if … if she forgot." She says this last without looking at Rachel.

Rachel reads volumes in the girl's body language and careful choice of words. So she walks up to Aaliyah and bends to her level.

"Save your money, hon. Your mama gave me loads, so don't you worry." She straightens the glasses on the child's nose.

Through the glasses, Aaliyah's worried expressive eyes relax. She nods simply and walks away from Rachel.

Rachel straightens up, then pulls out of her pocket the 200 dollars given her by Yvette that afternoon. As school let out, Rachel decided on the spot to spend the money on the two beautiful children who ran into their mother's arms rather than on her supposed dead ma.

To assuage her guilt on stringing the couple along, Rachel intended to spend the money on giving the children a good time – like going to the movies, to roller skate at Riverbank State Park, to museums, to the zoo, or wherever.

In considering the money now though, it will have to go for more practical items like food. She's wondering, why would the couple be lavishing her with money when there was nothing in the house for their children to eat? And why hasn't anyone called her to find out if she and the children have arrived safely home?

Reaching for justification, Rachel concludes that the couple is indeed so busy with the upcoming play certain basic obligations have fallen to the side and that is why she is desperately needed. Still …

Rachel reinserts the money in her pocket and runs down to the first floor in search of her coat. On her way there, she cannot shake the image of Aaliyah's worried and expressive eyes looking through her glasses.

| 9 |

Yvette does not have Aaliyah's expressive eyes on her mind as she rides the elevator up to her cousin's 11th floor apartment on West 57th Street in Manhattan. She told Rachel she had to run out to do some errands; whereas she told Marcus she would be spending the afternoon with Rachel and the children, to see that all were getting along.

He would not call her, nor would he call home to check on her. These are not his habits when deeply involved with work at the theater, so she has very little to worry about in terms of his keeping tabs. He trusts her implicitly.

Yvette hurries to her cousin's apartment. She is in constant motion, given there are other rendezvous to keep before the day is out. Her cousin Lily, a woman in her early 30s, lets her into the plush apartment while on the phone.

Lily is a full-time mistress of an investment banker who works on Wall Street. He pays the rent to the apartment, as well as all of Lily's expenses. She's on the phone with him now, coordinating which hotel downtown she's supposed to hook up with him in about an hour.

Lily kisses Yvette on the cheek then points to the center table in the living room. On that table sits two pill containers filled with prescription pain medication. Lily herself needs no such things in her system, but she fills the prescription in her name for Yvette.

"Yeah, baby, I know it," Lily says on the phone. She scribbles the address on a note pad as Yvette grabs the bottles and dumps into her purse. From her same purse, she takes out a handful of postcards advertising the play uptown. She gets Lily's attention, and indicates she's leaving the postcards on the table.

Lily nods. She will make sure the boyfriend figure attends and he will drag his well to do colleagues along. In this way, the investment community will represent uptown during opening night.

Lily gives her full attention to her love. "What you want me to wear, baby? Yeah, you wanna see me in that? You devil." She cackles good-naturedly as Yvette heads towards the door.

At the door, Yvette blows her cousin a kiss which Lily returns. Yvette shuts the door quietly while Lily continues on the phone, "Oh honey, please, I don't wanna talk about your nasty ass wife!"

Yvette's next stop is Terrence, an old high-school boyfriend. Their relationship in school was a dismal and painful failure, given their youth and immaturity. Remarkably, they survived to be best friends as adults.

Other than this friendship which Terrence values above all else, fortune did not smile too kindly on him when it came to love. Twice divorced, with five children combined from the marriages, Terrence is almost always in need of extra cash to make ends meet. Yvette helps out as much as she can – for example, sliding him 100 dollars cash for pills he gets for her.

She arrives to his work place in midtown, where he serves as head of security at a building. From behind the desk, he sees her approaching right on time. He indicates to a colleague he's stepping out for a smoke, then joins Yvette.

Outside, they walk away from the building, making sure not to touch. His colleagues are prone to watching such interactions and will rib him about it once he returns to his post.

Around the corner, Yvette and Terrence kiss and hug – the interaction is innocent, as a brother to a sister. He takes out of his breast pocket, three filled medication bottles which he hands to her discretely. She, just as discretely, slips him 100 dollars from the 300 in her purse. They walk in no particular direction as he lights a smoke and puffs it.

"Everything okay with you, babe?" she asks

He shrugs, then hands her the smoke. She takes two puffs then hands it back.

"I'm tired," he says. "I can't see the sun no more, you know." This is his way of saying he's tired of dealing with his two baby mamas and the five kids he's raising with them. The women are all about how much money they can get off him.

"It's gonna be alright, Terrence. You know that, right?"

He sighs. "I had a dream last night, Yvie."

"Yeah?"

"Yeah. I dreamt I had a heart attack."

She laughs, taking the smoke back. "Yeah, you keep smoking like this."

"For real," he says, laughing too and then becomes subdued. "I died, you know. Saw myself in the dream. Swear to God, it was the best sleep I've had. Then I woke up and had to get to work."

The thought of him dead makes her very sad, and she has to hold him.

"Don't worry, baby," he says tender. "I hang in there for you."

"For your kids," she says, letting him go.

Terrence finds himself wishing, as he's wished a million times, they had their shit together back when they were kids. Because he has too much respect for her and would never take advantage of their friendship, he knows their time has passed. She is married with two kids of her own now anyway and is committed to a man she would never betray.

She could not be entirely happy with Marcus, Terrence thinks, otherwise why is she taking this shit. She's hooked on the stuff, he knows, but like a true enabler – he believes, as she's led him to, that he's her only other supplier.

"You got them postcards?" he asks, aware by her body language she has to go.

She takes out of her purse the same postcards she left for Lily and hands to him.

"Give me more, babe. I'm goin' fill that house." And he will. He has followed her career on stage, appearing at every opening, with no less than two dozen of his personal friends and family – although he never takes either of the baby-mamas.

He will also pass the flyers out to the professionals in the building where he works, mostly lawyers, whom he has come to know over the eight years he has served there. In this way, the legal community will represent uptown come opening night.

Yvette hands him more postcards, as he requested, and gives him a peck on the cheek. She turns and heads towards the train. He watches her until she disappears in the crowd. He finishes the smoke and heads back to work, his mind on that heart attack he believes would solve all his problems.

For her next stop, Yvette is sitting in a booth at McDonalds. This particular restaurant is busy, as they all appear to be in west Harlem. There are the usual colorful folks – the semi-professionals pretending they don't frequent the fast-food chain, the rude and all too rowdy teenagers let out from school and the smattering of homeless folks occupying seats here and there and engrossed reading the paper.

Yvette arrived 25 minutes ago, and has already consumed four cups of coffee. The anxiety that Mindy might be even later is eating her alive. Mindy is, for the most part, on time. And when she's late, it's not for more than ten or fifteen minutes.

Mindy swooshes through the door right on the 15th minute of being late. She is a slightly overweight black woman who frequents McDonalds. It's Mindy's idea to always meet here so she can pick up an ice cream sundae (she's hooked on the thing). She will consume the sweet stuff behind the desk in the doctors' office.

Mindy is a receptionist and has worked in a private clinic owned by five partner doctors for five years. In that time, she has managed to gather a great many resources to "shift over" – for a fee, of course – to her small army of "high-end clients" – pill-popping middle class men and women, mostly women, who should know better. Everyone has their poison, Mindy concludes. Hers, for example, is McDonalds.

Yvette spies Mindy as she walks towards the counter to order the sundae. "Shit," Yvette curses under her breath. She's gonna make me sit here, Yvette is thinking, while her fat ass goes and gets her damn ice cream!

There's no reason for Yvette to be angry. This is what Mindy always does. And as always, Mindy will come over and pat Yvette on the back, ask her how she's doing and then return to the counter to get her order.

Sure enough, Mindy lumbers towards Yvette, a cheery woman who never gets angry for anything. Her name is actually Melinda, but she goes by Mindy to be different. She knows many black Melindas, her grandmother on her mother's side being one. Then two friends in college, and one of the doctors she works for – though a white woman.

"How you doing, girl?" Mindy asks, patting Yvette on the back. Mindy never apologizes for being late.

"Fine, girl," Yvette mutters, trying to mimic Mindy's cheeriness. "How are the kids?"

Mindy bursts into laughter. "Girl, stop! You know you don't give a damn about my kids!"

Yvette startles and looks around furtively. It's true she doesn't give a damn about Mindy's kids, can't even recall how many kids Mindy has. But did the woman have to be loud? Yvette does not want to draw attention to her table.

"How are yours?" Mindy asks genuinely. She loves all children – that is, before they become teenagers. They are terrors then. All of Mindy's three children are below the age of 10. She's not looking forward to their teen years.

"They're fine, thank you," Yvette says impatient. She doesn't like discussing her children with her, um, dealer? She still doesn't know what to call Mindy.

"You got the nanny yet?"

Yvette is surprised by the question. She has forgotten she sometimes confides in Mindy about details of her personal life. It's not that she wants to, it's just that Mindy is often generous after hearing such stories.

"Yes," Yvette blurts out distracted. Her mind is on the reason she's come. "She's from Africa. Her name's *Eefee*." Yvette hopes this will end the discussion.

"*Eefee*, huh?" Mindy disappoints her by saying. "That's nice. Be careful of them Africans though," advises the cheery woman. "You got to lock down the house, put away jewelry and stuff. She cute?"

"Cute? I don't know. I guess." Yvette really wants to be going.

"You guess?! Yvie, please. Don't you know the first thing you got to lock down is your husband?!"

Yvette sighs and looks out the window. She is not unaware of Marcus' proclivities. Because her grandmother raised her, Yvette was taught the virtue of tolerance when it comes to a husband. Her grandmother formulated many marital lessons during her 60 odd years of marriage to Yvette's grandfather who was no saint. The wise woman taught her granddaughter that when taking a man as a whole, his flaw of straying should not supersede his shining qualities. And to Yvette, Marcus has many shining qualities the greatest of which is, she is his number one.

What is equally important to Yvette is to maintain an atmosphere in the home whereby the marriage would be sustained, whereby her children would come home to a house in which there is a father and a mother. As a child who did not grow up with parents in the house, Yvette does not want the same background for her children. And so she has learned to tolerate Marcus' occasional need to stray. She understands it to be a need rather than a want. The distinction, though subtle, also makes it tolerable to her.

Yes, her husband is not a saint but the last thing Marcus would do – Yvette could stake her life on it – would be to commit adultery with his children's nanny right under the roof they all shared. And where would he find the time anyway? He is always at the theater, completely consumed and strung out by the pressures of the production. She recalls the last time she and Marcus made love was about a month ago and that was because she initiated it. He was so tired he passed out before she was done.

"I gotta be going, Mindy," Yvette says, hoping to prompt Mindy to give her what she came for. Mindy understands perfectly and asks, "You got my money?"

Yvette quickly pushes over 120 dollars, along with postcards of the play. Mindy puts the cash in her pockets, not bothering to count it – at least, not in full view of everyone. If Yvette expects Mindy to finally comply, she is sorely mistaken. Mindy picks up the postcards and studies them intently, as if looking through a microscope.

"These are real nice, Yvie."

"Thank you," Yvette responds, controlling the anger in her voice.

Mindy puts the postcards in her pocket and will distribute them among the doctors she works for and among the wave of patients she will see from now till opening night. And in this way, the medical and health community will represent. Mindy lumbers back to the counter to pay for her sundae with the money Yvette just slipped her.

Goddamn you! Yvette screams in her head, Give me the damn thing already! Yvette conveniently forgets the favor Mindy will be doing for her distributing the postcards. Yvette grips the coffee cup tight as she watches the woman at the counter. The coffee cup collapses under the strain. Fortunately, the cup is empty.

A bolt of pain suddenly shoots from Yvette's fingers through her wrist. Is it real or imagined, she has no idea. Doesn't really matter, since the pain is real enough. She opens her purse and roots for any of the pills she received from Lily and Terrence. She locates a container and discretely pours tablets into her palm. She throws the pills into her mouth, grinding them down to fine powder. She doesn't note their bitter taste in her mouth anymore.

Mindy arrives then – not with one sundae cup, but two. She graduated to two cups about a week ago, after concluding that one never really seems enough. She drops a folded newspaper next to the collapsed coffee cup on the table.

Yvette snatches the paper and looks through it. She sees the prescription pad within the folds. She sighs with relief as she inserts the pad into her purse. She gets off the chair and rushes towards the door, forgetting to say goodbye to Mindy. Mindy doesn't mind.

"Take care now!" Mindy calls to Yvette who is already out the door. Mindy decides to sit and finish one of the sundae cups. She will take the second back to the office, giving her co-workers the impression she only bought one.

Yvette fills her prescription at a drugstore in Inwood, though she has no business so far uptown. It's just that the drugstores closer to home have grown wary of her constant ins and outs. She spends the rest of the afternoon in Washington Heights.

She scribbles in cursive on the prescription pad she got from Mindy, her pain medications of choice. She then hands the prescriptions to her "boys" – local young men, mostly in their late teens, who walk into drugstores, hand the pharmacist the prescription, wait for the prescription to be filled, collect it and then hand back to Yvette waiting at the designated street corner.

For a half-hour's worth of "work" – which mostly comprises the wait period for the prescription to be filled – the boys earn 40 dollars each. She has only 80 dollars left after Terrence and Mindy, so she could only use two of the boys today. She does not give these boys any of the play's postcards because she does not want them in the audience looking up at her. She's not even sure they will come if she did.

As she waits at the last rendezvous spot, the Rite Aide store on 145th and Broadway, Yvette zeroes in on a group of teenage girls horsing around on the median island smack in the middle of the busy street. The girls are Latina – six of them occupy benches, while watching the seventh girl with a hoola hoop twirling around her waist.

The objective is to keep the hoop swinging round for the longest length of time. It is a strange thing to see in Washington Heights, amid the hustle and bustle of the early evening and amid the mostly Hispanic landscape. The hoop itself is bright pink, so that its color pops amid the grey and black worn by mostly everyone around.

Yvette watches the scene mesmerized. The girls holler with delight as they shriek words of encouragement to the seventh girl to keep on swinging her hips for the hoop to stay on her waist. The girl's face is screwed with intense concentration. Her arms swing out and flail at her sides. Her hips swing round and round, like a belly dancer.

She reminds Yvette of the aura she's been chasing all along – there was a time good health was a permanent condition. Peace and happiness were always there, not temporary fixes found at the bottom of an orange pill bottle. Yvette knows the respite she gains is nothing compared to the happiness she sees on the faces of the girls.

Eventually, the hoop cascades down to the girl's legs. Her girlfriends cheer and clap for she appears to have kept the hoop going the longest. Chatting merrily, all cross the light and pass by Yvette. She watches after them for a long time, as they head down the incline, towards Riverside.

When Yvette turns back to stare at the door of the drugstore, she is just in time to see Jose exit. He is 20, of average height, good-looking, a hoody over his New York Yankees cap, and walks with legs spread apart, to hold up his sagging jeans. He hands her the filled prescription – she already gave him the money when they first met up. Without saying a word, Yvette walks away from him.

Jose watches Yvette walking towards the subway station. Because she stops at the intersection to wait for the light, he trots over to her, holding his sagging pants as he hustles. When he arrives to her, she registers surprise to see him beside her since their business is already done.

"What's up, Jose?" she queries, slightly irritated. She does not like talking to her boys in such a public manner. Ever wary, she knows she has no business talking to anyone of Jose's character. What if someone she knows sees her doing it? Wouldn't it get back to Marcus?

"Hey, mami." The boy is fresh. She hates being called "mami" by these guys. But she's never told him her real name either.

"I've told you to quit calling me that." She wants the light to change already, so she can be on her way.

"So what's your name?" he asks for the umpteenth time.

"Mira," she answers for the umpteenth time.

Jose laughs. He likes the way she looks. She's a real sexy mama, although he would never try to get with her. He abstains from women who use, no matter what they use. He is beside her now purely for business purposes.

"Why you wasting money taking shit, mami. I can get you good stuff to make you feel real good, guaranteed. What you got there? It take the pain away, but it don't bring in the bliss."

She's stuck on the word *bliss.* It sends shivers up her spine. Yvette looks away from Jose and thinks of her children. She always thinks of her children's faces whenever she considers the good stuff. And she thinks about the good stuff at least once a day. But the faces of Aaliyah and MJ always surge forth, throwing the good stuff to the side.

"I gotta go," she manages nervously. She is nervous because next to her children's faces, for the first time, suddenly popped up the rosy cheeks of the seven girls and the hoola hoop between them. That was euphoria, that was bliss.

Jose reads her nervous tension as cha-ching, cha-ching. It is only a matter of time then. A natural salesman, he knows when to back off.

"I'm just saying," he says, a twinkle in his eyes. "Come see me anytime, aiight?"

The light changes. Yvette crosses. Before she descends into the subway, she looks back at him. She sees him standing there, a broad smile on his face.

| 10 |

Marcus returns home in time to tuck his children into bed at 8:30PM, surprising the children and Yvette. Marcus usually returns home close to 10. Yvette would have returned at 8 – this was back when they were still struggling with babysitters.

Now that Rachel is in the house, Yvette knows she is expected to return home with Marcus late at night. In anticipation of the coming crunch, she elected to take the day off to supposedly hang out with Rachel and the children.

Marcus came home, he said, to tell Yvette all about the gentleman he cast to play her husband in the play. Looking for an opportunity to pick a fight with him, she decides the topic worthy.

"What?" she asks, sounding incredulous.

Marcus is taken aback, the look of incense in her eyes surprises him. He thought she wouldn't mind, would even be elated.

"You cast someone else to play my husband?" She flicks the TV off with the remote control.

"But you said with me running things, it was all gonna be too much for me." He's taking off his clothes to go take a shower.

If she were not so bent on her own needs, Yvette would realize something is up because Marcus would never admit to such a weakness. The man believes he can do everything! Instead, Yvette's working over time to make sure he gets into that shower and stays there.

"Yes," she punctuates, getting out of bed to face him. "And you shouted me down cause you wanted to do it! You have to do everything!" She pokes at his ego, knowing it would make him defensive.

"Yvie, please. I thought you wanted this!"

"Why would I want this, Marcus? I got used to you in that role. Don't you think you should have consulted me about the decision? We're supposed to be partners in this thing, but it's clear you're running a dictatorship! You calling the place the Black Group Theater, but there's no group! It's just you! You should be calling it the Marcus Peyton One-Man Theater!"

"You know what?!" he retorts. She's played him just right. "I am the writer! I am the producer! I am the damn director! I can cast anyone I want to play whatever role! It's my damn vision!" His clothes completely off, he marches into the bathroom to soothe his anger under the showerhead.

Yvette waits until she hears the running water to make straight for his wallet. She knows when his mood turns like this, he will be in there for at least an hour. She takes out his bankcard, throws her clothes on, and rushes down the stairs.

She finds Rachel watching TV on the couch, says something to the effect she has to run out real quick, and then swooshes out the door. Rachel thinks nothing of it and returns to watching TV.

Outside, Yvette rushes to their local bank on Broadway. Out of breath, she uses the card to get into the branch, then withdraws 200 dollars from Marcus' account. She has her own bankcard and has her own separate account, but she has to be careful how she spends her money. She takes money from his account in small quantities like this because, as vigilant as Marcus is about keeping an eye on her money, he is slightly lax when it comes to his. Plus, with the expenses now associated with the theater, Yvette knows it would be easy for him to miss a hundred or two.

Inserting the money into her pockets, Yvette runs out of the bank and dashes up the incline towards Convent Avenue. Once in the house, she bypasses Rachel – still on the couch – to rush back up the stairs. If Rachel believes any of this is odd, she keeps this opinion to herself.

In the bedroom, Yvette replaces the bankcard in Marcus' wallet. She can hear the shower still running as she takes off her clothes and changes back into her nightgown. She reaches under the bed and retrieves the pill bottle tucked between the mattress and the box springs. She pours pills into her mouth, replaces the bottle under the mattress then throws herself onto the bed.

When Marcus exits half an hour later, she would be fast asleep. Still upset that she would challenge his decisions and indirectly his vision, Marcus puts on his PJs. He leaves the shirt unbuttoned so that his chiseled torso can be glimpsed.

He exits the room in a huff to go downstairs to get some water. In reality, he is going in search of Rachel, the reason he's home early although he will not admit this to himself. He hopes she has not turned in for bed, and is still sitting on the living room couch watching TV.

When he enters the living room, the TV is off and Rachel is no longer on the couch. Since he can hear her in the kitchen, he heads there. This is just swell, he's thinking. Since he's going in there to get some water anyway, he'll simply take the time to ask her how was her first day.

In the kitchen, Rachel is cleaning up the aftermath of her first official cooking for the Peytons. After she and the children ate dinner in the restaurant, they stopped over at the supermarket for Rachel to pick up grocery items.

Once back at home, she helped the children with their volumes of homework just as their mother walked through the door. Rachel left the kids with their mother to go into the kitchen to prepare spaghetti and meatballs. When Rachel was done, Yvette ate some of the meal and thanked her profusely for bothering to cook.

When Marcus returned home, Rachel decided not to clean up the kitchen just yet. She wasn't sure if he ate at home or at the theater. Seeing it was close to 10PM and he never came back down, she decided to clean up and put everything away.

She is almost done with washing the dishes when Marcus arrives. She is unaware of his presence at first since he lingers at the door, staring at her backside. She hums as she works – specifically, *Edelweiss* from *The Sound of Music.*

He stands there listening to her hum, enjoying the mood and the view of her perfectly round ass. Her hum is broken now and then with the actual lyrics of the song, "*... small and white, clean and bright ...*" She goes back to humming. *"... blossom of snow may you bloom and grow, bloom and grow for eveeeerrrrr ...."*

She goes back to humming, then, *"...bless my homeland forever ..."* She carries the last note into a long hummed note.

"That was really nice, Eefee," says Marcus, causing her to spin around. She's startled. "Sorry," he says. "I didn't mean to startle you."

"You didn't," she lies, her accent crisp and deep. The kitchen is shrouded in semi dark. The mood permitted the mournful nature of the song.

Marcus arrives to lean against the counter where she works. She immediately moves to the light switch and turns the light to full bright. She lingers near that area now, putting away the things she used to make the meal. She knows it's best not to stand in close proximity to him.

"How were the kids?" he asks innocently enough.

"Oh they were great!" she exclaims genuine. Marcus is pleased. He'd known she would say as much since his children have been no fuss to him and Yvette since they were born. They are his miracles. He does not believe he would be as effective in his work if his children are a source of concern in any way.

"And you girls, you got along fine?"

"We girls?" At first she's thinking Marcus is referring to her and Aaliyah, but didn't he already include the child when he asked about "the kids?"

"Yeah," he adds when he reads her slight confusion. "You and Yvette? She can be real fussy about other people taking care of her kids and all. I just hope she wasn't too much for you tagging along this afternoon."

Rachel stares at him for a beat, wondering which way to take. The fact that his eyes are roaming all over her body decides which road she should travel.

"She was no fuss at all," Rachel covers quickly. "Thanks for the money, by the way," she adds to change the subject. "She gave it to me."

"You're welcome," he says good-natured. "I bet 500 dollars goes a long way over there."

Rachel pauses again. Wow, the plot thickens, she's thinking. Yvette had only given her two hundred.

"Yeah," she says. "It'll go a long way. Thank you again."

"My pleasure," he adds, thinking of all sorts of pleasures that have nothing to do with money.

She caught his reference to pleasure and, of course, ignores it. She wants to ask him if he's hungry, but knows in the mood he's in, he is liable to interpret the question to mean something else. She does not want to invite double meanings in their banter, so instead she asks, "I made some spaghetti. You want me to dish you some?"

Marcus shakes his head. "I ate at the theater. *Louise* always orders dinner."

She doesn't know who *Louise* is and doesn't query him about it. The last thing she wants is to encourage elaboration of any kind. That would only keep him in the kitchen longer.

"I could use some water though," he requests.

"Okay," she says, taking the water jug from the fridge. She pours him some in a tall glass and leaves it for him on the counter. She does not hand it to him, not wanting their hands to touch.

"You miss your country?" Marcus asks, leaving the water where she left it.

"Yes, I miss my country."

"So how come you're singing the Austrian national anthem? Doesn't Nigeria have its own?"

She stops herself from rolling her eyes or shaking her head. He is wrong on so many different levels. Correcting him would require some elaboration though. Still, it's *The Sound of Music!*

"First of all, I don't have to be Austrian to sing a song about Austria," she explains saucy. Marcus realizes he likes her saucy.

"Second of all," she continues just as saucy, "*Edelweiss* is not the Austrian national anthem. The movie made it so popular everybody thinks it is. The country's official anthem is *Land der Berge, Land am Strome*. Literal translation? Land of the mountains, land on the river, written by Mozart."

"Wow," he says, astonished by her knowledge.

Rachel smiles sadly at the implication. As an African child, he never expected her to know such things. She inserts into the fridge the plastic container filled with the spaghetti sauce. She is very careful not to bend down because she knows he will be staring at her ass.

Marcus is, nevertheless, staring at that ass. "Can I have some of that?" He's not referring to the spaghetti.

Rachel gives him a deadpan look. Marcus meets her gaze without apology.

"Thought you said you already ate," she says accusingly. She thinks he's acting like a child now.

"What can I say? I'm hungry again," he says, not referring to food again.

"You also asked for water, you haven't touched that," she says, a tad insolent.

With mischief in his eyes, Marcus takes the water and drinks from it. She rolls her eyes this time. He thinks she looks cute doing that. Rachel brings the spaghetti back out of the fridge and locates a dish with which to serve him.

"By the way, how is it an African girl from a rural village in Nigeria got to see the *Sound of Music?"*

"You're asking that because you think we don't have televisions?" She means to insult him. She wants to establish a bad rapport between them to dissuade him from his silly advances. She has too much respect and love for his children to encourage a misstep. Why couldn't all men be like Chris, Jada's man, she's thinking.

Marcus shrugs. The idea of a TV in an African village never occurred to him.

"My village is only a few miles from the major township," she says. "It's in the town I got to watch the DVD, at a friend's house. I watched that movie about 500 times before I came to America. When I got here, I bought it from Blockbuster and kept on watching it."

"Did you bring it with you here?"

"No. It's one of the things I threw at the bastard when I walked out on him." She invites the topic of the make-believe cheating fiancé and her actions against him to let Marcus know she doesn't take shit from men.

"Wish I'd been there." He ignores her threat. "I'd love to see you wild like that."

She avoids adding anything to this line as well, thinking that maybe, if she says nothing more, he will say goodnight and leave her to finish her work. She adds pasta sauce on the dished spaghetti and takes the plate to the microwave.

"Thanks for cooking," he adds after a while, since it doesn't look like she wants to talk anymore. A shame – he likes hearing her accent, the way she sounds all proper and stuff. It's funny what an accent will do.

"Um, regarding cooking—" the subject reminds Rachel to ask about the cooking allowance. After she and the children ate at the restaurant and after buying the grocery items, she has only 60 dollars left. "—will Yvette be giving me cooking allowance?"

Rachel is careful how she posed this question. Something is going on with Yvette and money, any idiot can see that. Since she doesn't know what it is and since it's not her place to imbalance the family's rhythms, she does not want to clue Marcus in on it – at least, not until she herself knows what's going on for sure.

One thing is clear, if Yvette will be giving her money for the household, that money will most likely be coming up short. And the last thing Rachel needs is discrepancies if she will be handling any of the family's cash.

For his part, Marcus is thinking, God she's so cute. Who says *cooking allowance*?

"No," he answers, to the question of who will be giving Rachel money. Yvette is very bad with money – this is a fact, the reason he controls the family's finances. The way the couple rolls is this: Marcus deposits a set amount into Yvette's account every month. That amount is for her personal use. Every other expense – the household and now the production – comes out of numerous accounts he's set up.

At the beginning of their marriage, they had a joint personal account that Yvette controlled. He'd given her full reign of it because he had foolishly believed that's what a man is supposed to do – he grew up in a household where his father simply handed his mother his paychecks every two weeks. His mother ran the family finances with the shrewd acumen of a corporate accountant. Bills got paid, retirement funds got put aside, and every one received weekly stipends, including his father. There were never fights or nasty words about money.

This was not the case with Yvette. In only one year, she nearly drove them into bankruptcy with her frivolous spending. Marcus took the bull by the reigns and restructured their entire financial life. He put her on a strict budget and looked over her account statements with the vigilance of a hawk watching over its young. She is not to go over that budget since he has calculated her monthly needs down to the cent.

"Yvette won't be giving you money," he answers Rachel. "I will be ... giving it to you," he finishes in a horny voice.

Rachel gives an involuntary chuckle. His lines are so bad she concludes he's been married so long he doesn't even know how ridiculous he sounds.

Marcus is amused by her amusement and asks, "What?"

She says nothing, merely shakes her head. Quiet descends again, just in time because the microwave beeps. She takes the dish out and places it on the table for him.

It's true, Marcus is not really hungry, but he intends to eat the food anyway.

"Goodnight," she says and heads out.

"Wait!" he calls her back. "Don't you wanna know what I think of it?

"The food tastes great. The children and Yvette told me."

"My opinion doesn't count?"

She wants to say, I don't care about it. But decides to get it over with by sticking around. He samples the food, takes his time chewing and savoring each mouthful.

"It's very good," he pronounces at last, so she about-faces and heads for the exit.

"How do you say 'light' in your language?" he calls after her out of nowhere. "Which tribe are you from anyway?"

Rachel turns around, regards him with disdain. "You mean *ethnic group!*" she states with emphasis."

"Sorry. Ethnic group. Sure."

"I'm Igbo."

"Ah yes," he says, as if he is familiar with the Igbos. He is not. "So how you say 'light'?" he repeats.

"*Oku*. Why?"

"*She Who Bears Oku*," he says to himself. "I don't know. It doesn't sound right."

"What're you talking about?"

"It's the play I've written, for the performance?" Looking at her eyes, he can tell she's intrigued. She returns slowly to where he is.

"What's it about?" she asks, forgetting the thing about not seeking elaboration.

Marcus smiles and spends the next hour telling her about it. He feels like a college senior all over again, trying to impress some freshman girl in the cafeteria.

"So how's she so good at combat?" Rachel can't help but ask at the end of his summary because at her core – despite the fact she's trying to bury that part of herself – she is a dramatist. "*Light*'s been home all this time tending to the kids," she reminds Marcus, as if he's forgotten that part of the story.

"She just knows how, that's how."

"You're asking too much of the audience, Marcus." He loves the way his name falls out of her mouth – the "r" is totally silent.

"Why don't you have her husband teach her?" she suggests.

"He came home maimed, remember?"

"Yes, but it wouldn't have to be anything elaborate. We just need to see that someone taught her how to fight otherwise, it's gonna be hard to swallow."

She knows the word is a mistake as soon as it leaves her mouth. She sees his eyes transform with, no doubt, images of all sorts of things he can get her to swallow.

"He can hobble about the stage or something," she rushes on, "as he's teaching her to fight. That scene would be crucial because you don't have too many scenes with *Light* and her husband. The audience needs to see he cares for her, that he'll be worried about her out there at war – in short, that she is his one true love. There would be no greater image of how much they love each other than a husband and wife interacting on stage together like that."

Marcus has completely forgotten about the spaghetti. He wants to have this girl. She is smarter than anything he imagined, and carries herself with an immense dignity. His desire for her overwhelms and suddenly frightens him. This would be no casual fling, he can see that. Only Yvette has ever made him feel the way this girl is making him feel now. He would totally lose himself in her. He can see that now.

God, what am I doing, he asks himself, noticing for the first time his PJ top is unbuttoned. He appears an ass to himself.

Marcus puts the utensil down and pushes the plate to the side. All that he has worked for, the intricate web of love and family he and Yvette have sewn all these years would come tumbling down.

Marcus has had affairs within the marriage before – meaningless one-night stands with actresses he's directed or actresses who want to be cast for this or that role. They've been white, black, Asian, Latin – you name it, he's bedded it.

None has ever held a candle next to Yvette, however — except, well, maybe this girl. But would he really be able to throw 11 years of marriage out the window? Just like that? Just because she yelled at his ego this evening? And Yvette was right about the significance of the husband role.

Marcus wrote the relationship of *Light* and her husband based on his relationship with Yvette. At 31 when he met Yvette, he was already somewhat renowned in the tight-knit New York City black theater circle, having written and produced half a dozen plays that were received well by the critics and audiences alike.

Yvette was a 25-year old struggling actress who walked into his audition one day. He first bedded and then cast her in the play he was producing at the time. Then followed a whirlwind courtship that succeeded in making her his wife a year and a half later. He married her because, quite frankly, he fell deeply and madly in love with her – just like *Light's* husband with her.

He wrote himself in the play to be her husband as a sort of celebration of their marriage. The play's debut will be January 4th, which would be the 12th-year anniversary of his marriage with Yvette. Yet, here he is, making a total fool of himself with his children's nanny! Even if the girl were compliant, would he really have her in this house where his wife and children lay their heads at night? What was he thinking?!

Marcus looks up at Rachel. Their eyes connect for a long moment as he tries to banish desire from his. From where she stands, Rachel sees the transformation she hoped for. All her talk of husbands and wives, really, had nothing to do with the play. She wanted Marcus to remember Yvette and all that he stands to lose.

"Your wife and children live here, Marcus," Rachel says softly, echoing the thoughts already swirling in his mind.

"I need the job," she says, driving the point home. "But I will not give my soul for it. That needs to be understood from the very beginning, okay?"

She does not wait for his response before saying "Good night" for the final time. She heads for the door. When she gets to the light switch she asks, "Leave it on?"

"Turn it off," he says quietly. "Thank you."

Rachel turns off the light and walks out of the kitchen. Darkness falls on the room and on Marcus whose face is colored red with shame.

When he manages to crawl into his bedroom half an hour later, Marcus sits at the edge of the bed staring at Yvette's tired face. For a long time, he sits there marveling at the familiarity of it. She is and always will be his future, the woman his theater is built around. She is the mother of his children besides and his queen, for better or worse.

Marcus eventually crawls into bed. He wakes Yvette and tells her he is sorry he cast someone else to play the husband role. He will find some other role for the actor.

She tells him not to do this, that he is already overworked taking care of everything else, that she is sorry she blew up like that, that she will work with the actor, but knows he will be sub par compared to him.

To his words he wanted to take the role as a celebration of their love, she holds him tighter and says that working together as they do is a celebration, in and of itself, of their constant and unwavering love for each other. They make love after that, though she falls promptly back to sleep before he is done.

| 11 |

The next coming days and weeks in the Peyton household are filled with content for Rachel. The couple pays her 500 dollars a week. She has no idea if this is large or small for her services, but she saves every penny and is grateful for her room and board and for the company of the children.

Her day begins early. She wakes the children and feeds them breakfast, then takes them to school. She returns to the house to do whatever housework she sees is necessary. No one said housekeeping is part of her duties but no one objects either.

Rachel does the cleaning and the cooking to keep herself busy. Besides, with her around, Yvette has abandoned all attempts to keep up with the housework. When not at the theater, the woman keeps mostly to her room, or sees to her yoga routine on the first floor. She gives Rachel complete reign over the children, which the children – Aaliyah in particular – do not seem to mind, but which Rachel finds very odd.

After doing housework and needing to avoid being cooped up in the house all day, Rachel makes her way to the local library to research career paths on the Internet. The Peytons are connected to the Internet but the computer is located in Marcus' study. Rachel is keeping to her plan of avoiding Marcus and his space as much as possible – even though he spends most of his time in the theater.

As to her research on the net, Rachel is bent on discovering a new direction for her life. She knows all about nursing – the default career of the immigrant black woman. She stands to make a lot of money as a nurse but there's the issue of blood. She always faints at the sight of it, so maybe not something in the health profession.

She could be an elementary school teacher since she's very much enjoying her time with Aaliyah and MJ. Research confirmed she would need to finish college and become certified. She could enroll at City College. She wonders if some of her credits from Columbia would transfer. But would she be happy among 25 rowdy elementary school children?

Then again, she could become a banker, like Jada. But wouldn't that mean some serious overtime and dealing with the public? She wonders if she has the patience to deal with complaints on a daily basis – Jada reported that's all she ever got working at the bank. No need to stress about it, Rachel concludes. She will keep all her options open since she has some time to make up her mind.

She initially planned to stay with the Peytons till December but decided to stay on till the spring. Things are going very well with them, especially because Marcus began to behave like a sensible father. She is putting away all the money they're paying her, and plans to use it as down payment for her own place. She is sure that by spring she would find alternate employment.

She thought of reconnecting her cell phone but thought against it. Someone from her past might call when one of the Peytons is around. So to stave off that potential awkwardness, she put her cell phone away and decided not to contact anyone from her old life until she is good and ready.

Another reason she spends all her time in the library is to avoid having to wander around Harlem. The Peytons are located somewhat away from her old hunting ground of 125th Street. She avoids 125th

Street altogether in order not to bump into anyone she knows. She called Jada only once to tell her she got the job and to let her mother know she is okay. Jada promised to relay the message to Anne.

After the library, Rachel returns home in the afternoon to prepare lunch and or dinner for the household. Then at 3PM, she picks up the children and off to karate they go. They return home to a nutritious dinner, then homework, then bed.

On the weekends, she takes the children to the movies, to the skating rink, to play- dates, or to whatever else activity their little hearts desire and their parents approve. She really feels like *Maria von Trapp* now – although, instead of caring for a brood of seven children, she only manages two.

With all the running around, Rachel easily loses the 11 pounds she gained while at Jada and Chris'. Yvette does not notice the weight loss, though Marcus couldn't miss it. He wanted to say something about it, to compliment Rachel, but knows intuitively he better not. To say something would be to let on he's aware of her body and he is trying his best not to notice it.

Rachel's body with the weight was supple and full, making her face appear childlike. And now, her features sharpened, making her look more woman than child. Her waist thinned even further, her boobs and ass became more pronounced. If there ever was an hourglass, she fit that image perfectly.

Overnight, it seemed to Marcus, she turned into the most beautiful thing he has ever seen, more beautiful, he is disappointed to see, than Yvette. So because he keeps mum about her body, he finds other ways to let her know he is mindful of her presence – innocent ways.

For example, Rachel returned home from the library one day to find a DVD copy of *The Sound of Music* on top of her bed. With a neat script written on a yellow sticky pad on the face of the movie, Marcus bade her enjoy herself while the children were at school. She graciously thanked him for the movie on the same sticky note, then stuck the note on the door of his study. She did not enter the space.

That evening, she sat the children down on the couch after their homework was done and introduced them to the cherished classic. Aaliyah immediately fell in love with the story, unlike MJ who had a low tolerance for it. He said sitting around singing silly songs was gay.

To Rachel's question of, What do you know about being gay? The boy retorted, That's when two boys are kissing! To Rachel's follow-up question of, What does that have to do with *The Sound of Music*? The boy looked at her blankly then shrugged.

What MJ does delight in doing is teaching Rachel the basics of karate. She shared with them the possibility that she might end up being a karate teacher. MJ laughed out loud, while Aaliyah gave one of her winsome smiles that Rachel loves to see. So, while Aaliyah spent night after night on the couch engrossed in the musical, MJ insisted that Rachel do exactly as he commands throwing kicks and punches in the air, all while letting out piercing screams that emanate from her gut.

Every Monday morning, Marcus hands Rachel an envelope filled with cash for the household expenses. She is careful with the money, spending as he instructs and handing him receipts in the same envelope when he hands her a fresh one the following week. Her interaction with him is crisp and to the point. They say very little to each other, only relaying and receiving necessary information – no chitchat.

Then on another day after returning from the library she found his play on her bed. He left yet another sticky note, asking her to read it if she had the time and to kindly give him input on this or that idea. Her suggestion to show *Light* learning how to fight from her husband had been brilliant, he told her on the sticky, and he has already incorporated the suggestion into the story.

Truth be told, Rachel had been thinking about the story since Marcus summarized it for her that first night they were together in the kitchen. She was captivated by the drama – not so much the idea of it. Women wanting to fight in battles where they are denied is nothing new. However, Marcus' spin on it is different.

He set the action in Africa, for starters, where he created an intricately layered conflict between two regions simply known as the Green Lands – for their rich soil – and the Orange Lands – for their mettle. *Light* is a member of the Greens. Marcus went further to create dynamic characters imbued with complex motivations. He then masterfully filled each character's journey with insurmountable obstacles that would, nevertheless, need to be surmounted before goals can be attained.

Rachel got all this information from his simple summary of the play. Since that night, she has not been able to get the drama out of her mind. She's been wanting to read the story for herself, but did not know how to directly ask him for it. So in a way, Marcus did her a tremendous favor by leaving the manuscript on her bed.

Rachel immediately got to work. She was not able to put it down until she was done in an hour and a half. She immediately read it again then praised the work in subdued tones that communicated professionalism more than awe. She made some suggestions, using the yellow sticky notes from the pad he provided for her to use.

She stuck the notes between the pages of the play then left the play in his study this time. She reasoned she could not leave the manuscript pasted to the door. It was the first time she had entered his study. She's never been in the couple's bedroom either. There is unspoken understanding Yvette would clean that room and the study if needed.

In Marcus' quiet space, she lingered after placing the manuscript on his desk. She took note of the numerous books on his shelves – all great pieces of literature: representing the far reaches of the earth. There were the Russians, the English, the Africans (of course), the Asians, the Americans, and everyone else in between.

She also took in the forgotten exercise equipment, and his numerous African drums (though *Malika* was not there). The room made her feel at peace and she found she rather preferred it to its owner. She realized also she preferred Marcus the writer to Marcus the man. She touched nothing in the room and eventually left.

A few days later, she found the play again on her bed and was surprised to see he took most of what she had suggested – the most important was to give *Light* the ability to command animals and nature. No African story would be complete without animals and nature, she mentioned. Giving *Light* these abilities, also, made her even more powerful against the enemy.

Rachel wrote to him saying she would understand if, due to budgetary reasons, animals could not be incorporated. He wrote over her sticky note regarding the budget that he appreciated her concern about money, but that it would not break the bank to hire more actors who would portray the animal characters.

They went back and forth like this – talking between the pages of his play, long after all her suggestions had been considered, long after all the edits had been made and long after the revisions were revised.

Mostly he asked about Africa, requesting details of the landscape, details of this or that custom, meanings behind this or that action. Then the notes segued into personal questions about her likes and dislikes – what books she read as a child, who are her favorite authors, what is her favorite color.

She did not answer these questions and ceased responding to the ones that followed – also personal. Finally, he wrote one last time – a single yellow sticky stuck in the center of her bed. He apologized if he had offended her – that was never his intention – then thanked her for all her input in making his play better.

He ended by inviting her down to the theater anytime to see how production is moving along. Rachel did not respond to that either.

| 12 |

Rachel throws the back door wide open, revealing a backyard overgrown with even more clutter than when she arrived to the Peytons' one month ago. She's been toying with the idea of becoming a gardener. She decided not to follow any of the conventional paths. What appeals to her are professions that have nothing to do with sitting in an office.

She took the children to the Bronx Zoo and the Botanical Garden last weekend. The idea to become a gardener dropped into her head as she and the children marveled at the colorful array of flowers from all over the world. It was either that or become an animal wrangler. Given the Peytons' available backyard, she decided to first give gardening a chance before considering whispering to animals.

She walks over to the shed, a shanty-type cottage tucked at one corner of the yard. In there, she sees gardening tools. Before she died, Yvette's grandmother was fond of poking around in the yard. She had grown simple vegetables she served at meals. Rachel is determined to prepare the yard for something similar.

The library furnished her with the knowledge of how to plant and sustain simple plants and vegetables. But first, the ground had to be tamed. The Peytons have used the space as a sort of dumping ground for old toys, pieces of unwanted furnishings, boxes, and other odds and ends.

In the shed, Rachel locates a pair of sturdy gloves. She puts them on and gets down to the business of preparing all the trash for the dumpster. Yvette said she could knock herself out and discard everything. Rachel intends to do just this.

She works all morning separating the recyclables from the regular trash. She already knows the sanitation schedule for when the trash is supposed to be put out to the curb. Marcus volunteered to do that much. All she has to do is pile the debris neatly. Upon return from the theater, he will drag the dirt out to the curb.

By noon, Rachel is done. She can see the ground now. The grass is beaten and dead, brown in color. She is not perturbed. She knows exactly what has to be done to resuscitate the soil and get going on planting her seedlings.

She pulls up the dead grass and weeds, which she collects and inserts into black plastic bags she dumps next to the garbage that's going out to the curb. Because the ground is rock hard, she goes in and out of the house with buckets of hot water that she pours to soften the ground. She uses a small shovel to dig the earth, creating rows in which she drops seedlings.

In no time, she is dirty from head to toe. Sweat is pouring off her forehead to mix with the dirt. By mid afternoon, she is done. She has planted flowers and basic vegetables, which she hopes will sprout despite the onset of fall. She goes back into the house for a quick shower and a bite to eat before going to pick up the kids.

By the washing machine, she takes her clothes off and throws into the washer. She's clad only in her panties and bra, and is not worried about being semi-nude because she is alone in the house. And anyway, she would hear the footsteps on the stairs before whoever got to the floor.

Next, comes the scarf covering her head. Since arriving to the Peytons', Rachel's hair has remained a natural afro that she keeps tamed with scarves. The particular scarf she just took off misses the washer's mouth and sails off to behind the machine.

Amused by her missed jump shot, she goes to the back of the washer to retrieve the scarf. She pushes the hamper away and looks behind the washer. She is puzzled at what she finds back there. She gets down on her knees, sticks her hand all the way behind the machine. She pulls out an inordinate amount of orange pill bottles.

Rachel stares at the bottles in non-comprehension. She notes that quite a few have labels with Yvette's name. But most have labels with names of people she's never heard of. During her cleaning spree of the house, she has had occasion to find these bottles here and there, behind nooks and crannies, one or two, always empty. She'd assumed they'd simply fallen to the wayside, on their way to be discarded. She's never thought anything of it. But here before her are over 20 bottles, all filled with pills.

She recalls occasionally being startled into wakefulness in the dead of night. Stumbling out of her room, she has found Yvette scurrying in the dark, always near the washing machine and dryer area. The woman will apologize profusely for waking Rachel, saying she couldn't sleep and needed to engage in some yoga exercise. Rachel never thought anything of that either. She will shut her door and stumble back into her room to fall back to sleep.

Rachel walks over to the dryer now, sticks her hand behind it and retrieves about two dozen orange pill bottles. She knows she doesn't have the time to contemplate the mystery. She has to be on her way to get the children. So she puts the bottles back where she found them, replacing the hamper beside the washing machine as she had found it.

She throws her scarf into the wash and begins a wash cycle. While under the shower in the bathroom, she thinks about Yvette and the medications she has found. Is this why Yvette always seems so distracted, totally out of it? Rachel assumed this was because the practice to get her ready to be *Light* is just that rigorous.

Even while watching the children practice their karate kicks, Rachel's thoughts are on Yvette and the implication behind what she found. At home, Rachel sees to the children's bath, feeds them dinner, battles through math computation and reading comprehension, and then tucks them into bed. She retires to her own bedroom to wait.

Sometime after 1AM, she hears the sound she knew would come – the sound of Yvette by the washer area carefully moving the hamper. Rachel quietly crawls out of bed and to the door where she stands for some time, her hand on the doorknob.

Yvette stiffens when she hears Rachel open the door. She quickly swallows the pills in her mouth while simultaneously throws the empty pill bottle into the hamper. She grabs a handful of dirty clothes and stuffs them into the washer.

"Yvette?" calls Rachel, pretending to have been very much asleep.

"Hey girl," Yvette answers, in a cheery voice she's putting on to sound normal.

Rachel is beside her now, staring into the woman's eyes. She notes Yvette is avoiding looking at her directly as she pours detergent into the washer.

"Why're you doing laundry? It's after midnight."

"Well, you know, girl, I kind of feel guilty not helping you out once in a while."

"That's what you're paying me for," Rachel answers softly.

"Technically—" Yvette rushes on, trying to control the moment. "— we only pay you to take care of the kids." She laughs nervously, not at all in control of the moment.

Rachel doesn't say anything, is only looking at her. This makes Yvette even more nervous. "Did I wake you?" Yvette asks, just to have something to say.

Rachel shrugs and says, "I have to use the bathroom. Why don't you leave that, I'll take care of it." With that, she goes into the bathroom. When she exits minutes later, Yvette is gone – and so too are all the pill bottles behind the washer and the dryer.

| 13 |

Rachel is caught off guard at how different she feels walking on 125th Street. Was it only in June that she and Jada walked this same route on their way to lunch at the park? There is the hair-braiding saloon where she entertained the crowd singing the *Mother Abbess* song *Climb Every Mountain*.

She wonders if the African woman who braided her hair the way Bo wanted it for his birthday that day managed to get out of the shelter with her baby. She hopes mother and child are doing well. Rachel no longer needs her hair braided since going natural. Even now, a tie-dye scarf circles her forehead, putting order to her bushel of tresses.

There was a time her energy flowed with the rhythm of 125th Street. She spent all her available hours on the strip, going from one shop into another. Now she feels uncomfortable walking through it all. The crowd is too thick, the cars too many, the traffic too loud. How much she has changed.

Rachel wants to get out of the flow so she crosses over to 126th Street, walking parallel to 125th Street, until she gets to the theater on 5th Avenue.

In the tiny office – the theater's center of operation – Marcus and Theo, the business partner, are screaming their heads off at each other. Theo, a 40-year old black man, appears older than his actual age and certainly appears as if he is older than Marcus. The bald spot atop Theo's head and the paunch on his belly do not help. He developed the unattractive paunch due his dislike of physical exercise of any kind, and due to his years of sitting behind tables, conducting business for this or that theater. He is behind the desk now as he and Marcus go back and forth.

"I can't believe you invited that jerk, Theo!" Marcus says while pacing. Just as he can't stand Luis because Luis is a gay black man, Marcus cannot equally stand Theo because Theo is a gay black man. And like for Luis, he also has a secret moniker for Theo: *Thelma* – of same *Thelma and Louise.*

"He's a critic, Marcus," Theo states. "Of course I invited him!" Theo has the ability to multi-task and so busies on the computer while simultaneously sparring with Marcus. He's sending e-mails to a variety of list serves in connection with the upcoming play. This is the monthly reminder that the play is only two months away. People should buy their tickets if they haven't already.

"The man is condescending and rude," Marcus retorts. These are behavior traits Marcus is very familiar with since he is often condescending and rude. "No matter what I've written, he's shown time and time again to pan it."

"Marcus, David Cross is someone we can't afford to slight." Theo suddenly raises his hand towards Marcus, indicating quiet, then he taps the blue-tooth phone affixed to his ear.

"Really?" Theo says on the phone. He is very excited. "Cool!" He hangs up with the caller and addresses Marcus. "Just got word the invite's on the Mayor's table. He'll be in early tomorrow, so we should get some kind of word by end of day."

Marcus' eyes light up. "Awesome, brother man!" he says. He resisted the temptation to say, "sister girl!"

He resisted the temptation because, one, he dare not ridicule *Thelma* to his face as he does *Louise* because he needs *Thelma* more than he needs *Louise*. Two, *Thelma* is hardly effeminate and besides – *Thelma's* boyfriend is one of New York City's Finest, a buffed hulking detective by the name of Vinny Esposito. Vinny and *Thelma* have been together for more years than Marcus and Yvette have been married. Marcus is certain that should he begin ridiculing *Thelma* – well, Vinny would not like that. And Marcus is intimidated by Vinny.

Just then, Yvette pops her head through the door and says, "Can I talk to you, Marcus?" She disappears back out before Marcus can answer. He promptly follows.

Out in the hallway, Yvette paces. Marcus walks up to her.

"What, babe?" He asks cautious. He knows she's not clicking with the actor he chose to be her husband. If the bad blood between them continues, he will be forced to cast another actor.

"Did you sleep with her?!" Yvette asks out of nowhere. She's in his face, staring into his stunned eyes. For a moment, Marcus believes she's talking about Rachel. But he realizes, that can't be. His spirit has given up the girl.

"Huh? What?" he asks for clarity.

"You know what I'm talking about!" she exclaims, spit flying. "I'm talking about Vicky, goddamn it! Did you sleep with her?!"

Vicky is the understudy, a lovely woman with an acting resume as lengthy as Mt. Everest is high and only 27-years old. Marcus cast her yesterday.

"I don't think I should dignify that with a response," he states, insulted.

"Stop tripping, Marcus. Just tell me, okay. I want to know what I'm up against."

"Yvette," he says and not *Yvie.* "Pull yourself together and get ready to run your damn lines with Mason!" Mason is the actor playing her husband.

Just then, Luis, the intern arrives in a rush. "Sorry to interrupt, lovebirds," he calls out to them. "The soldiers are ready, Marcus."

Marcus stares Yvette down before he marches off, leaving her deflated. She was so sure he was sleeping with the girl. A bolt of sudden pain shoots up Yvette's spine, making her stand rigid, like a soldier she's soon to play. Luis takes note.

"You all right, Yvie?" he asks concerned.

"Yeah sure, Luis. Thank you for asking."

"*Louise*!" calls Marcus from somewhere unseen.

The intern startles. He has an amazed look on his face. "Did the nigga just call me *Louise*?"

"He always calls you *Louise*." Yvette says, aware she's starting trouble and not caring. "At home anyway," she finishes.

"You know what, he can kiss my motherfucking ass!" Luis about-faces and marches out of the hallway like a diva.

The pain on Yvette's back intensifies, causing her to visibly wince. Moving like the devil, the pain races down her spine and jumps to her knees.

Speak of the other devil – Vicky Bowman rushes into the hall, breathless from running from the subway. There was some malfunction on 96th Street. She is a mere 5 minutes late, but it's her first day and obviously she wants to make a great impression.

She is as tiny as Yvette and nearly as yellow-skinned. Aside from her acting chops, Marcus chose her as the understudy for these similarities she shares with Yvette and the reason Yvette believed he had to have slept with her before casting her.

By accusing Marcus to his face about it, Yvette is quickly forgetting her grandmother's rules about tolerance when it comes to a husband – especially the most important: if you suspect your husband of cheating and you've searched within yourself and conclude you absolutely cannot tolerate it, it's best to catch him in the act rather than accuse him to his face. This will piss him off, especially if you are wrong. But these days, the drugs in Yvette's system have made her slightly off kilter, have raised her paranoia and have lessened her reasoning faculties.

"Hi, Yvette!" Vicky says, breaking into Yvette's thoughts. She takes Yvette's hand before Yvette offers it. "We met yesterday," Vicky says in a high-spirited tone of voice. "I'm sorry, I was just so thrilled I got the job, I didn't get a chance to talk to you. Let me say, it's an honor, a total honor, to be working with you!"

Vicky's genuine graciousness touches Yvette. "Thank you, Vicky," Yvette says, offering a subtle smile. "It's a pleasure to meet —"

"Oh no no no! The pleasure's all mine!" Vicky appears to be one of those people who won't let you finish talking before jumping in.

"Um, okay, well, see you on the sta —"

"Yes, yes, yes! On the stage. Cool!"

Yvette hates her already. She walks towards her private dressing room, while Vicky rushes off to the general female one.

In her dressing room, Yvette crunches pills she got out of her purse. She watches her face in the mirror, but it's Vicky's eager face she sees staring back at her.

Two soldier factions rush towards each other from opposite ends of the stage. One side wears dark green tongs, the other dark orange tongs – and that's all. There are 40 men altogether, 20 for each side. Muscles rippling, the men crash into each other, expelling grunts. They push and shove, the objective being for each side to push the other as far back as it can.

"Stop, stop, stop!" Marcus calls from downstairs. Luis occupies the first row of seats. He watches the action on stage, jotting notes in a huge binder that contains the play. He is also, of course, salivating over the toned flesh of the men on the stage.

Marcus quickly takes the steps leading onto the stage proper. The men disengage. They are out of breath, with sweat pouring down torsos. Marcus addresses the green soldiers, men of the Green Lands.

"Green soldiers, you're the good guys! Push 'em off the stage!"

"Whoa, whoa, whoa!" says Orange Soldier 1. "You mean literally off the stage?"

"Yes!" says Marcus, his eyes wide and bright with the drama of it all.

The orange soldiers, as one, look at the drop from off the stage.

"Y'all got insurance, right?" says Orange Soldier 2, nervous. "I'm gonna sue if I break anything." His brethren laugh.

Marcus is not amused. He waits for the soldiers to get serious.

"You serious?" asks Orange Soldier 3, dead serious.

"You're not gonna break anything!" says Marcus, trying to control his temper. "It's how you fall off! Okay watch." He indicates one of the green soldiers to engage him. The soldier and Marcus grapple at each other, then the soldier pushes him off. Marcus sails off the stage, landing firmly on his feet like the seasoned acrobat he is.

The orange soldiers look down at him skeptically. They suddenly bunch up together to whisper conspiratorially.

Marcus turns around in disgust and comes to an automatic stop when he sees Rachel sitting all the way in the back. "Eefee?!"

She waves at him unenthusiastically. She had hoped not to be noticed. In fact, all the soldiers, along with Luis, turn to look at her.

"*Eefee*, everyone," Marcus introduces her. "My kids' nanny."

The men acknowledge her with slight nods then return to what they're doing.

"Is this a break?" Green Soldier 1 asks Marcus.

"Okay, take 10," Marcus responds. The soldiers walk off the stage, while Marcus returns his attention to Rachel. "Why don't you come up to the front. You'll see better from up here."

Rachel thinks if she doesn't move, he'll insist. So she gets up and moves to the second row, sits behind Luis.

Marcus arrives to the first row, remains standing to talk to her. He knows better than to sit beside her. Who knows what the intern would think. Luis, meanwhile, is staring back at Rachel.

"Hi," he begins good-natured. "I'm Luis. Luis! L-U-I-S!" he spells loudly, for Marcus' benefit. "I'm the head intern around here though you'd never know it, the way I'm treated. How're you?" He extends a manicured hand.

"I'm fine, thank you." Rachel shakes the proffered hand, deciding she likes Luis.

"Girl, I just love your accent," he says, acting all gossipy. "Where you from?"

"Nigeria."

"He don't treat you like no African, does he?"

"What the hell is that supposed to mean, Luis?!" Marcus interrupts irritated.

"Well, at least you got my name right!"

"You know what?" Marcus has just about had it with the intern. "Why don't you take advantage of the break."

"If you say so, massa." Luis rises and goes in search of Green Soldier 1 whom he has a mega crush on. He intends to charm the guy's cell number off him.

"Sorry about that," Marcus apologizes. "He's an ass."

"He's only looking out for his African sister," Rachel says. She's following on her plan to be in disagreement with Marcus as often as possible – although in truth, she does not believe Luis is an ass. He's funny, actually.

Marcus is not annoyed by her defense of the intern, far from it. He notes a twinkle in her eyes – God, she's adorable, he's thinking – and knows she's playing bad cop, good cop. She would be the good cop.

"Where's Yvette?" Rachel asks. She does not like the way Marcus is looking at her. And anyway, Yvette is the real reason she has come. With her newfound information, Rachel will never look at Yvette the same way.

At Rachel's mention of Yvette, Marcus is brought back to the whole unpleasant moment they shared a few moments ago. The thought had never crossed his mind to look at the understudy in the way Yvette insinuated – although Vicky is just the type of woman he might have traded bodily fluid with in exchange for a part in the production.

His lack of interest in such a fine morsel, he deduces, could only be because of Rachel. But was it not for Yvette he banished Rachel from his thoughts? Is it not for Yvette that he is now restraining himself against sitting next to her?

Yet there was Yvette, pacing in the middle of the hallway, with a look in her eyes that assumed he has already cheated and querying him about it to his face! Anger rises in Marcus like bile. He struts to the second row whereupon he plops himself on the chair beside Rachel.

Rachel shifts her body slightly away from Marcus. She does not think it's a good idea him sitting so close to her. It would be very odd, though, to get up now and leave two seats between them.

"Did the school call or something?" he asks. He noted her physical shift away from him and understood its implication. The question served to engage her in a topic along the lines of her employment. He hopes it would make her feel more relaxed.

"No," Rachel answers quickly, not wanting to worry him about the kids. Her body language also relaxes which Marcus gleefully notes.

"The school didn't call," she's saying. "I was asking about Yvette because she's the star and I noticed she wasn't part of the practice just now."

"Oh, well, she usually enters an hour from now," Marcus answers. "She's probably in the back running lines with someone or some such thing." He realizes he doesn't give a damn where Yvette is at the moment so he changes the topic from Yvette to something closer to his heart. "Did you see any of that? On the stage, I mean?"

"Yes," Rachel nods. "Are actors always so … disagreeable?"

He sighs, "Sometimes you get divas – yes."

She smiles, which he is happy to see. "Can I make a suggestion?"

"Please!" He has come to value her thoughts.

"Will drums accompany the clash?" she asks, deep in thought.

"Yes."

"The soldiers can fight and dance. How they dance will serve as metaphor for the age-old battle. The drumbeat could stop suddenly. I don't think they have to jump off the stage if they fall on the stage floor. To have it work, they'll all have to fall at the same time."

"Wow," Marcus says incredulous. "Did you ever think of becoming a writer?" He does not wait for her response because he rushes off to gather the men. It's just as well for what could Rachel say?

Three hours later, *Malika's* drumbeats resound in the hollow space. Marcus is drumming her, with three other drummers beating on similar drums. The drummers are down stage, while on the stage itself, the opposing factions throw themselves at each other, engaged in a dance/fight that rivets Rachel at her seat. The image also rivets Vicky the understudy. She watches off to the side on the stage.

Yvette suddenly bursts through the dancing throng in front of her men – the green soldiers. She throws herself on the orange soldiers, who catch her in midair and throw her back into the arms of her men. The enemy hops and thrashes, punches and shoves the green soldiers who falter and fall back, cowering in fright.

Yvette falls to her knees, beseeches her men to engage the enemy alongside her. Her men will not follow so she abandons them and throws herself once more upon the enemy. She is outnumbered, however. The enemy pounces on her, throwing her to the ground. They rip her clothes off, leaving her covering her naked breasts with her hands. Soldiers assault her, simulate lewd sexual acts upon her.

Her men can take it no longer. They roar and attack the enemy. Yvette's men locate her on the ground, raise her, clothe her and hug her, then ambush the orange soldiers. She makes her way to the front of the line and too attacks. They push and strain, grunt and howl against the resistant enemy, moving them to the edge of the stage. The drums stop suddenly and in the blink of an eye, the orange soldiers hit the ground.

Luis, in the audience seats, and Vicky, on stage, break the dramatic silence by jumping to their feet cheering and clapping. Marcus stares at Rachel with wide-eyed wonder. Desire for her courses through his body to lodge itself at the center of his groin.

Rachel, for her part, has her eyes only on Yvette. She sees Yvette quietly slink off the stage.

Yvette hobbles painfully into her dressing room. She opens a drawer and pulls out her purse. She takes pills out of a bottle and throws them into her mouth. She takes a seat on a stool. She's thinking about Vicky sitting right there on the stage floor waiting for her to falter.

"You were great," Rachel says from where she stands at the door. Yvette nearly has a heart attack seeing her there. The pill bottle is still in her hands so she immediately puts it away in her purse.

"Um, thanks, Eefee." A myriad of thoughts is going through Yvette's mind. Rachel's presence appears very odd to her, even if to congratulate her.

Rachel shuts the door behind her. "It's pretty bad, huh? The pain? That's why you take the pills?"

"What? What did you say?! Yvette is incredulous. She heard the questions but she believes she didn't.

"I said," Rachel repeats as calm as ever. "The pain must be pretty bad, that's why you take the pills?"

"What the fuck are you talking about?" Yvette is angry. Her bones are creaking, and she wants to take more pills – instead, she is being queried by the damn nanny! This is what she's thinking as she gets off the stool to throw her purse into the drawer. She slams the drawer shut.

Since Rachel does not answer the question, Yvette hisses, "Go home!"

Instead of going home, however, Rachel comes face to face with Yvette, surprising Yvette. She puts her hands on Yvette's face. To an onlooker, it appears she might kiss Yvette. She stares into Yvette's eyes with tenderness.

"Pills don't bring you peace, Yvie." Rachel says softly. "They'll only bring you down. You'll lose everything you and Marcus have ever worked for. I know you don't want that."

Yvette is staring at her amazed. She's thinking of denying everything, but sees in Rachel's eyes it would do no good.

The air goes out of Yvette and she is suddenly tired. "No," she agrees with Rachel. "I don't want that." Unbidden tears suddenly fill her eyes and spill.

"So stop taking them okay," Rachel says as she cleans Yvette's tears away.

"But I need … I them," Yvette argues.

"No, you don't." Rachel is firm. "Everything you need is inside you, Yvie. What I saw out there today, that was incredible, that was you. Reach inside yourself and see it too."

Yvette sniffles and wipes off more tears.

"I busted my ankle in March," she says at long last. "I fell off that damn stage. It was during the construction. The whole place was falling down on our heads."

"And the ankle now? How is it?"

"It healed … but then came arthritis."

"Aren't you too young for that?"

"It runs in the family. My grandpa could hardly walk by the time he died."

"And you're still dancing?" Rachel is incredulous.

"They're gonna have to carry me off that stage!" Yvette exclaims.

They chuckle, looking at each other fondly.

"You need treatment, Yvie." Rachel states, all kidding aside.

"And how do I keep that from Marcus? He'll yank me from the play, give it to that bitch understudy." Rachel startles hearing the curse.

"I'm the only one who can do it, Eefee!" Yvette says somewhat hysterical, worrying Rachel even more. "He wrote *Light* for me!"

"Get a hold of yourself, Yvie." Rachel pleads. "Everything will be okay."

"We've got everything riding on this play, Eefee," Yvette says, a little calmer. "We borrowed against the house!" She looks panicked just thinking about it and instinctively reaches for the pills in her bag.

"Are you kidding me? Give me that!" Rachel snatches the bottle and shakes it. It's almost empty. "Just how many of these things do you take a day?" she asks worried.

Yvette looks away.

"How many?!"

"50, 60, 100. I don't know."

"Jesus Christ, Yvie!" Rachel is horrified. "It's a wonder you haven't collapsed!"

"I'm careful!"

"You're not gonna be standing come opening night!"

"I saw *This Is It*! Mike was great!"

"Mike is dead! From an overdose!"

Yvette clams up and looks away.

"Marcus should know, Yvie. There's still time to get off this shit and continue the play." Rachel's not actually certain about that, but she's not sure she can say nothing after what she knows now. Her worst fear is that Yvette could overdose. How would she be able to look the children in the face – Aaliyah through her glasses – knowing she did nothing to stop their mother's death.

"No, no, no, Eefee!" Yvette protests vehemently. She runs to the door and bars it, certain that Rachel is about to walk out to go to Marcus. "Please, Eefee, don't! I'll stop. I swear to God I'll stop. Let me do it my way."

"How?" Rachel asks, perplexed that Yvette is barring the door. She's not really thinking she can stop me from walking out that door, Rachel thinks.

"I got to wean myself off, that's how!" Yvette is rambling. "I'll take less and less every day, till I get off. I swear to God. I can do it!"

"You can't. You need help!"

"Then help me, Eefee! We'll do it together. I'll give them to you, all of them!"

Yvette pulls herself off the door and runs about the room. She retrieves pill containers from all over the place, hidden in nooks and crannies, behind furniture and the walls. She shoves them all into Rachel's hands – close to 40 pill containers. Yvette then grabs her purse and pours the entire contents on the table. There are some six containers on the table that clatter to the ground.

Eyes wide, Rachel stares from Yvette to the pill containers all over the place. This is why she wasn't able to find any in the house once Yvette moved them from the behind the washer and dryer. Rachel searched all over the house, including in the master bedroom, Marcus' study and the cluttered basement. She found nothing because Yvette moved her stash to her dressing room in the theater. Clever.

"That's all of them?" Rachel asks.

"Yes."

Rachel does not readily believe her.

"I swear!" Yvette sounds convincing, so Rachel gets down on her knees and gathers all the fallen containers. Yvette stares on with longing – a look that's suddenly interrupted by someone knocking at the door.

"Hey, Yvie!" It's Marcus. The women react simultaneously as fear amplifies both of their eyes. Yvette gets down on the floor and begins assisting Rachel to stuff containers back into the drawer where Yvette's purse had been.

"I'll be out in a minute, honey!" Yvette calls out to Marcus, adjusting her voice to sound as normal as possible.

Outside the door, Marcus is not so patient. He turns the knob and enters. He finds Yvette seated on the stool with Rachel standing above her, brushing her hair. This age-old image – two women bonding over hair – should fill him with the warmth and fuzzy aura it's supposed to invoke except he's angry at one woman and finds the other irresistible. He talks to Yvette even though Rachel is whom he's thinking about.

"Can you come out to the stage, honey, I've got some directions."

"In a minute, baby," Yvette says, giving him a wide smile that seems misplaced on her face. Marcus doesn't even notice. He exits. The women let out a sigh of relief.

"Thank you, Eefee," Yvette says genuine. Rachel gives her a simple nod.

Yvette rises to her feet, heading for the door. There, she stops and faces Rachel. Rachel reads Yvette's body language, sees the way she's wringing her hands together. She knows what's coming and waits for it.

"Um," Yvette begins, anxious. "Can I have one? My back is, um …"

"No." Rachel says resolute. Her eyes are dark and piercing. Yvette has never seen this darkness in Rachel's eyes so she turns around and flees the dressing room.

| 14 |

Marcus thinks about the girl especially in the shower. He thinks about her all the time actually, but the shower is particularly special. The moment serves a dual purpose – he cleanses himself as well as plays with himself.

The hot water soothes him, untangles tense nerves, and brings his anger and adrenaline down. He wasn't aware of the first time he started doing it. He just looked down one day and saw his hand massaging his shaft. It felt very good to do that so he continued, leaning against the opaque bathroom tiles at just the right angle that the water also falls on his erect penis.

His eyes are usually shut as he imagines it's the girl's hand there. In his mind's eye, he watches her get down on her knees to wrap her lips around his balls. He throws his head back, a moan or two escaping his parted lips. He is not afraid of Yvette hearing him since the water falling creates a buffering sound that absorbs his moans.

When he can stand it no longer, his imagination moves the girl from his groin to creep up his belly button. He imagines her implanting kisses on his torso, then his neck, then his parted lips.

Needing to release, but never in the shower, he climbs out and goes in search of Yvette. These days, she is more wiry than usual, and he finds she climbs atop him with an urgency similar to when they first got married.

It is not Yvette he sees when they make love. The girl's face and scent now consume the moment so thoroughly, he keeps his mouth tightly zipped for fear of uttering her name in the throes of passion. After love, he falls into a deep sleep during which he finds himself drumming on *Malika* as the girl alone dances for him on the stage.

In this recurring dream, the girl's ass ripples and gyrates so invitingly, he finds himself abandoning the drum altogether to come and dance behind her. He is her husband now, and she is *Light.* The girl backs into him, bumping against him to the degree he loses all reason and he has to insert himself inside her from the back. Thus joined, the sound of *Malika* beating buoys him and the girl to a rising crescendo that ends with him flowing all over the bed sheets.

How to act around the girl becomes his singular most directing force – how to act around her and yet appear as if nothing is out of place. She suffuses his very pores so thoroughly she is the only thing he smells, the only thing he sees, the only thing he hears.

Knowing her fondness for scarves, he finds himself acquiring these on his way to and from the theater, from the numerous shops that dot the 125th Street shopping strip. He leaves the scarves on her bed, but come his return from the theater, he finds them left atop the table in his study. She returned the seven he purchased for her in this manner before he gave up and gifted the scarves to his daughter who put them away in a drawer and never wore them because Aaliyah does not care for scarves.

On the Mondays when he hands the girl the bulging envelope filled with the week's cash allowance, he makes certain to touch her hand, leaving his to linger on hers for as long as he can. She always, politely, disconnects the moment. These days, she takes the other end of the envelope, no matter which side he's holding to extend it.

He puts extra cash in there for her with a note to spend the money on her personal needs. She always returns the envelope with the receipts of how she spent money on the children and always returns the extra cash he meant for her.

He is saved from self-combustion by the very fact she is in the theater every day. She arrives with Yvette, or comes soon after. She hangs out in the audience seats, watching everything that occurs on stage with the eyes of a hawk.

It takes incredible restraint for him to keep focused on the actors dressed as animals jockeying for space, or on the soldiers throwing their spears, or on the art director's color scheme to recreate a jungle, or on the understudy Vicky's resilience and powerful struts as she perfectly recreates Yvette's movements, or on his Blackberry with news from *Thelma* that the tickets are going briskly – the play's almost sold out – oh, and the Mayor is confirmed to attend.

Marcus is thrilled that everything is going swimmingly well. Even Yvette's recent strange behavior does not perturb him. One minute she's soothing wounded soldiers, the next she's pulling him aside to complain that she's feeling negative energy from Vicky, and the very next moment, she's apologizing for everything.

Marcus justifies the mood swings to jitters. This is the biggest role of her career. She is understandably bouncing off the walls. What's important to Marcus is that the girl is in the house. Her presence has a way of soothing him. In his own way, he performs for her. He is loud and commanding, wanting to seem even more directorial.

During breaks, he asks her this or that suggestion about what she's seeing. Her comments are always on point, continuing to be brilliant. Of late, though, she's ceased giving her opinion altogether – mostly acquiescing to whatever choices he makes.

When the girl is not at her usual post next to Luis – she sits besides him in the front row now – Marcus will find her in Yvette's dressing room, helping Yvette with her lines, or her costumes, or her hair, or just plain chatting. He thinks Yvette is monopolizing the girl and is not happy about it.

The girl rushes off close to 3PM to go get the children, and will not be seen again until he and Yvette arrive home close to 10, when it appears she cleans the kitchen. While Yvette showers, he makes certain to arrive to the kitchen to keep her company.

Then he noticed she switched her routine to shut down the kitchen ever before he and Yvette return to the house. He will not follow her to the first floor because, well, that would be obvious.

And so he finds his anger festering and growing, causing him to spend more and more time in the shower, where he imagines the girl's on her knees, her lips wrapped around his balls.

| 15 |

Rachel is engaged in the greatest challenge of her life – being at the center of a junkie's universe. She knows she's way over her head acting as a clinical psychologist to Yvette's awesome problem. Rachel's research on the matter yielded more information than she could ever fully comprehend. *Maria von Trapp* never had to deal with this!

The first thing Rachel did was bury all of Yvette's pill containers behind the shed in the backyard. She dug a hole large enough to hide a baby and threw the bottles in. She did not let Yvette know where she buried the treasure, so to speak, and had no fear Yvette would ever find the pills. No one went to the backyard. To make certain no one would, Rachel neglected the yard and let it return to its former ruined status. As a result, her plants and vegetables wilted and died.

Then one day, she sat the woman down in the kitchen. The kids were at school and Marcus was away in the theater. Over a cup of chamomile tea, Rachel made it clear that once the current pill rations ran out, Yvette would acquire no more.

She exacted that promise from Yvette and another: Yvette is not to cheat in any way, shape or form. Cheating includes – but is not limited to – acquiring new pills in secret, remaining in contact with her dealers or substituting any other harmful substance in place of the pills. If Rachel found out, the contract would be done.

Rachel reduced Yvette's pill popping to half from jump, then to 20, then 15 and finally to 10. They coasted on 10 for a while, supplemented by the herbal roots and medications Rachel also researched to soothe and heal arthritis more naturally.

Yvette followed this regiment religiously for the sake of her children whom Rachel never ceased talking about. She told Yvette that MJ is soon to ascend to the next color belt in karate – orange; that Aaliyah no longer pushes her glasses up her nose; that MJ did a somersault on skates at the skating rink the other day; that Aaliyah doesn't so much skate as glides; that MJ secretly loves a girl in his class; that Aaliyah wants to grow up to fall in love with an Austrian sea captain – she did not mention the fact that Aaliyah also wants to grow up to be a nanny like *Maria von Trapp* and *Eefee Okoli!*

Rachel encouraged Yvette to come on adventures with her and the children – whenever she could get away from the theater – and so they have all been to the movies together, to dinner in local restaurants, and even to roller skate. Yvette refused to step foot onto the rink, however, for fear of falling on her ass. So she sat on the bleacher section and watched her children and Rachel going round and round.

Rachel encouraged this interaction with Yvette and her children to help Yvette keep her eyes on the prize. She believed there was yet hope for Yvette. Yvette had not been so far gone as to sell her children to obtain her pills. And as such, hearing about and interacting with the kids would only bolster her resolve to work really hard to stay clean.

Conversations about the children naturally segued to Yvette's own happy childhood with her grandparents. Her grandparents made her the center of their world, doted on her, and encouraged her wild imagination. They were her first audience members as she pretended to be a myriad of characters she saw on TV. They enrolled her in acting classes before she went to kindergarten and attended every school play she was ever in. Her happiness was forever broken, however, when she learned at 12 of her mother's suicide.

All along, Yvette believed her mother died in her sleep as her grandmother had told her when she was 4-years old. Rather than be angry with her grandmother, Yvette channeled that anger towards her mother. She felt her mother abandoned her by throwing herself onto the train tracks. Her mother should have stayed to dote on her as her grandparents did.

Anger towards one parent soon turned to devastation about the other – when at 16 she learned of her father's murder. For years after that, she imagined her father hanging from that rope on the tree, his neck broken at a crude angle, like she had seen in pictures of lynchings done to black people way back when.

Yvette spoke of her dreams to be a legendary screen actress but felt she had to give it up to be a good partner to Marcus. She then veered to her love for and respect of Marcus. She spoke of falling in love with him the moment she laid eyes on him. He reminded her of her late father in that she likened Marcus' desire to spread his stories into the world similar to her father spreading God's word into the world.

She spoke of Marcus in such an exalted tone and can do no wrong attitude that Rachel inwardly sighed. She forgave Yvette for her blindness towards Marcus whom she was barely tolerating. Love is blind, isn't it, Rachel supposed. She had been blind towards Bo, hadn't she? Had she not believed Bo loved her to pieces?

Rachel followed Yvette to the theater to carefully administer the ration of pills and to soothe Yvette's aching muscles with hour-long massages in the dressing room. Yvette mainly needed medication after each practice routine and almost always to help her sleep at night.

Rachel often wondered: if Yvette overdosed in her sleep – or anywhere else for that matter – would she, Rachel, not be dubbed the accomplice? Would she not have aided and abetted? Wouldn't she be spending some quality time behind bars? And so she followed Yvette around all the time to keep her safe.

Yvette is determined to stay off the drugs but the craving is greater than her will to sustain the wish. Though she does not share this with Rachel, she believes it was a grave mistake to try and wean her off the medication – what with the pressure of the looming performance.

At the same time, she knows that due to that pressure, she would most likely be increasing dosage. And if dosage were increased, wasn't there always the possibility of an overdose? She does not want her children to go through what she did at the loss of her parents. But God, the pain of withdrawal is far worse than the pain of the hunger.

At the moment, Yvette sweats in bed. Marcus lies beside her. She makes sure she's not touching him. She is entirely drenched and imagines the entire bed will soon be soaked. If the mattress fills with sweat, would it wobble like a waterbed?

She needs to get off the bed. She tries to move and finds she is not able to do so. She appears to be paralyzed from her neck down. This is only in her imagination, however, and it calls to mind the recent bout of dreams she's been having – where she's lying on subway tracks, unable to move and a train is bearing down upon her.

With determination, Yvette rolls herself off the bed and crashes onto the ground. Marcus stirs but remains asleep. She lies on the ground as quietly as possible until she can hear him soundly snoring. She drags herself on the floor till she gets into the bathroom. There she raises herself with tremendous effort with aide of the bathtub. Sitting on the tub's edge, she wonders if there is any medication somewhere in the medicine cabinet she and Rachel might have missed.

Yvette and Rachel returned home early on the day they made their pact. She watched Rachel ransack the house, looking for any and all remaining painkillers. Yvette eventually assisted in the search, so they turned up a small handful, hidden in the basement – a great place for such things given the clutter down there. After locking the door, Yvette relinquished the basement's key to Rachel.

Now in the bathroom, Yvette knows there are no pill bottles here – Marcus never seems to suffer from any physical ailments that require even an aspirin. Still, there has to be something. She knows she's about to cheat, but her body is tingling all over, the sure signs of excitement at the mere thought of a fix.

She knows she's supposed to go wake Rachel – this is part of their pact whenever she feels this way. Because Yvette has already consumed the tenth and last pill for the day, Rachel would whip together some herbal concoction she got the guy at the Chinese store down the street to recommend. The mixture usually involves raw ginger.

Yvette hates the taste of raw ginger. Ever since she was a child, her grandmother gave it to her to drink – mixed in hot tea – to chase away her flu and colds. Rachel's ginger and the natural remedies only dull the pain, but do not entirely chase it away. What Yvette would really prefer is a couple of tablets of Vicodin.

Yvette drags herself to her feet and heads to the medicine cabinet. Opening it, she glimpses what she expected – toothpaste, shaving cream, male and female razors and mouthwash. She's done it before, when she foolishly allowed herself to run out of pills. She grabs the mouthwash now, then swallows the entire content of dark blue liquid.

The burning sensation courses down her throat and into her belly. She feels immediately lightheaded but knows the feeling will pass in a little while. She stops sweating at least, and the pain in her body subsides. Even life is returning to her legs. She jumps to her feet and does an impromptu tap dance.

Yvette returns to the bed. She's about to climb into the covers when her phone vibrates on her nightstand. It's 2:30 in the morning. She wonders who would have the nerve to call her at this time of night. The ID states the caller is "private." Everyone knows bad news comes late at night. She takes the call because she is still a member of a large and extended family, though her immediate family members are dead.

"Hello?" Yvette speaks cautiously into the phone.

"Hey, mami." It's Jose, one of her supplier boys.

"Jose?!" Yvette blurts out amazed. No supplier has ever called her.

"Haven't heard from you in a while, mami." Jose is saying as Yvette runs quickly back into the bathroom so as not to wake Marcus.

"Why you calling me?" She can feel her anger rising. If he calls her *mami* one more time, she's gonna curse him out.

"Just wanted to know if you okay."

"It's three o'clock in the fucking morning!"

"For real?"

"Jesus!"

"Hey, you need me to get you something? You wanna stop by tomorrow?"

"What the fuck is wrong with you, boy?! You don't call me, I call you!"

"Yeah, but you know what? I was minding my business lying right here then I got to feeling the universe talking to me, you know. It told me to call you."

"The universe, " she says deadpan. She thinks he might be sampling some of that good stuff.

"Yeah, mami, you need something from me? None of that regular shit you be taking, I mean the good stuff?"

"God damn you, Jose!" She is furious. "I've told your fucking Dominican ass to quit calling me *mami*!"

She hangs up, exits the bathroom, storms into bed, throws the covers over her head, and lies there in the dark thinking about a teenage girl on a median island in the middle of Broadway swinging a pink hoola hoop round her waist.

| 16 |

There is a writer in Hollywood who wrote a screenplay seven years ago. He spent those years running about Hollywood land, looking for someone to produce and invest in his movie. The search proved fruitless and just when he was about to quit the business, a famous director read the screenplay and wanted to produce the film.

The famous director lent his name to drum up investors and sure enough – the investors lined up, so long as famous actors would act in the movie. Lo and behold – because the famous director asked them to – famous actors lined up to be in the flick. When it came time to pick a director, the famous one suggested to tap the writer because the story is so unique, he felt only the writer could do it.

The writer was overjoyed for he had secretly wanted to direct the movie. With little directing experience under his belt, however – having only directed music videos – the writer was not going to stand in the way of someone else directing his baby. And now, all his dreams were coming true.

Fast forward to today. There is one key element left to the production – the lead role is yet to be cast – enter Yvette. The writer, now director, is her cousin Jam, named *Jam* for his love of grape jelly back when they were kids. Oh, and they are each other's favorite cousin.

Yvette meets up with Jam in her cousin Lily's plush apartment – Lily, the full-time mistress of the investment banker and sister to Jam. At the moment, Lily is away downtown, in an equally plush hotel, her feet up in the air and her head hitting the bed's headboard as the boyfriend figure rams his tiny prick of a dick into her vagina.

Yvette's mouth is literary hanging open after Jam brings her up to speed on why he wants to cast her as the lead in his movie. He is sitting across from her, backed all the way in Lily's lazy boy, one leg crossed over the other. He has a wide grin on his face and waits for the expected, When do we leave for the Bahamas?! – the location in which the entire movie is to be shot.

Instead, Yvette squeaks out, "Why me?"

"Baby girl," begins Jam – he always calls her baby girl, even though she is three years his senior. "Why not you? This is the break you've been waiting for. Didn't I tell you it was gonna happen? I just never saw I'd be the one giving it to you."

"But, but, but," Yvette stammers. "Meryl Streep will be in it! Jada Pinkett Smith too! And, and, and Bruce Willis! Why can't Jada play me?!"

Jam is momentarily taken aback. She's not responding the way he had seen it all in his head.

"Baby girl, I explained all that," he explains patiently.

A long time ago, Yvette financed Jam's relocation to LA with money she stole from Marcus. She had to steal the money because Marcus and Jam never got along, stemming from neither having respect for the work of the other. And because of this, there was no way Marcus would approve of any resources to keep Jam pursuing his dream. So Yvette began siphoning money out of Marcus' account to send to Jam out in LA – risking her marriage for her beloved cousin.

Even Jam's sister Lily did not believe in him enough to loan, let alone give, some of the surplus the investment banker threw at her on a monthly basis — although now, Lily has changed her tune given Jam's lucky break. She is his greatest fan these days.

Jam is not stupid, however, and sees right through his get-over sister. His relationship with Yvette, on the other hand, is one of profound love and admiration. He never forgot Yvette's generosity when he was a nobody, so he is happy to return the favor now that he's a somebody.

"The role calls for a new face," Jam is saying to Yvette. "And remember, the character is brutally killed at the end. No one wants to see Will's wife killed at the end. The producer and all the investors saw your reel. They think you're amazing. They've given me the green light to consider you."

Yvette is looking at him wide-eyed. Jam mistakes this for shock when in fact her thoughts are on the two pill containers in her purse. Believing Yvette was also coming over to pick up pills, Lily left two medication bottles filled with pills on the table.

Yvette grabbed the bottles immediately upon arrival, before Jam got out of the shower for their meeting. Jam knows absolutely nothing about her dependence on the stuff. Yvette plans to get rid of the pills as soon as she leaves the apartment – that's what she's telling herself anyway because she wants to keep her promise to Rachel.

"When do we leave for the Bahamas?!" Yvette finally asks. Seriously – the infinite possibilities of the opportunity Jam is offering finally take a hold.

"Not the Bahamas right away," Jam answers, pleased that she's finally reacting like someone whose entire purpose for living is about to come through. "We leave for LA tomorrow. You have to come read for the part, but I have every confidence you'll nail it, baby girl. I practically based that character on you!"

"You did?" Yvette is touched.

"Uh-huh, then it's off to the Bahamas sometime after Christmas."

"For how long?" she asks, holding her breath.

"One month at most."

Yvette's heart stops beating. She opens her purse, uncaps a medication container and swallows two tablets. She notes Jam's eyes narrow at the sight of the pills.

"Headache," she answers his unspoken query.

"Oh," he says relaxing. So the news is too much for her, he's thinking. He suspected as much. Neither of them says anything for some time. He thought after the initial shock, she'd be a whirl of movement to get going. Yet, she's just sitting there.

"Um, don't you need to go home to pack or something?" he asks perplexed.

Yvette looks out the window, at the clearest view of the Manhattan skyline she has ever seen.

"I can't, Jam," she finally says. "Marcus and I … we got the, um, play …"

Jam pulls his body to the edge of the lazy boy. He peers at her intently, waiting for the punch line to the joke. He knows about Marcus' play, of course. However, he is one of those filmmakers who feel the screen is far more superior to the stage. Plus, he despises Marcus.

"I'm talking Meryl Streep, baby girl," he says, speaking slowly – as if she's deaf and therefore needs to read his lips. "Back when we were kids," he continues. "She's all you ever talked about."

Yvette feels like bursting into tears. God's doing this to me, she's thinking. The movie's production would have to be smack in the middle of the play's opening run. God is continuing to punish her for offenses she doesn't recall.

"How about the understudy?" Jam probes with a voice laced with mounting irritation. Like any Hollywood writer/director full of ego, the idea of a practically unknown stage actress not wanting to take the lead role in his studio-approved movie never crossed his mind.

"What's her name?" Jam asks, understanding he needs to lead her to make a decision that would be best for her.

"Vicky," Yvette responds, acting like a child answering a parent.

"Vicky." He repeats. "That's what she's there for, right?" he pushes.

Hope springs in Yvette's eyes.

"Either that," Jam continues, "or get Marcus to move the play till after you're done with the movie." It never occurred to Jam to consider moving his production date.

Yvette waits for Marcus to get out of the shower to break the news to him. He has been in there for over an hour, his habit of late. She justifies it as the byproduct of the stresses associated with the play's production. She knows in her heart what she will say tonight will blind-side him but feels compelled to tell him.

There is yet a way they can both have what they want. Pushing the play's production, as Jam had suggested, is out of the question – even Yvette knows that. Opening night tickets are already sold out. No, the play would go on right on schedule –even with someone else as *Light*, particularly if that someone were to be Vicky.

Yvette admits now, of course the understudy is great. She's so great she's been a threat. Vicky can stay on the role while she runs off to the Bahamas and does the film. There may even be pockets in there where she can return to New York and do days as *Light.* And after the movie wraps, she will return to play *Light.*

Jam will give her till tomorrow afternoon to confirm if she will be on the flight to LA that evening. He implied, though he never said it, if she missed the flight, she can kiss the role goodbye. Yvette understood perfectly and therefore has every intention of making that flight.

Marcus ushers out of the bathroom, beads of water on his skin, the towel around his waist. She can see in his eyes he wants to have sex. It's been every night for the past week or so. They go at it like animals, each unwittingly receiving from the other a type of remedy to temper personal demons.

One look at Yvette, however, and Marcus knows he rushed out of the shower for nothing. He is immediately let down, though he is prepared to pretend he doesn't notice. He throws the towel to the ground and she notes his erect penis, curved at the tip, as if beckoning her to come here. Marcus climbs on top of her, his finger already pushing her panties aside. He detects she's not wet, so he takes his hand out and spits into his palm.

"Marcus, stop," Yvette says curt. "I have to talk to you." She pushes him away, and rolls out from under him. He sits up in bed, his legs spread apart so she can see him at all times. He hopes the talking is quick so they can get on with it.

"What?" he asks, equally curt.

She does not answer right away, preferring to be on her feet and pacing. This new habit of hers of pacing is getting on his nerves.

"I saw Jam today," she says very cautious.

"Yeah?" he asks suspiciously, reading the caution in her voice.

So she saw the Hollywood big shot wanna be, he thinks. He knows that when they were kids, Yvette and Jam nurtured dreams of making it in Hollywood. Whereas Yvette gave up that dream for him, Jam pursued it. No wonder she's in a solemn mood, he concludes. Jam no doubt reminded her of the other life she gave up. Damn that prick!

Marcus draws his legs together, understanding his dangling penis seems suddenly inappropriate given the tone in the room. "What's up with him?" he asks, hoping Jam's not doing well.

"He got 50 million dollars to do a film."

"Say what?!" Marcus is intrigued. "Who the hell gave him that kind of money?"

"People who believe in him."

Silence suddenly falls in the room. The implication resounds throughout the four walls. Marcus decides not to take the bait. He says absolutely nothing.

"He wants to cast me in the lead." She hopes he'll catch her excitement.

He does and ignores it. "Why?" he asks without thinking.

"What do you mean why? I'm an actress!"

The fury in her voice cautions him to step lightly. At the same time, he is prepared to overpower her. He doesn't know where this is going, but he is prepared not to lose. He has grown wary of her picking unnecessary fights with him lately, although this one can hardly be called unnecessary.

"What I mean is," he begins, his tone sure and steady. "You haven't acted for the screen in a long while." His way of staying in control is to throw her shortcomings to her face, to sew doubt.

"No thanks to you." She's pouting and crosses her arms across her chest.

"When does he need you?" he asks. He finally understands this is where they are going and so decides to get there before she does. As he knew it would, his directness disarms her. She falters.

"I, I was thinking," she's floundering. "It could all work out." She sits beside him on the bed and in her eyes he sees desperation. He makes sure that his eyes broadcast threat.

"When, Yvie?!"

"Soon," she whimpers, avoiding his terrifying eyes. "The audition's in LA, he wants me to leave with him tomorrow night. After that, production begins around Christmas in the Bahamas, for about a month."

Marcus suddenly relaxes. Oh, he's thinking, he thought the battle would take longer to win.

"I'm sorry, honey, I'm sure it wasn't easy to turn him down." He gets off the bed and to the drawer to find his PJs. He could live without sex for one night.

"I didn't turn him down," she states matter of factly.

It's not what she says, it's the way she says it. Looking at her from across the room, Marcus realizes the battle wasn't done after all. Nevertheless, he decides to play it as if it's already won. He puts on his pajama pants.

"He's a dick for springing this on you right now, baby. I'm sure you told him we've got the play. Do you want me to call him and tell him you can't do it?"

"I'm getting on that plane, Marcus." Her eyes are intense and unwavering.

Marcus takes note of her demeanor as he regards her coolly. "For what possible end, Yvette?" he asks at long last.

"Don't ask me questions you already know the answers to!" she snaps. "Everything is gonna work out. Vicky will cover for me until ..."

He sprints towards her with such speed, she never saw him coming. He grabs her by the arms, towering over her. "Vicky?! The damn understudy!! She's good enough for you now?!"

"Let go of me, Marcus!" She pushes him away.

"They're all coming to see you, goddamn it! The Mayor! All of New York!"

He had wanted to add, They're all coming to see me too! It's my reputation goddamn it! Instead, he decides to make this all about her. "For you, Yvie! They're all coming to see you!" He sees the panic in her eyes and goes for the jugular. "Everything we have is riding on this, baby! We borrowed against the damn house, for godssake!"

He is loud, beside himself with unparalleled anger. He cannot believe what she's saying. He cannot believe they're even having this conversation. It's the craziest thing he has ever heard.

"You talking crazy, woman!" he punctuates with finality.

"Hush, baby, hush!" Her hands cover his mouth against his ruckus, her eyes full of all kinds of hurt. "I want this, Marcus, I want this! This is a great opportunity. Nothing bad is going to happen. The play won't fold, we won't lose the house. It will all work out, you'll see. We can do both, we'll find a way!"

Marcus is suddenly filled with darkness. He feels it rise from deep within him, flaring into a cloud that swallows his eyes and engulfs his head. Before he knows what he's doing, he shoves Yvette away from him with all his might.

Yvette flies across the room, bangs into the closet door and spills to the floor. The impact is such her head had hit the door. The pain to the back of her head is so excruciating, unconsciousness threatens to envelop her. She is as surprised at Marcus' action as Marcus would be if his anger were done. It's not. He's just getting started.

He sprints towards Yvette and easily lifts her off the ground. He throws her onto the bed where she slides across the sheets and comes to a sudden stop against the headboard. Marcus is upon her again. His hand finds its way round her throat, while his other hand he lifts above his head, balls into a fist, and readies to strike.

"Marcus!" Yvette yells terrified. He is unrecognizable to her. His one hand is stalled in the air because his other hand round her neck is squeezing the life out of her. Yvette coughs and rasps for breath, fighting him with all her might.

Marcus' spirit calmly asks him what he thinks he's doing. In considering the question, awareness suddenly drops into Marcus' eyes and he sees himself choking Yvette to death. He lets go immediately, as Yvette cowers in terror, coughing and wheezing. Marcus gets off the bed and rushes out of the bedroom.

Yvette bursts into tears. She runs to the door Marcus just exited and locks it. She rushes to her purse and takes out the pills from Lily. With shaking hands, she throws three capsules into her mouth, then rushes to the very closet she'd been thrown against and pulls out a small overnight luggage case. She starts throwing her things into it, weeping uncontrollably all the while.

Outside the door, Marcus paces. His chest rises and falls rapidly as a myriad of images swim in his mind's eye — confusing images of his mother cowering in terror on the ground as a figure looms above her.

Marcus does not understand these images, even though the images seem strangely familiar. A succession of them rush past now: his mother bleeding from a gash on her forehead, his mother trying to run under a bed, the figure pulling her out and throwing her about as if she's a rag doll.

Marcus feels faint and leans against the wall to keep from falling. "Take it easy, take it easy," he sings to himself. In fact, it's his spirit trying to calm him down. Marcus sees Yvette wheezing for air, his hand round her throat.

"Shut your eyes," his spirit commands. So Marcus shuts his eyes immediately, distancing himself from the image, as well as the images of his mother running for her life. The man chasing her is none other than Marcus.

| 17 |

Rachel finishes showering and throws the shower curtain open. She comes face to face with Marcus standing at the door of the bathroom, shirtless. Stunned, her reaction is swift – she steps back, grabbing the shower curtain closed. She stands in the tub, water glistening off her body, her heart beating fast.

"I'm sorry," his voice is steady, unrushed. "The door was open."

"I'm quite sure it wasn't." She wants to make her voice sound as steady and as unrushed as his, to treat this moment as casual as possible.

"Sorry," he says again. She's not sure if he's sorry for invading her privacy or sorry for lying about that invasion. She waits for signs he's leaving. She hears nothing.

"Yes, Marcus?" She did not want to say, Do you need something? His presence says it all. Marcus does not answer.

"Shit," Rachel says under her breath. He has crossed the line tonight. She will have to leave this house – apparently, sooner than she had planned. The question is when? Now? Tomorrow? In two weeks? After the play opens? When?

She hears him enter, let the toilet top down, then take a seat on it. She doesn't know what to do. She is getting cold standing in the tub, but she dare not reach for the towel, hanging on the rung right outside the curtain. She thinks it best no more of her naked flesh should be seen by him, even if just an arm. She also wants him to know she will not exit before he exits.

If Marcus knows this, he is prepared not to act on it. He remains on the toilet, his mind numb. He is trying not to see the image of his mother throwing pieces of furniture at someone slowly approaching her.

"Marcus?" Rachel calls him again. He startles a little. He had completely forgotten about her. "I need to, um, I need to come out."

"So come out," he says wearily. "I won't bite."

Rachel says nothing and of course, does not exit the tub. He didn't really think she would. He sighs heavily, leaning his forehead in his hand. He sees his hand round Yvette's neck again and quickly pushes that image away from his mind.

"Yvie is going to Los Angeles," he mumbles. "To audition for some movie."

"That's good, right?" Rachel asks. She can take being wet no longer. She reaches outside the curtain and quickly grabs the towel. He is amused by her action as he continues talking.

"Good for whom? We've got the play."

"Oh, so they're happening at the same time?"

"Yeah." He sighs again.

"There's no way to fit them both?"

Showing an openness remarkable for him, he answers, "I don't want to."

"Why not?"

He has no answer for this.

"Marcus," she calls him again, in that way she has of pronouncing his name with the "r" silent. He finds his entire being tuned to what she's about to say.

"Do you love your wife?" she asks softly.

Marcus considers it a strange question as he is in the space with her whom he covets. Rachel's ample, well-formed boobs, glistening with water, flashes in his mind's eye. He wishes she had not been so quick to draw back the shower curtain. So to her question of whether he loves Yvette, he finds he cannot answer. So she answers for him.

"I know you love her, Marcus. And because you do, you are going to support her." Though she is only 24 years old, Rachel knows that sometimes you have to tell a man what to do, particularly if he wants to have sex with you. This is what she calls using her womanly wiles to good use.

"You know very well this is very important to her," she continues. "Ask yourself this – if the situation were reversed and this were important to you, she would have your back. Please let her go for the audition. If she passes it, you are going to work together to find the best way to do both things. Maybe it will work, maybe it won't. She needs to see you trying to make it work though. Sometimes this moves a wife, moves her very much. She might even be the one to decide to give up the movie."

Marcus suddenly throws the shower curtain open, startling Rachel. Fortunately, she has the towel wrapped round her body. She looks into his eyes and sees pure and adulterated hunger to fuck. She decides on the spot she will leave the Peytons after Yvette returns from Los Angeles. She will give her two weeks' notice then. But first, she has to get Marcus out of here.

"Marcus," she calls, her voice calm and steady. She makes sure her eyes on him do not waver. "Please leave."

Marcus does not move so she takes her voice up a notch.

"Now!"

The sound is sharp and piercing, like a clap. This seems to do the trick. It breaks him out of his trance. He actually startles as uncertainty and fear reflect in his eyes. He backs away until he gets out the door.

Rachel quickly climbs out of the tub to lock the door. She is not entirely certain Marcus is not behind it. She takes a seat on the toilet and looks down at her hands. She sees they're trembling. She will remain seated there until dawn.

That night, Marcus knocked quietly on his bedroom door and whispered sincere apologies to Yvette that got her to unlock the door and let him in. In bed, he held her tight and wept more apologies that moved her to clean the tears that fell out of his eyes. He told her she could go ahead and go to Los Angeles, that she can come back whenever she wanted. Yvette showed great maturity in not telling him she was already packed and did not need his permission to go anywhere. He continued to say that whatever the outcome of the audition, he would support her. They would sort it out.

They made passionate love afterwards, all night long. Unfortunately, it was Rachel whom Marcus saw as he rammed his pelvis against Yvette's vagina. Even when Yvette moaned his name, it was Rachel's voice he heard saying, "Oh Marcus! Yeah, baby! Oh Marcus! Marcus!" — the "r" in his name silent as usual.

Only when they were done did he realize it was Yvette lying asleep in his arms and not Rachel. So he took the opportunity to pray to God and to all his forebears that Yvette would blow the audition and return home to his arms where she belongs.

As it turned out, God and all of Marcus' forebears paid attention to his prayer that night. Yvette blew the audition so badly, she embarrassed the hell out of Jam, who was sitting with the famous director, turned producer, who had given him the opportunity.

She knew she was blowing the scene as she was reading the lines. It might have been the blinding headache she was suffering, emanating from the back of her head that had slammed against the closet door when Marcus threw her across the room.

In the end, the role went to the famous director's 28-year old daughter who, one year later, was nominated for an Academy Award for the role. The daughter did not win the award that year, but the role is considered her breakout part. She went on to star in other high-profile movies that elevated her star in Hollywood to A-status level.

After the reading, Jam immediately loaded Yvette onto a plane back to New York with comforting words to the effect that, Don't worry, baby girl, maybe next time. Call me when you get back home.

In a daze, Yvette promised she would, then boarded the plane and proceeded to weep all the way home. She did not call Jam when she got to LaGuardia, nor did she call Marcus to say she had arrived home two days earlier than she said she would.

Yvette headed straight uptown, met up with Jose who finally sold her some of that good stuff. She ran downtown and holed up in a cheap motel on Long Island City where she proceeded to inject heroin into the main artery running beside her Achilles tendon.

Lying on the bed in the seedy room and listening to the hissing radiator somewhere in the shadows, Yvette finally finally feels like that teenage girl on the median island on Broadway, twirling a pink hoola hoop round her waist.

| 18 |

Life at the Peytons' moved in slow motion in the week after Yvette came back from Los Angeles. She told Marcus she had carefully thought about it and concluded her marriage and her family are far more important than any Hollywood career. She told him she wanted no further distractions against focusing on the play. Marcus was overjoyed and spent all of that week pampering and treating her like his one true queen.

The only damper on things was Rachel's two-week notice. She informed the couple she was going back to her cheating fiancé who has relocated to Maine. She's been in contact with the man who has seen the error of his ways. He wants her back in his life and would spend the rest of eternity making up for the pain he's caused her.

Yvette pretended to hit the roof at the news. The truth is, she needed Rachel gone to feel comfortable to fully indulge herself in her own home. She beseeched Rachel with false entreaties to reconsider, not to believe the fiancé, a cheating man is a cheating man. Rachel held her head high and did not change her mind.

Yvette next tried to use the children – her departure would break Aaliyah and MJ's little hearts. Rachel felt guilty but reasoned it is because of the children she is leaving. Their father is in danger of committing a transgression in her name. In case the marriage fell apart, she did not want to carry the responsibility of home wrecker.

Rachel did not say any of this to Yvette, of course, merely explained that the children will become used to whomever else they hire to care for them. She did ask Yvette to let her be the one to tell the children in her own way.

Yvette agreed to that but continued to lobby against Rachel's departure. She used her condition as the last resort – asking Rachel not to leave otherwise she might fall off the wagon. Rachel responded by saying she has every confidence in Yvette against her falling off. She would even swear on her dead mother that Yvette would do no such thing. Yvette swallowed the lump in her throat and said nothing more.

Marcus did not, of course, believe the bullshit Rachel spun for her reason for needing to quit. He knows she is leaving because of him. He considered it against his pride to ask her to stay, so he didn't. But he found himself sulking and pouting at the mere thought of her impending departure.

Finally, one night, with Yvette in the shower, he makes his way down to the kitchen to find Rachel, to ask her to stay. Like on that first day he met her, he will be a gentleman again. He will give her that promise which he intends to keep – at least, he'll try. He does not find her in the kitchen, nor anywhere on her floor. Seeing that the light leading into the basement is on, he goes down there and that's where he finds her.

Rachel is rooting among knickknacks stuffed in the space for a small suitcase she saved back when the Peytons' backyard was in its initial disarray. The suitcase was to be thrown to the curb when she came upon it. She asked Yvette then if she could have it and Yvette said yes.

Rachel tucked the suitcase in the basement that day and promptly forgot about it – until now. Since arriving to the Peytons' in early September, she has acquired quite a few clothes and other personal items.

The suitcase would be just right to fit everything in. First though, she has to extricate it from where it is lodged between all sorts of things.

"Hey, let me help," Marcus says, coming down the steps to quickly assist. His manner is polite and gracious.

"Oh it's okay," Rachel says nervously. "I got it. Really, you should go back up!" She knows she doesn't want to be alone with him at any time, let alone in a tight space like the basement. He ignores her and helps anyway.

Marcus pulls the suitcase out for her and out pops a scarf which hits the floor. He recognizes the scarf as one of the ones he had purchased for her back when he was acting like a love-struck schoolboy.

Embarrassed beyond belief, he bends to his knees and picks up the scarf. That's when he notices there's something wrapped in its folds. He opens the scarf and there discovers a rubber tube, a syringe, an old spoon and cocaine powder in a clear plastic bag. The syringe clatters to the ground, at Rachel's feet.

Horrified, he gets down to his feet a second time and picks up the syringe. He rises, his eyes ovals of amazement that he beams towards Rachel. She reads accusation in his eyes. Accusation turns to horror.

"What the fuck!" the man retorts. "You're doing this! In, in my home?!"

"What?" she asks, staring at him stupidly.

"That's why you didn't want me down here, right?!"

"Marcus," Rachel is amused now. "You can't be serious. That's not …"

He strikes her face with such force, red spots actually appear in the darkness of her consciousness. Her body slams against all the junk and everything comes cascading down, causing her to fall. He pulls her up and throws her against the wall that's closest to the steps leading out of the basement.

"Marcus!' she screams incredulous. She sees the faint outline of his figure bearing down upon her in a menacing way, so she spins around and stumbles up the steps and out of the basement.

Marcus pursues her, grabbing onto her feet right before she gets to the top step. She spills into the first floor, beside the bathroom she uses. When the darkness of her consciousness clears and reality blooms, it's to see his face only inches from hers. Insanity has screwed his features so that he might as well be someone else.

"You fucking bitch!" she hears him screaming from a distance even as his hot breath washes over her. "My children live here!"

"It's not … mine," Rachel whispers, as self-preservation kicks in. "It's got to be Yvette's!" But how could it be, she's thinking disoriented. The door was locked.

"Yes, and Jesus Christ is white!!" Rachel has no time to ponder the expression because Marcus lifts her to her feet and throws her against the wall next to her bedroom.

"Stop, stop!" she screams. She wants to sound convincing, knows it's important to do so. But her voice is shaky and trembling. She cannot believe what is happening.

"Your fucking wife's a fucking addict!" She is pleased her voice sounds stronger this time, not filled with the terror that's making her faint.

Of course, the African accent is out the window. She herself is unaware she's dropped it. And if Marcus noticed her sudden American sounding line, he doesn't care. He raises his hand. She sees the blow before it comes so she pivots her face. Vanity will not let her allow him to hit her face a second time, so the blow lands on the side of her head. He curses out loud for he had meant to strike her face. He pushes her against the wall, to secure her against it, then pummels her body with his fists.

Because Rachel's true nature is to fight when under attack, she raises her hands to defend herself. She digs her fingernails into the flesh of his face, leaving streaks of blood in her wake. Marcus does not utter a scream or even a yelp. Instead, he grabs her hand and nearly breaks off the fingers when he bends them back.

Rachel screams. The pain is unbearable. He quickly covers her mouth. She bites down on his palm, forcing him to let go. She runs through the yoga studio and towards the steps leading out of the space. He is upon her before she can get there. He twists her arm unnaturally behind her, then wraps his hand around her neck in a chokehold. He throws her against a wall a third time.

His hand around her neck prevents her from breathing. Her eyes bulge and Rachel knows he means to kill her. This knowledge, as unbelievable as it sounds, fills her with such terror, she bursts into tears.

"Marcus please!" She means to beg for her life, but the words did not actually come out, his hold on her neck makes it virtually impossible for words to escape.

Marcus pulls her off the wall, swings her round and round, building momentum before releasing her to spill on the exercise floor. Rachel falls hard, on her boobs which hurt like hell. She lies there breathing heavily, relieved to find she's at least alive. He will go away now, she thinks. Dear God he will go away now. Be still.

Despite Marcus' attempts to assault Rachel as quietly as mice move within a home, all the noise ushers Yvette. She runs down the steps, and comes to a sudden stop seeing Marcus unbuckling his belt while standing over Rachel.

"Marcus!" Yvette begins horrified. "What are you doing?!" There is that man again, the very one that had assaulted her not too long ago. As then as like now, she does not recognize Marcus in this person.

"Hey, baby," Marcus says to Yvette, not bothering to look at her.

Hearing Yvette's voice, Rachel finally believes the ordeal is over. There's no need to lie still any longer, so she attempts to sit up. Marcus suddenly swings out his foot and strikes her on the back. Rachel yelps.

"Stop!" Yvette screams.

"She's been shooting up down there, baby." Marcus deadpans.

"Shooting up?" Yvette is confused. "Huh?"

"Uh-huh. Found her shit in the basement. It's over there." He indicates the drug paraphernalia on top of the washing machine. He had brought the scarf up with him.

If Marcus' eyes were on Yvette instead of on Rachel he would see the truth of what Rachel blurted out minutes ago. As it is, he is busy slipping his belt off his pants.

"What, what you gonna do?" Yvette asks terrified, her eyes on his belt.

"What needs to be done."

Marcus swings the belt over his head and brings it down on Rachel's body. Rachel howls.

"Please stop!" Yvette pleads. She takes a tentative step towards Marcus, wringing her hands nervously. "It's enough, okay."

Marcus looks at his wife, gives her a deadly look that roots Yvette to the spot.

"She said the shit's yours!"

Yvette's breath catches. If Marcus sees the truth in Yvette's wide eyes this time, he doesn't let it change his course. "She's something else, huh?" he says, and faces Rachel again. He swings the belt once again and brings it down on her back.

Rachel screams. She can feel the swollen welts rising on the flesh of her back, her neck, and the back of her head – everywhere the leather belt makes contact.

Yvette squirms. "She's gonna call the cops!"

"Who's gonna believe an illegal goddamned African!" Marcus roars. As if for emphasis, he brings the belt down on Rachel's butt.

Rachel crawls towards her room, the only direction she can think to go since Marcus and Yvette are blocking the stairs. He follows her slowly, nailing her to the ground with each whip of the belt.

Yvette can't take it anymore. She takes the steps two at a time and fleas the first floor. She runs up to the children's room to see if they are awakened. MJ and Aaliyah are resting peacefully.

Meanwhile, Rachel has finally gotten to the door of her room, and reaches for the knob. Her hand cannot reach it, however, and she is too weak to rise. Marcus himself throws the door open. He steps over her and enters, then drags her in and throws her on the bed.

Rachel remains as he has thrown her – on her stomach. She is delirious with pain, going in and out of consciousness. She hears the door slam shut, hears his footsteps approach. Her body tightens with anticipation. She expects the belt at any time. Instead, she feels his hands push down her pants and feels his hands drag down her underwear.

Take it, take it, goddamn it! she thinks. Take it and leave me alone!

For a long time after that, Marcus does not make a move. She thinks maybe he's changed his mind. He will get off the bed. She expects to hear his footsteps as he walks back out the door.

She hears nothing of the sort – instead, she feels him suddenly stand up on the bed. She does not dare to look to see what he's doing. There is no need to see for what Marcus Peyton does next becomes all too clear – he pisses on her.

The hot stream of yellow filth splashes onto Rachel's ass. The stream finds its way through her butt crack, defiling her anus and soiling her vagina. The wetness combines with her broken flesh, searing her mind with dazzling pain. The stream steadily moves off her butt, directed by Marcus to zigzag across her back.

Anger, the likes she has never known, clouds her thoughts and overwhelms her. Rachel blacks out as the urine flows atop her head, then trickles its way down her face and into the corners of her mouth.

| 19 |

From Marcus' perspective, the girl's amused face is what did it – not that he could've ever forgiven her for doing drugs in his home. But to be amused about it?! Anger, in the form of a fast-moving cloud, blinds his eyes and engulfs his head – same as it did the night he went after Yvette. And same as that night, he is unaware of when he does it. He strikes Rachel with all his might, an impact that sends her flying into clutter.

The riddle unraveled right there and then. Marcus Peyton is a domestic abuse survivor. As a child, he witnessed his biological father named Hector Newman constantly beat up his mother — Hector's physical resemblance to Marcus is such that side by side, they could be mistaken for identical twins. When Marcus turned 6, his mother could take no more and fled into a shelter.

She eventually earned her GED, then a college degree and married the man Marcus would call his father – a loving unassuming man who taught Marcus how to play drums, and who taught him everything about the respect of woman. The family would grow to include four more children, and all lived happily ever after. Well, sort of.

When Marcus' fist connected to Rachel's face, he found his spirit lifting to the air. And there he remained, watching himself assault the girl. Marcus finally understood the confusing and chaotic images he's been seeing recently in his mind's eye. Apparently, he'd completely forgotten those terrible images from his childhood. He'd even forgotten about Hector, the boogeyman of his first six years on earth.

His fight with Yvette ushered forth the floodgate, ushered forth the nightmare his consciousness and spirit disposed of to the point of non-existence. Now, Hector's face was as real to him as the faces of his children. Not only that – Hector's mind as well. Marcus understood that Hector had beaten up his mother for the absolute thrill and rush of it – a thrill and rush Marcus understood very well because he felt them now.

Underneath the thrill, however, was blinding rage. He had held the girl pure of heart, had nothing but the utmost of respect for her. But underneath it all, she was just another fiend no good crack head — to Marcus, every drug user is a crack head. What was particularly unpardonable, he had come down to ask her to stay!

So the drug items he found permitted the rage, permitted his fist against her face. If she's nothing more than a drug addict then it's okay to certainly treat her like one. That's what he told himself anyway. But the real reason Marcus Peyton was as mad as hell was because for weeks, the girl rebuffed his advances, tantalized him with her steadfastness. The more he pursued, the more she denied his charming self.

Who does she think she is, he fumed? Was he not the one who found her all alone crying in the park? Was he not the one who convinced her to stay in America instead of return to Africa to become nothing? Was he not the one who gave her the idea to get the roommate to pretend to be the ex-boss to get the job? And was he not the one who agreed to give her the damn job?!

He felt vindicated with each instance he threw her against the wall. In his mind, it was her fault he was treating her so. Yvette burst in then, as he was unbuckling his belt. He might have stopped – he was suddenly ashamed of himself, ashamed of this brute of a man who was in fact his biological father, a man he loathed, feared and wished dead with each breath he took as a little boy.

The fear Marcus saw in Yvette's eyes, however, instantly energized him, made him forget about whatever shame he was feeling about being like Hector. Marcus wanted to declare to Yvette that he was the man, that she would never choose Jam or whoever else's worth or need above his. All the choices she made from here on out must be okay with him. She would dare not pursue them otherwise. He communicated all this in his stare and saw her cower. So Yvette fled.

Marcus dragged Rachel onto the bed. He was completely charged and turned on. His spirit continued to watch from up above as he saw himself pull down the girl's pants and underwear. He wanted to fuck her, the need was pressing. He wanted to rip her ass apart with his dick and knew more than life he would enjoy it too.

He unzipped his pants, removed his already hardened member when his spirit above asked a simple question, "Suppose she's diseased? She is a crack head."

Marcus froze. His spirit asked a follow-up question, "You're not gonna fuck her without a condom, are you?"

"Um, no." Marcus was certain of that. Then he answered the spirit's unasked question. "Nah, there's none in the house."

"So you gonna run to the drugstore and get some?" his spirit mocked.

"Hm." And just like that, the need was gone. The girl wasn't worth it after all.

"What you gonna do now?" his spirit asked.

An answer flashed in Marcus' mind, in the form of an image – Hector pissing on his mother after one particularly brutal beating. The man had been drunk and weaving about – hence, his urine stream was also zigzagging. This was the last act suffered by his mother before she fled with her son into the shelter.

So Marcus jumped to his feet atop the bed. His penis was already in his hands. It was the easiest and most satisfying thing in the world to let loose a stream of pissing hot urine onto Rachel's buttocks, back and head.

His spirit watches him now near the end of the stream, as Marcus bounces his penis around, making sure that the last droplets of piss fall on Rachel's head. While up above, his spirit begins the slow descent to rejoin his body.

The reaction is immediate as soon as his two elements merge. Marcus is suddenly filled with horror, loathing and guilt. He cannot believe what he has just done. He pulls his pants up and jumps off the bed. Frantic, he searches for his belt and sees it lying on the floor near the door.

As he slings his belt through his pants' loops, his eyes flicker towards Rachel whom it just occurs to him has not made a move since he threw her on the bed. Her great mound of a butt juts in the air indecently for her underwear is midway down on her calves. Is she living or dead, he does not know. He sees his entire life, his entire future, everything he has ever worked for come crumbling down.

What have I done?! he shrieks in his head.

His spirit answers calmly, "I told you not to do it."

"You told me shit!" Marcus says out loud. He turns to flee and runs right smack into the door.

End Book 1

Book 2

Coming Soon!

Read the Intro Chapter to Book 2 on:

www.vigilchime.com